VIKING
Mystery
Suspense

A Long Reach

ALSO BY MICHAEL STONE

The Low End of Nowhere

A Long Reach

A STREETER MYSTERY

Michael Stone

VIKING

VIKING
Published by the Penguin Group
Penguin Books USA Inc., 375 Hudson Street,
New York, New York 10014, U.S.A.
Penguin Books Ltd, 27 Wrights Lane, London W8 5TZ, England
Penguin Books Australia Ltd, Ringwood, Victoria, Australia
Penguin Books Canada Ltd, 10 Alcorn Avenue,
Toronto, Ontario, Canada M4V 3B2
Penguin Books (N.Z.) Ltd, 182–190 Wairau Road,
Auckland 10, New Zealand

Penguin Books Ltd, Registered Offices:
Harmondsworth, Middlesex, England

First published in 1997 by Viking Penguin,
a division of Penguin Books USA Inc.

1 2 3 4 5 6 7 8 9 10

PUBLISHER'S NOTE
This is a work of fiction. Names, characters, places, and
incidents either are the product of the author's imagination or
are used fictitiously, and any resemblance to actual persons,
living or dead, events, or locales is entirely coincidental.

LIBRARY OF CONGRESS CATALOGING-IN-PUBLICATION DATA
Stone, Michael.
A long reach/Michael Stone.
p.   cm.
ISBN 0-670-86166-9
I. Title.
PS3569.T64144L66   1997
813´.54—dc20   96-21141

This book is printed on acid-free paper.
∞

Printed in the United States of America
Set in Minion

To Dominick Abel

Acknowledgments

The author would like to thank and acknowledge
Carolyn Carlson, Pat McCullough, Clifford
Irving (belatedly), Nancy and Dan Dupler, all of
my fellow mystery writers who gave me a hand,
Ann Mygatt for pretending to like my writing, all
the terrific mystery store owners who have
helped and supported me (especially Tom and
Enid Schantz, Ed and Pat Thomas, Shelly
MacArthur, Shirley Beaird, and Richard Katz),
and last but not least, the hardest-working man
in show business: Matthew Bradley.

A Long Reach

1

Merton "Buddy" Hinckley wouldn't tell you the truth if you set his hair on fire. As a small-time contractor, he treated his customers like lice, and he had more process servers after him than both Clintons combined. Streeter was so mad at him that he was doing this one for free. His partner, Frank Dazzler, had talked him into serving the garnishment papers. Streeter usually avoided serving process. At twenty-five bucks a pop, you could easily make less than minimum wage. Fortunately, as a bounty hunter for Dazzler's Bail Bonds, he seldom had to do it. But then an Army pal of Frank's from Korea had mentioned a scammer who'd conned his aunt out of nearly four grand.

"It breaks my heart to see her," the friend had said. "Old Clara always dreamed about adding a little sewing room on the back of her house. So this cowboy contractor named Hinckley comes along while I'm outta town and waltzes her into forking over thirty-eight hundred and change. In advance, no less. Was he peddling a line of manure? Does Michael Jackson love little kids? Anyhow, Hinckley comes out to her house for half a day, knocking holes in a wall like he's getting down to business. Then he disappears, and we can't find him for months."

They sued Buddy and won a judgment plus punitive damages. But he didn't pay a penny and they all knew he almost certainly was still out there running the same hustle on other people. Clara's attorney got a garnishment order, meaning that a chunk of whatever the builder was earning should go to her. But the order would be worthless until it was hand-delivered to Hinckley.

Frank played on Streeter's compassion and sense of fairness. They'd been partners for ten years and Streeter was the best skip tracer in Denver. Still, the bounty hunter was reluctant until he dropped in on Clara to pick up the papers. That's when he got mad. It was so endearingly pathetic, the way she walked him to the back of her house and showed him the boarded-up holes. She described in slow detail how she'd envisioned the sewing room that would never be. When she finished, a solitary tear worked its way down an ancient cheek as creased as a used lunch bag. Then, in a voice suddenly hard, she added, "When you serve this shit heel, Mr. Streeter, please kick him one in the grapes for me."

Patiently, he explained that the service was as far as he'd go. Clara nodded and let out a resigned wheeze. "Whatever you think is best."

Now, turning north off 14th Avenue onto Colorado Boulevard, Streeter thought of how he'd all but given up. Hinckley, a paranoid boozer in his late forties, lived in a secured building. His wife and son screened all calls, as well as any visitors who got past the locked lobby. Buddy didn't have a regular work schedule and he kept his truck in the closed, underground garage. It could take weeks of surveillance to catch him coming or going.

On a hunch, Streeter had read the court file. In the financial-disclosure portion, Buddy had listed a 1953 Ford sedan valued at six hundred dollars that he intended to sell. He gave its location as a Conoco station on the East Side. When the bounty hunter went there, the antique Ford was parked in the rear. Still for sale. Streeter asked if he could talk to its owner. The manager said that that wasn't possible, but that he himself was authorized to handle the deal. Buddy was cautious to a fault. Acting indignant, Streeter wrote his phone number on a slip of paper. He said he'd pay nine hundred cash money for the Ford, but only if he could talk directly to the guy holding title.

Three weeks went by and no response. Then, early one morning, a strapped Buddy finally called him. Streeter said his offer was still good, provided Buddy'd meet him at the station for a test ride. Reluctantly, the contractor agreed to be there at ten. At precisely three minutes to the hour, Streeter pulled his brown Buick into the driveway. As he moved toward the office, a man in sagging blue jeans and a filthy green windbreaker walked out. Streeter stopped his car but left the engine running, then grabbed the papers from the seat next to him and stuffed them inside his suede jacket.

"Mr. Streeter," Buddy said as he approached, holding out his hand. A grin was plastered across a face aged by Camel non-filters, sun, and house bourbon. "Howdy."

Streeter got out of his car and stood tall to accentuate his full six-foot-one-inch frame and all two hundred twenty pounds. He dwarfed the contractor, who now stopped a couple of feet away, his smile fading. Streeter glared into Buddy's rheumy eyes. A whiff of alcohol, perspiration, and fear came from the little guy. Looking at the mass of man in front of him and the anger in his eyes, Buddy sensed that the sale was in trouble.

"These are for you," Streeter said as he pulled out the papers and handed them over. Buddy took them, his mouth silently opening. "Compliments of Clara," Streeter continued. "And if I ever hear of you pulling a stunt like that again, I'll be disappointed. You understand? *Very* disappointed. I'm sure you don't want that."

Keeping his eyes fixed on the smaller man, Streeter got back into his car. When he stopped at the end of the driveway, he glanced in his rearview mirror. Buddy was frozen in the same spot, his mouth still open, staring at the garnishment order in his hand. He stood there like that for a long time after the Buick left.

As Streeter drove back to the renovated church he shared with Frank, his anger cooled. By the time he walked into the first-floor office, he was almost cheerful. That feeling didn't last. On the desktop was a note on a yellow legal pad. It read: "Street, Carol Irwin called. I gather someone's trying to kill her. She'd like you to discourage him from doing that. If you get a chance, give her a holler. F."

2

At first it reminded her of a small, fuzzy hand moving under its own power. It had a certain choppy grace. Carol almost laughed, but instead she let out a nervous snort. This was one huge tarantula. She'd never thought she'd see one up this close. Being a tax lawyer, why would she? Carefully, she looked at the spider while holding the jar up to the light. Its hair seemed so soft. Touchable. Suddenly it jerked, rolled itself into the shape of a cue ball, and turned away from her. Indifferent or maybe just trying to hide. Carol put the jar down and stepped back from her desk. Slowly, she brushed her hands together like they were sticky.

Between the note now in her briefcase—an idiotic poem, actually—and the tarantula, the message seemed obvious. That being she was a dead woman. The spider wouldn't get her. It wasn't meant to. But the man who presumably sent it would. He being Kevin Swallow. And he'd take his own sweet time doing it.

Early that morning, Carol collected the spider and the poem, and called the police. The two uniforms took forever getting to her apartment in central Denver. Typical, she thought as they strutted through her cluttered home, frowning. Judging. Lingering over the full ashtrays, the overflowing clothes hamper, and the unmade bed. Dirty dishes stacked nervously in the sink. All the while subtly scoping an aloof and chain-smoking Carol Irwin. They tried to be cool, but she made them right away. Then she spent an hour answering their questions. The young officer with thinning blond hair and a closely trimmed beard came on as particularly concerned.

"Maybe we could get together for coffee sometime," he told her just before they left. "We could go over your case and discuss the best way to approach it." He tried to hedge his move by sounding official. Clearing his throat, he ran an unsteady hand over his receding hairline. "Tactical-wise, that is."

"Tactical-wise, huh?" Carol studied him. "How old are you, Peaches?"

"Twenty-seven." He now tried to sound loose but could only manage shaky. "And my name's Jeff." As an afterthought he added, "Barrows."

"Twenty-seven. That makes you what? About nineteen in actual guy years. Maturity-wise, that is. Call me when you make captain." Carol disliked all cops, regardless of rank. Still, he looked so disappointed she added in a softer tone, "Look, Jeff Barrows, I'm involved with someone. Don't take it personal."

When they left, she called and gave her message to Frank. Streeter got back to her just before noon and they agreed to meet at three. Carol had been engaged to him almost seven years ago and they were still friends. Or, rather, they became friends after the breakup. Their separation was brutal, accusatory, and tear-drenched. The tears and accusations were hers, but neither of them had behaved well. All that was history now. Not that they were close. More like the exchange-discount-birthday-cards-and-stilted-phone-calls, have-dinner-twice-a-year kind of friends.

Driving to her office, Streeter was skeptical. When she'd asked him if he'd do a job for her, the stutter of crying burst through the receiver like gunfire. Carol's tears. They always got to him.

She wept unlike anyone he'd ever known, seemingly on command. "I swear, that woman cries at card tricks," Streeter had once told Frank. "I've never seen so much liquid coming from one little person."

Could he work for her? They'd done all right in the old days, though he was never impressed with her legal skills. Because Colorado has no licensing for PIs, Carol used the ex–football player as an investigator back when she was still practicing criminal law. He'd hunt down witnesses or do interviews where there might be trouble. Just the intensity in his deep-brown eyes and the bulk of his shoulders and forearms kept people from getting out of line. Not that he'd ever hurt anyone unnecessarily. Still, Streeter had plenty of backbone. You couldn't deal with the kind of punks he routinely handled and not make smoke once in a while.

"I'm glad you made it," she said, showing him into her office located in a so-called Denver Square: a large two-story turn-of-the-century house. It was about four blocks east of the state capitol. "I might have sounded unhinged on the phone, but cut me a little slack, okay? It's not every day someone threatens to kill me."

Streeter knew that Carol was a woman of intense feelings and random mood swings. Her being "unhinged" under these circumstances was no surprise. All he said was "Let's hope not." They gave each other a perfunctory hug. Her perfume hit him in a soft, warm wave. It was a new brand for Carol and he couldn't quite place it.

He sat down across the desk from her. Though he hadn't visited the office in years, it was as he remembered. Messy places never seem to change. It reminded him of a dorm room for law students cramming for finals. There was one window, partially blocked by thick accordion file folders on the sill. Files also lined the floor along a wall. Stacks of legal papers competed for space with an ashtray and half-full Diet Pepsi cans on the desk. The credenza behind her was crammed with manila folders, office supplies, Styrofoam coffee cups, and books.

Carol herself was a sharp contrast to the chaos around her. She was dressed in an elegant white silk blouse with a short black skirt, and black nylons and pumps. Only bloodshot eyes and nervous hands revealed any stress. Just like her to stay gorgeous no matter how much her insides twitched. She had long chestnut hair, streaked handsomely with gray. Those few strands were the only signs of approaching middle age. Her eyes were dark brown and her lashes, thanks to a plastic surgeon she'd once dated, were a permanent, thick black. Although educated and professional, Carol looked more like a sultry cocktail waitress. She was pushing thirty-seven and shapely by virtue of good genes, not a healthy life-style. There was a subtle, smoky sexiness about her. The only imperfection was the scar from a deep cut on her left hand, which she tended to keep down at her side.

She had cold, cynical street smarts after years of representing crazies and thugs in a criminal-justice system whose treatment of her ranged from condescending to flirty to pissed. Still, there was a frail bitterness just below her surface. Streeter had seen it often. Unappealing, it could quickly and inexplicably erupt into rage.

"Are you still playing Trivial Pursuit?" she asked, referring to one of his hobbies. Her voice sounded snotty and she immediately regretted it.

"You're still playing lawyer," he shot back.

They were both quiet for a moment. Carol spoke first. "Truce. I didn't mean to say it like that. Really. This threat has me pretty wired. Let's start over, okay?"

He nodded. "Someone wants to kill you? Just relax and take it from the top. Who, what, when, where, why. Tell me everything."

Carol grabbed a cigarette from a crumpled pack of Merit

100's on her desk and lit it. She sat back and drew the smoke into her lungs like it was pure oxygen. When she exhaled, she leaned forward. "I'm pretty sure I know the who. A killer I represented five, six years ago. Kevin Swallow. I know for a fact he's murdered several people over the years. I represented him on a double homicide. He was convicted but he got out of prison on a technicality. He blames me for having to go there in the first place and now he wants revenge. That's the why."

"How do you know all that?"

"I talked to another client of mine who was in prison with Kevin down in Cañon City. Evidently he told the client about his plans some time ago. He knew it would get back to me. Half the fun for Kevin is my worrying about it before he strikes."

Streeter nodded and adjusted himself in his seat. "How'd he threaten you?"

"He left a note and a calling card. That crazy bastard put this in my mailbox." She reached into a side desk drawer and pulled out the jar with the tarantula. "He's always been a freak for creepy animals like snakes and lizards."

Streeter held the jar up near his face. "It's called a rose-hair tarantula. They're not very poisonous, but I bet it got your attention." He set the spider on her desk.

"I'm impressed. All that reading you do pays off." She nodded. "It sure did get my attention. There was a note, too. A stupid poem. He really means business, Street."

"What went wrong with his case?"

"He thinks I blew it for him. See, he was charged with two homicides for a car bomb he put in a Mercedes belonging to a local orthopedic surgeon. Dr. Theodore Mallory. Teddy Mallory. It was big news back in '90."

"I read about it. Some kind of domestic battle, wasn't it?"

"That's the one. The doctor's wife hired Kevin to take Teddy out of the game. He was about to file for divorce and leave her flat broke. She didn't care much for that. Unfortunately for her, she told Kevin she didn't want to hear any of the details. When he planted the bomb he didn't know she'd be in the car with the good doctor that day. Two counts of murder one. He might've gotten away with it except that a neighbor saw him screwing around with the car and followed Kevin to where he was parked. The old man got a license-plate number. One thing led to another and eventually he made Kevin in a lineup.

"I got the case on a court appointment. Amazingly, Swallow had no prior felony convictions—arrests but no convictions—so he could take the stand. Juries hate it when a defendant doesn't testify. The only reason you don't let a client take the stand is prior felonies. And the only way the DA can introduce them is to impeach a defendant once he testifies. Juries hate defendants with priors even more than they hate ones who don't testify. But in the end, Kevin didn't take the stand. At least not in the second trial."

"Second trial?"

"Yes. The judge separated the cases into two trials. Kevin took the stand in the first one but he was found guilty. Now he had a felony conviction. I appealed, but while we were waiting, the second trial started. If Kevin testified in that trial, the first conviction would get in, so I kept him off. He was found guilty again. Then it got weird. He received life for the second murder. Later, the first conviction was overturned. Then Kevin got a new lawyer, who appealed the second conviction due to incompetent representation. The incompetency came from my not letting him take the stand. It was a good decision at the time, but when the court overturned, technically Kevin had no priors. He could've testified. My not letting him was grounds for a new trial. By then the old neighbor had died and the deputy DA was crippled in a car accident near Aspen. Both counts went down the tubes and now Kevin's free with no felonies on his sheet."

"So you really did the right thing and his new lawyer twisted it into a technicality to spring him." Streeter shook his head. "Swallow can't blame you for that. Hell, he should thank you. You gave him grounds for the appeal that got him out."

"That's one way to look at it," Carol said. "But Kevin didn't like going to prison. All he thought about was revenge on anyone he blamed for putting him there. He's a sadistic, cold-blooded killer, and if he wants to get you, nothing'll stop him. *Nothing.*"

"He's that tough?"

"He's that resourceful. Killing from a distance is his specialty. Like that Mallory car bomb. 'I got a long reach when it comes to that kind of shit,' is how he put it to me. Inarticulate but effective. He's a wizard with booby traps and planting bombs."

Streeter considered that while Carol smoked in silence. "So police protection might not be too helpful," he said. "That's why you wanted to see me?"

"It is indeed." She put out her cigarette and studied him. She'd always liked the way he carried himself. Streeter was forty-three, but looked to be in his mid-thirties. He slouched, but in a way that made him seem loose and confident. His hair was thick and brown, and he wore it long and straight back with short sideburns. The ends fell neatly a couple of inches over his shirt collar. His cheekbones were pronounced and high, his skin was tan. She'd always thought their children would have been exotic. He also had endless sources and more street connections than most cops. "That's exactly why," she continued. "I'd like you to find this nut case. The cops will keep an eye on me, and I think we have a little time before he makes good on his threat."

"What makes you say that?"

Carol reached to her briefcase on the floor and pulled out a folded white paper. "This poem. Kevin likes thinking he's clever." She tossed the paper across her desk.

Streeter picked up the paper and read:

To err may be human but to forgive is absurd,
You erred by a damned mile,
And the jury got the last word,
The others on the list will pay with their lives first,
While you watch, pondering your fate,
And end up paying—in death—the worst.

"If he kills as well as he writes, you're safe," he said. He slid the paper back at her. "It's like a depraved Burma Shave ad. Who're the others on the list?"

"I guess he's referring to the people who worked on his case. My investigators: Steve Gagliano and Brian Cullen. The deputy DA's not worth the effort anymore, but the cop who arrested him is. His name's Cleveland Watts and he's a chauvinistic slob. He's semiretired and dabbles at being a private eye. The police are calling everyone who had anything to do with the case and warning them."

"So he's made up a hit list and you're last. Why do you get to wait?"

"Like I said, knowing Kevin, he wants me to suffer for a while."

"That part could be bogus to make you feel safe. He could come after you first."

"I doubt it. Kevin has a lot of faith in his abilities and he's always been up front with me. Generally, he's a pathological liar. Hell, in the Mallory case the cops talked him into taking a polygraph and he actually flunked his own name. Can you believe that? They asked if he was Kevin James Swallow and he said 'Yeah.' The needle showed he was lying. He just looked at the operator and said, 'Well, who the hell do you want me to be?' In some ways, Kevin doesn't even know what reality is, but he was honest with me. I think he wants to impress me with how proficient he is."

"Proficient at killing? A Mark Chapman–Jodie Foster situation with a new twist."

"Sort of. He wants to let me know that he still has that long reach."

"Do you have any idea where he might be? Any relatives? Friends? Job prospects?" Streeter stood up.

"Friends? I doubt if he has any. No relatives that I know of, either, and he's not in the job market. At least not for the kind of job you read about in the classifieds." She bent over again and pulled a file folder from her briefcase. Then she stood up and handed it to him. "Not much, but that's all that I have on Kevin. It's old, from his trial. And he wasn't paroled, so he's not required to stay in touch with the state."

Streeter leafed through the file. "I'll see what I can find out." Then he glanced back at Carol. "You might consider getting out of town for a while, just to be safe."

"Maybe. Eventually. But I want to stick around for now." She pulled a check from her top drawer and handed it to him. It was for three thousand dollars. "This should get you started. For your time and expenses. Let me know if you need more."

"Okay. How recent is this picture?" he asked as he looked at the small mug shot from the file. A deep frown distorted Kevin's features.

"It's from when he was first booked into jail. He used to be quite handsome, but who knows how much he changed in prison? That's the only picture anyone has."

With her standing next to him, Streeter again could smell her new perfume. It came to him: Calvin Klein's Obsession. Looking at her now, he felt protective. Where women were concerned, Streeter always had a strong streak of chivalry. "Carol, I know we've had a tortured history together. Our breakup wasn't easy on either of us. But I'd hate to see anything bad happen to you."

"I was hoping you'd feel that way, Street. Keep me posted."

3

Cleveland Watts was a man of routines so stern, he made the Third Reich seem laid back and goosy. At 7:45 A.M. each weekday he walked into his sparse PI office. He'd worked there the past two years with all the clock-watching rigidity of a retired public employee on a solid pension. Four hours of paper shuffling and phone calls and it was time for lunch. Then he'd hit the streets for an afternoon of "field work." At five o'clock he'd head over to Washington Park for a stroll. Finally, at six straight up, he'd go home for dinner. His weekends shook loose a little, but not much.

Even his lunch habits were consistent. Monday was Chinese food. Tuesdays and Thursdays, he brown-bagged it. Every Wednesday, he'd meet his brother for Italian. But Fridays were his favorite. That's when he'd order ribs delivered from a place on South Colorado Boulevard near his office. His wife and his doctor had both told him to change his fatty Friday habit. Nearly old enough for retirement, Cleveland was seventy pounds overweight. "I'm not fat, I'm just eight inches short for my weight," he'd tell his wife. Funny guy, that Cleveland. He was subject to heart palpitations that squirmed like baby rats in his chest. But he dearly loved his ribs and he'd rather take a beating than give them up. He figured he earned that greasy slab of beef and sauce. If they wanted to take it away from him they'd have to pry it from his cold, dead hands.

Kevin Swallow couldn't believe it. Cleveland's routines made Kevin's job so easy he almost felt embarrassed. "For chrissakes," he told Gina Gallo on Thursday night. "This makes washing the car look like work for the space program. I've never seen anything like him. Bet the man even pisses on schedule."

"You shouldn't complain," Gina responded, looking up from the toenail she was coating heavily with plum polish. "It's not like you lose credit if it ain't a big hassle. You just want this guy to go down. Who cares how easy it is to do him?"

Kevin nodded. "But this is going to be such a snap it doesn't hardly seem fair."

She scrunched her face into a pained half-smile, half-frown. It was her way of indicating astonishment. "Well, come on, Kev. This one really ain't hardly fair when you think about it. We didn't even send the poor guy no poems warning him."

The "this one" she referred to would take place the next day. Gina would enter The Bayou Rib Shack at eleven-thirty. She'd tell the counterman that, rather than them delivering, Cleveland had asked her to pick up the ribs, seeing as how she was headed over to his office. Then she'd give him a big tip so he wouldn't call Watts to verify. Once she got back at the car, Kevin would put several grams of belladonna powder in the extra sauce Watts so loved. He chose the toxic dust in deference to his own drug days, when he'd take the psychedelic to hallucinate. Even in much smaller amounts and with his stomach pumped, Kevin had almost died of an overdose.

"Good old belladonna," he told Gina that Thursday night. "Might as well give the old fart a little thrill before he checks out. This could finally loosen him up some. Course, belladonna won't fool anyone—it's easy to trace. But I want people to know it's murder. That way, the rest of those jerks we're after'll have something to think about."

Gina just smacked a huge gum bubble, gave him her normal, barren stare, and shrugged. "Whatever you think's best, you bad boy. I just want to get these people taken care of." With that she turned her attention back to her toenails. Fake gold bracelets clanked like bar dice on her wrists as she worked. "Just make sure you don't wear anything too stupid. Know what I mean, honey? Wear that blue workshirt and some jeans. Promise me."

Kevin glared at her. "I promise," he said, rolling his eyes with the forced drama of a child. He hated it when she talked down to him about clothes. It wasn't as if she was walking the fashion runways of Europe. He'd met Gina shortly before Christmas, half a year after he got out of prison. It wasn't her clothes that attracted him. They'd met in the bar she worked at just outside of Evergreen, about thirty miles west of Denver. Gina lived nearby in a house her mother had left her and she only dated dysfunctional misfits, ex-cons, and other pissed-off losers. Those were the only men who, as she put it to a girlfriend, "make me twitch, if you follow my thoughts."

No, it wasn't her clothes that had attracted Kevin. Gina had three strong selling points.

First, her attitude. Although noticeably flighty in the old brain department, she had a burning anger that made up for it. She let him know their first night that there was little in life she considered morally repugnant or too vicious. And she jumped at the chance to help him get revenge.

"Count me in, Big Balls," she moaned, breathing gin fumes savagely into his ear as they lay in her bed. "You got yourself one flat-out rebel-woman ass-kicker here. No one's safe from us. You just count me in, sir."

In more sober moments since then, Gina had waffled a bit. But Kevin kept her in line by convincing her that their targets deserved what they were getting and by hinting at marriage. That and an occasional threat of violence.

The second thing he liked was Gina's setup. Money in the bank and a secluded house made her perfect. The place was one of the few pure ranch styles in that part of Evergreen. If it were any more sparse and rectangular, it'd be on wheels. Gina wasn't big on interior decorating, either. The entire inside was done in blocky, yard-sale Mediterranean furniture, swag lamps, and Formica. It had all the sad, tired charm of an AA clubhouse. But Gina kept it neat and she was one hell of a cook.

Finally, there was her looks. She had jet-black hair and a dark, dangerous face. Too round and flat to be called pretty, but, with enough makeup and her oversized lips, Gina had a raw appeal. Although only thirty, she was aged from partying and her body was soft from inactivity. But Kevin enjoyed her sizzle, and he knew he'd never fall for her. Another love affair was not in his plans.

"Good," she now said of his promise. Gina knew that if he was left on his own, Kevin might dress loud enough to draw attention. Not that he wasn't an incredibly attractive man. That he was. Women always noticed Kevin. True, his face had a square, Midwestern vacuousness, but there was a tenacity and ruggedness about him. He always looked like he was on the verge of uttering an insult, an expression Gina found irresistible. Steel-blue eyes, dirty-blond hair and beard, and a thick neck added to his ominous appeal. "We don't need any busybodies from this old guy's office building identifying you because of some weird stuff you pulled out of your closet," Gina concluded, again looking up from her toes, and smiling patiently.

Kevin was melted into the couch across from her. A TV remote control dangled from one hand, a bottle of Dr Pepper was clutched in the other. Because of a spectacularly nervous stomach, he'd vomit like a deranged pig if he had so much as one beer. "No, we don't," was all he said as he turned his attention back to *Friends*.

When they got to the Rib Shack the next morning, Kevin waited out back while Gina went in. She handed the counterman a twenty to cover an $11.84 tab. Once back in the car, she gave the food to Kevin. He sprinkled the dark-purple powder over the sauce and on the ribs. It blended in with the deep, brownish-red goo of the sauce. He'd decided to take the order to Watts himself. Kevin had added forty pounds of prison muscle and a ZZ Top mustache and beard since his trial. His hair was much longer, and after corrective eye surgery in Cañon City, he'd shed his glasses. Looking so drastically different, he was sure that no one he'd met before prison would recognize him. Making this delivery would prove that theory.

Watts paid little attention to Kevin. Instead, the old man focused on the invoice and frowned, as he did every Friday. Then he pulled out a ten-dollar bill and three ones, also as he did every Friday. Cleveland Watts never tipped more than 10 percent in his entire life. "Keep it," he told the new deliveryman. Then, pulling food from the steaming bag, "Is there plenty of extra sauce, like I asked for?"

"Plenty," Kevin said without enthusiasm as he inspected the tip. He looked down at the blubbery detective and snarled, "Enjoy."

When he was alone, Cleveland poured the sauce over his huge slab and dived in. He ate furiously, without interruption, and was done by twelve-twenty. As he went down the hall to the bathroom, he noticed a bitter aftertaste that he couldn't recall from previous weeks. He assumed his system was just reacting angrily to his eating so fast. But later that afternoon, as he drove to Washington Park, Cleveland kept blinking. His eyesight was blurred, his mouth and skin felt dry. By the time he parked and started walking around the pond at the north end, he could feel his heart pounding and he was becoming disoriented. He stopped at a wooden bench and sat down. His heart was racing by now and he could barely see. Several ducks on the ground near him fluttered their wings, but he didn't notice. Everything seemed distant and dreamy. Soon his heart was pounding audibly and he thought his chest would explode. Then he slumped forward and fell off the bench. He hit the ground, stone dead, before anything blew up.

4

"Kevin's not screwing around, Street." Carol's voice rose into the phone. "He killed that ex-cop I told you about. Not that Watts' dying did any major damage to humanity as a whole—the guy was a jerk. But he didn't deserve this."

Streeter frowned. "When did it happen?"

There was a pause. Carol took a deep breath. "Yesterday, Friday afternoon at about six. It's been on the news. They found the body in Washington Park. I talked to someone I know in the coroner's office this morning and he said that at first it looked like a heart attack. But now they're pretty sure it was a toxin. They don't know what kind. Not that it really concerns me. Or Watts, for that matter."

"Poison. I wonder how Swallow got to him?"

"They're not sure. It had to be something he ate. It'll take a while to sort it all out."

"How you holding up?"

Another pause, then, "I'll manage."

"Are you alone?"

"The police sent a uniformed officer to my apartment at about ten. We're at my office now. Until they figure this thing out, they'll have someone stay with me day and night. Let's hope it doesn't take too long." She was quiet for a few seconds. "I don't mean to hound you, but have you had any luck in your search yet?"

"I've got feelers out there, but so far nothing. Look, I know this is very upsetting, Carol, but try to be patient. You've got police protection now."

"Big deal."

The bounty hunter rolled his eyes and sat back. He could picture Carol: half terrified, half snarly. "It's not perfect, but the police are better than nothing. At least it'll slow Kevin down and make him think. Maybe he'll get cold feet."

Streeter was in his partner's office in the church he and Frank jointly owned and had converted into two living units and a couple of businesses. He'd been home all morning and was about to go grocery-shopping. From down the hall, he could hear the front door opening and shutting. Must be the noon karate class letting out. Streeter lived in the huge upstairs loft, and Frank's office and apartment shared the first floor with a feminist self-defense school called the Womyn's Workout Space.

"From what you told me the other day, I thought we had time," he continued. "I also wondered if this clown was serious. Looks like he answered that last one for me. From now on, Carol, finding Swallow gets my full attention. Work's a little slow anyhow, and I've got a few ideas on where to look."

"Good." She sounded calmer. "We shouldn't take anything for granted. He may have me planned for last, but I don't want to take chances."

"Me either. Listen, I'll call around and see what I can find out." Streeter stood up and arched his back as he spoke. "If I hear anything, I'll let you know."

"Okay. I'll be in the office until about five and tonight I'll just be at home."

"You sure you're all right?"

Yet another pause. It sounded like she had her hand over the receiver and was talking to someone. Finally, "Yes, I'll manage. The cop they sent seems to know what he's doing, which is more than I can say for most of them."

Streeter tried to imagine what it would be like to guard Carol hour after hour. "Be kind to the man. He's just trying to help."

After he hung up, he was too preoccupied to go shopping. He walked outside. Autumn would begin the next day but it felt hot as midsummer. To the southwest about a dozen blocks, the base-ball stadium, Coors Field, sat empty. The Rockies, in the last week of the regular season, were out of town. Streeter flashed on Watts. His death meant that Carol's interpretation of the poem was fairly accurate. It also meant he had to act. He walked back to the office, picked up the phone, and punched in Linda Parnell's number. He'd first met her two weeks earlier, when he was working a traffic-accident case. The bounty hunter had gone to a station house in North Denver to interview the investigating officer. But he was soon distracted by the woman in a gray skirt talking to a female cop and drinking coffee at the front counter. Linda looked to be in her early thirties, five feet eight inches tall, and slim. Her hair, long but in a work bun, was the color of black silk, and she wore black-rimmed glasses. On her they looked terrific, fronting eyes a shade lighter than her hair. Her smile could melt a Dove Bar.

When he finished his interview he approached her. Watching the female cop walk away, he made an inane crack about being "a sucker for a woman in a uniform." Linda looked him up and down and said, "The lady who lives next door to me works at the Wendy's in Glendale. Dynamite uniform, Wendy's. I'll get her phone number for you."

Streeter grinned. "That *was* a pretty lame opening line. You must hear things like that about ten times a day."

"About that." Linda's face softened with a hint of a smile. Not actually friendly, but encouraging. They talked for fifteen minutes. It turned out she was a psychologist on retainer with the DPD to counsel officers. Streeter asked if she'd meet him for a drink. Four days later, they got together at a restaurant in central Denver. After a few glasses of wine and much casual flirting, he walked her to her car. Then they sat inside of it and necked like college kids. Streeter loved the way she kissed. Before he left, she gave him her home phone number and they decided that seeing each other again was one solid idea.

"Hello," her voice now came over the receiver. She sounded formal.

"Linda? It's Streeter."

"Hi there." Her tone brightened. "What's up?"

"Well, I wanted to say hello and I also wanted to ask you a couple of questions. Sort of job-related. You mind?"

"That depends on the questions." Formality crawled back into her voice.

"I need to find out about a guy who fell over dead in Washington Park yesterday. Cleveland Watts. He's a retired cop. You know anything about that?"

"Watts. I met him once. He was on the job when I started here, five years ago. A good cop, when he wanted to be. Which wasn't nearly often enough to justify a full-time salary, from what I heard. Strictly old-school. A regular ass-kicker, particularly with people of the nonwhite variety. About as evolved as a lump of pizza dough. I had an appointment this morning with a detective and he mentioned Watts' dying. I gather he was poisoned. Why are you so interested?"

"It's a long story. Meet me for coffee later and I'll fill you in. How about The Market, down on Larimer, at three?"

The brighter tone came back. "Sure."

Larimer Square is a block-long section of ornate Denver architecture with pricy boutiques, restaurants, brew pubs, and The Market: a coffee shop and designer deli with tables spilling out onto the sidewalk. With the nice weather, Larimer was mobbed. All the tables were full when they arrived, so Streeter suggested they go next door to Josephina's restaurant for a drink. Linda had on a short denim skirt and a white T-shirt.

"So tell me, cowboy," she said as they sat at the L-shaped saloon bar nursing their beers. "Why all the interest in poor old Cleveland? Was he a friend of yours?"

"No. I never met him." Streeter took a sip from his glass and studied Linda. "It's a bizarre deal that has to do with a woman I know who was involved in a murder case that Watts worked on years ago. There's good reason to believe that the same guy who did Watts is coming after other people, including her."

"Who is she?" Linda tried not to sound too interested.

"An old girlfriend of mine. She hired me to track down the guy who may have killed Watts and threatened her."

"In case you hadn't heard, that's why we have cops. They go get the bad guys."

"I read that somewhere. She's getting police protection, but she still wants me to nose around." Linda nodded and took a sip of her beer, but said nothing. Streeter continued. "He's a killer she represented who got out of Cañon City a while back and now he's looking to nail her for screwing up his case. Kevin Swallow. Your detective friend know any details on Watts?"

She stared at him for a moment. "The way I heard it, the poison was probably in the food he got from a rib joint. Apparently, a woman came in yesterday at lunchtime and said Watts asked her to pick up the order. The cops are very interested in finding this lady. They're getting the word out about her in case anyone saw her leave the rib place. It should be on the TV news tonight."

"A woman? They have any idea who she is?"

"The rib-joint guy said she looked like either a high-end hooker or a low-end aerobics instructor." Linda paused. "You didn't know about a female accomplice?"

He shook his head. "We assumed Swallow was alone."

"This woman who hired you was an old girlfriend, huh?"

Streeter nodded with a quick grin. "Now, that's *really* a bizarre deal."

"I've got time."

"Her name's Carol Irwin. She's a lawyer who used to do criminal-defense work until she burned out. Trial pressures got to her, so now she does mostly low-key stuff like contracts and taxes. She's doing okay, I guess. We were sort of engaged."

"Oh? Where does one buy a 'sort of' engagement ring?"

"Okay, officially engaged. It didn't last long. We had one of those highly charged relationships. Neither of us behaved too well. I don't want to blame it all on her, but Carol's wound pretty tight. She's hard to deal with on a daily basis."

"How so?"

Streeter took another sip. "She's incredibly intense. Never lightens up. And she's got this thing about loyalty. You're either a hundred percent for her or a hundred percent against her. Very draining. Plus, she holds a grudge longer than the Mafia. We broke up years ago." He finished his beer.

"With your track record of—what?—four failed marriages, you hardly need another wife. What was the attraction to Carol?"

Streeter nodded to the bartender for a refill. "She's quite beautiful and has a great body. Pretty smart, too. And there was something vulnerable about her that I found appealing. She had a way of getting to me. Plus, she can be very affectionate. Very passionate . . ." His voice trailed off.

"Now we get to the real reason. Hot sex."

"Out of this world. Let's just say she was intense about everything. You mind if we change the subject?"

"Fine with me. You live around here, don't you?"

"About a mile to the north. Up in the low thirties, near Curtis Street. My partner and I fixed up an old church. We live and work out of it. Frank Dazzler, the bondsman. You may have seen the place. It's got a red neon 'Jesus Saves' sign hanging over the front door. The thing doesn't work anymore but I think it's cool. In fact, the whole place looks like a little castle. We call it Fort God."

"Interesting. You like living in a fort?"

"It feels safe. With the jerks I run into, there's nothing wrong with being fortified. Plus, the church has a colorful history and I've always liked Lower Downtown."

"Who wouldn't like LoDo? A new ballpark and all the development. This place is a riot. Art galleries, sports bars, fancy lofts. Not to mention property values through the roof."

"I suppose that's nice, but I miss the old LoDo." Streeter shrugged. "You know, those funky rat-hole bars and that lonely-warehouse, after-midnight feeling."

"You're quite the little bohemian." Linda finished her beer and nodded to the bartender for another.

"Have you and Frank been together long?"

"About ten years. I trust him with my life and the feeling's mutual. He's older than me and I think of him almost as a father." Streeter waited as the bartender set her beer down. "I met him when I was working as a bouncer at a country-music joint. He came in one night looking for someone and we got to talking. Right on the spot, he offered me a job. Working with him's been good, but sometimes I wonder."

Linda waited for him to finish the thought. Finally, she asked, "Wonder what?"

"If it's what I really want out of life. I love Frank, but there's times I look at him and ask myself if I want to end up like that. Sixty-five years old, living with some guy in an old church. Banging heads with felons and conning assholes to serve them papers. There's got to be more to life than that. I don't want to get too heavy here. It's just that lately I've been asking myself if there's a better way to live. More civilized, for starters."

"A home in the suburbs and a few kiddies? The whole nine-to-five deal?"

Streeter looked hard at her. "Let's not get carried away. I'm not that unhappy, but it's just that sometimes I wonder where I'm headed."

"You're trouble all the way around, Streeter. That history with women alone is enough reason to get me running, not to mention a midlife career crisis. The term 'heavily conflicted' comes to mind."

"So, why aren't you running?"

She smiled and stretched casually. "I'll have to think about that. We might want to get together again and explore it further."

He liked the way she moved, the way she carried herself. Confident. A sense of being in control yet still relaxed. Curious without being nosy. Even her glasses added to the effect. "Whatever you say. You're the shrink."

5

"There you are, Big Guy," Frank said as he walked into his own office Monday afternoon. Streeter was sitting behind the desk studying notes he'd just written on an envelope, concentrating so hard he seemed to be in pain. "I been down at Division Fourteen since nine o'clock with this total mother of a bond-revision hearing," Frank continued. "Four hours plus in a death struggle with the judge and those court jesters, the lawyers. On top of all that, we end up with *nada*. No revision, no nothing. I got to tell you, Streetmeister, this is one hell of a way to make a living."

Frank was bushed, sweaty, and looking forward to flopping down in the leather swivel chair he'd bought at roughly the time gas was three gallons for a buck. But that would be difficult, since the bounty hunter was already sitting there. So the bondsman lowered himself into the smaller chair across the desk. Frank's office was an uneasy blend of wood-veneer and plastic furniture coexisting with the rich mahogany built-ins and thick, flowered carpeting appropriate to a rectory. It was bright thanks to an enormous, arched stained-glass window on the west wall. By late afternoon it had a rainbow feel to it as the sun poured through the deep purples, reds, and yellows.

Streeter kept studying the envelope. Finally, he glanced up.

"You look tired, Frank." His mind was still focused on the conversation he'd just had with Carol Irwin. "Where've you been?"

Dazzler stared across the desk and just muttered, "Shopping," while waving his hand feebly in that direction. "Anything new on Irwin's case?"

Streeter looked hard at him. Frank was a decorated Korean War veteran and an ex–sheriff's deputy of twenty years. At first glance he seemed as rumpled and tired as the wilted tan linen suits he favored. But he had those lively blue eyes and a quick smile. His hair was still surprisingly dark. It was thinning only slightly and he kept it long and neatly combed back.

"It's getting more crazy, Frank. Watts is killed last Friday and then Carol gets threatened again. Swallow left a dead cat this time. You believe that?"

"A dead what?" Frank shifted forward. "The hell you talking about?"

"Somehow, yesterday, he got into Carol's office and left her another one of his dopey poems. She read it to me over the phone." He glanced down at the envelope. " 'One down, how many more to go? Just enjoy the wait.' To make his point he left a dead cat, cut down the middle. First that spider and now this. Personally, I've never been a very big fan of felines, but come on."

"How'd he get into her place?"

"Picked the lock. It's one of those Denver Squares up on Capitol Hill. East of all the government buildings. She doesn't have an alarm system in yet. Smart move in that neighborhood, but, then, Carol never was much for details."

"What the hell's his problem," Frank said slowly, "he can't just kill people? He has to make a production out of it? Bet Irwin's about ready to blow through the ceiling. You got any idea where Swallow is?"

"I've been talking to people all weekend. Called or visited

everyone who might know about an ex-con. Bartenders all up and down Colfax and Broadway. Former cons, bondsmen, pawn-shop guys, probation people. Hell, I went out Saturday night and talked to most of the hookers we've written up. Showed his mug shot, too. Even been spreading Carol's money around. I told everyone that he's traveling with a woman, too. This morning I talked to our computer friend Stevey down in Castle Rock and had him do a trace. Guys like Swallow don't take out loans or set up any bank accounts, but why not give it a try? All that, and nothing." Streeter built up momentum and volume as he talked. "I'm starting to wonder if he's even in Denver. Maybe he's not the one we're after. Maybe someone else is pulling this crap and trying to make Swallow look like the man. He should have been spotted by now. Not that I'm quitting. This guy's got to turn up eventually."

Frank watched him closely as he spoke. "The cops are with her, Big Guy. You might wanna consider not giving it such a high priority. Working this close with Carol Irwin and all. We don't want another Story Moffatt situation here, do we? By the way, are you still seeing that woman?"

The bounty hunter flashed a grin. Story was a former client whose case had led to several people dying as well as to a decent financial payoff. It also resulted in him and Story having a passionate if choppy fling together. "Naw, we broke up."

"It was a mutual decision, I trust."

"Right." Streeter's head pulled back slightly. "We mutually decided she never wanted to see me again. Don't worry, Carol's different. All business. Starting up with her romantically again is not in the cards. But I have to admit, when I see her, I still get a little jazzed. Maybe I'll always have a blind spot where she's concerned. Maybe I can't be totally objective. You know me and women. Carol and I had some hot times back in the old days and she's one great-looking lady." He thought for a moment. "Actually, I'm surprised at how well she's holding up. A guy breaks into her office, leaves a dead cat, and still she doesn't fall apart. The old Carol would have gone Oklahoma City on us."

"Yeah, that's about her style, as I recall," Frank said. "Totally unglued at the drop of a hat. Not that you never gave her any good reasons to be upset."

Streeter thought about how close he'd come to marrying Carol. That near miss alone was reason enough to cut down his drinking, which he did after their split. He'd cheated on her. Something he'd never done before. Or since. It was a quick, joyless roll with her best friend. He felt guilty for months afterward, and not just because she found out about it. Carol was furious, of course. But to his surprise, she eventually mellowed and even initiated a friendship.

"That wasn't my finest hour," he admitted. "I still cringe when I think about it. We had our problems, but sliding around like that was no way to deal with it. Especially when I'd said I'd be monogamous."

"You were monogamous, Street. Just that you weren't fanatical about it."

"There's an unusual spin. Anyhow, I've met someone I'm interested in."

"Who's that?" Frank perked up.

"A lady shrink named Linda Parnell. She works with the police, among others."

"What's she like?"

"I'm not sure yet, but she can take care of herself. Thirty-three, bright, funny, nice-looking. All the right curves, as they used to say in your day. But a little distant. Linda has a way of studying people like she's always doing an evaluation. It can be unsettling. The other day, we met to talk about Watts and I ended up babbling about my problems. She seems to have a good approach to work, though. It's important to her, but she's got a life outside of it. Sort of the Anti-Carol in that regard."

"Just keep your head screwed on this time, okay?" Frank looked concerned. "Take it slow and easy."

"We haven't done anything except neck in her car. Very passionate, and she seems to like me. But don't worry. I've got a feeling I'll be too busy with Swallow to be seeing much of Linda for a while."

6

As he approached Denver from Greeley, to the north, Steve Gagliano was in a foul mood. He saw the infamous "Brown Cloud," Denver's shroud of sooty air, draped low around the skyline. That didn't help. Then he focused on where he was going. Denargo Market. It's an old industrial-warehouse area festering under the I-25 viaducts on the near West Side. A client's receptionist had called him that morning and told him to meet the lawyer on Huron Street, at a small furniture factory next to an abandoned Shell station.

"Mr. Hillebrandt would like you there by two o'clock," she had told the private investigator. "He has two new cases for you and one of the clients works in that building. The three of you should meet there."

"Shee-it," Steve muttered under his breath. He hated that part of town. It was practically impossible to find street addresses there. Only a small fraction of Steve's clients were in Denver, since he had moved to Greeley a few years earlier. But even before the move he had a hard time finding his way around downtown in general, much less a screwed-up area like Denargo Market. Still, Hillebrandt was an all-too-rare quick-pay client. Although he grumbled, Steve knew he'd make the trip.

"One case, an agg assault, took place in that furniture factory, and he wants to walk you through it with the client," the receptionist had explained with obvious irritation. "Will there be any problem with that or do you want me to tell Mr. Hillebrandt you're busy and he might wanna find another investigator?"

"Let me talk to him." Steve didn't recognize her voice. Probably a new hire, he thought. Almost like she was reading from a script. Despite her attitude, she sounded young and sexy. Possibly Hispanic. He'd have to get the lowdown on her from Hillebrandt.

"I'm afraid that's impossible," she responded. "He'll be in Denver District Court until just about two. But he should be calling in for messages. If he's a couple of minutes late, don't worry. Just go to the door nearest to the gas station and walk in. The client'll be working and he probably won't hear you knock. His name is Dwayne Carter and he's expecting you."

Her instructions sounded like something out of the Hardy Boys, Gagliano thought. "All right, all right. Tell Hillebrandt I'll be there. He would have to pick a hot day like this, wouldn't he, honey? So late in the year and I bet it still hits ninety. Maybe higher."

The receptionist hung up without saying another word.

When Steve saw Coors Field looming up on the left, his spirits rose. He pulled his leased Mercedes off the highway and drove past the stadium for a closer look. The Rockies' new stadium went up quickly and on budget. A far cry from the grossly extravagant Denver International Airport, which came in millions of dollars over cost and missed its initial opening date by about a year. Speaking of overbudget and out of time, Steve could use a little boost himself. Business was slow and he lived a life-style where that particular pace wasn't welcome and couldn't last long. He hoped that the cases Hillebrandt had were big ones. Maybe federal court appointments. They tended to drag on for months, if not years. His meter would run the whole time and he could easily pad out his invoices. The government. He shook his head. Nothing more than a damned slot machine that paid every time you yanked the lever.

He drove slowly past the north side of the park. Set near the middle of town, it looked like it had been there forever. The designers gave Coors Field plenty of blue-collar charm while providing state-of-the-art conveniences that customers demanded. Fans, Gagliano thought bitterly. Players and the owners both dump on them with strikes and tickets costing more than a round trip to Spain. Still they turn out, cash in hand, like zombies who get nervous if they walk ten feet without seeing a vendor.

Steve headed down 20th Street and then wound his way toward Denargo. He cursed periodically, never feeling sure of his sense of direction. When he got below freeway level, he squinted for numbers on the odd side of Huron Street. Most of the buildings didn't have visible addresses, so he looked for the boarded-up Shell station. When he saw it he pulled in and glanced at the decaying building next door.

"Shee-it," he mumbled; it was one of his favorite words. Hillebrandt's Volvo was nowhere in sight, even though it was almost twenty minutes after two. Steve got out of his car and walked to Carter's building. There was a metal door off to the side that opened almost directly into the Shell lot. Must be the one the receptionist told him to use. Even though she said don't bother knocking, he banged on the door twice out of habit. He waited a couple of minutes, standing off to the side like he'd seen cops do on television. Then let out a quick "Fuckin' Hardy Boys" under his breath.

The twelve-gauge was adjusted to hit him in the middle of his torso. It was set fairly low, for Gagliano stood only five feet five. What Kevin couldn't have anticipated when he placed the trap was that, just as Steve opened the door, an obese brown rat would run over his shoes. That caused him to jump across the threshold nearly a foot off the ground and twist to his right. The elaborate entrance ended the kill-shot possibilities, although it didn't leave Mr. Gagliano feeling any too good.

Kevin had rigged a simple trip wire from the door to the shotgun trigger. There was no trouble with the gun going off on cue, and the aim stayed true. But Gagliano came flying into the room at such a weird angle and height that the load hit mainly his upper left thigh. Close enough to his groin to leave some incredibly unromantic scars, but not so close as to change his gender.

Gagliano screamed twice before he hit the ground. The burn on his left leg was excruciating. With all his remaining strength, he crawled to his car, leaving behind a trail of blood that looked like he'd dragged a slaughtered chicken. When he got there, he phoned 911 from his cellular. Within seconds after giving his location, he passed out. The only thing his muddled mind could reason up as he slid into unconsciousness was how that new receptionist had given him the wrong directions. He'd tell Hillebrandt not to make her permanent if she was going to keep on screwing up like this. It was inexcusable, no matter how sexy her voice was.

7

Golf is truly evil, Streeter thought as he sifted through the church basement's storage area, next to his weight room. There were tools, snow tires, skis, cleaning supplies, and other stuff he seldom used. Like that bag of Spalding golf clubs. He'd bought them fifteen years ago, when he'd made a serious run at learning how to play. But within two seasons, he'd lost interest. Golf isn't like simpler games, such as bowling or volleyball. Those are for "fun." But a golf swing is a skill you must learn. If you don't, you're destined to relentless heartache and deep humiliation. You have to practice and take lessons. Streeter wasn't much for either, so he stored his clubs and only hauled them out occasionally to hit balls at the driving range. Like now, meeting Linda at Wellshire. He'd called her that morning and she said she was going to practice her short irons after work. She asked him to join her.

Wellshire, formerly a private golf course, now open to the public, is a moderately challenging course on the border between southern Denver County and Arapahoe County. Streeter met Linda in the parking lot just before five. It was cool and cloudy. He wore a white Western Michigan University sweatshirt and blue jeans, which Linda almost matched with faded jeans and a powder-blue sweatshirt. Her raven hair was in a ponytail that came to the middle of her back and she wasn't wearing glasses.

"You want to make it more fair by coming blind?" he asked as they walked to the range. "We should be about even with your glasses in the car."

She shot him a glance. "I have contacts, but I could be blindfolded and still outdrive you, Streeter. Golf is my sport and I'm really hot near the green. How about you?"

He shrugged without looking at her. "I don't put enough into the game to be hot anywhere. But I like coming out and hitting rockets once in a while. Golf courses are beautiful even if the game tortures me."

They bought a large bucket and set it between their tee mats. Thirty feet in front of them the ground dropped off into a lake, so it was hard to tell what kind of roll you'd get. Linda set her first ball off the tee, pulled out a five-iron, and took a practice cut. She was steady and smooth, with a full backswing. Head down, body quiet. Then she stepped up and knocked the ball straight, maybe a hundred thirty yards. Maximum for a five-iron. She *could* be blindfolded and outdrive him. For his part, Streeter settled on hitting three-irons off the tee. He had better control of irons than woods, and a three still gave him distance. His motion was smooth but short, with little backswing. It kept his shots straight, though not particularly long. Less chance to embarrass himself.

"Gagliano's shooting yesterday was all over the news," he noted. "But the cops aren't linking it to Watts or Swallow."

Linda looked up from her ball and shook her head. "I know. I had coffee with a Sergeant Haney today. He said all they have so far on that is Irwin's speculation. They're not even sure it was Swallow. Apparently, a lot of the cops don't think Carol's very reliable. Besides, there's no physical evidence linking Swallow to anything."

"I know, but come on. This can't be a coincidence. Why not just plaster his picture all over the front pages? Maybe they could flush him out. I'm sure Haney at least wants to talk to the man."

"He said their old mug shot of Swallow could be practically anyone." She drove another long shot, this time with a seven-iron. Then she looked at Streeter. "Don't forget, if it was Swallow who delivered the ribs, Watts looked right at him and probably didn't recognize him." Her voice hardened. "How's Irwin doing?"

Streeter bent down to put another ball on the tee. When he straightened up, he leaned on his iron. "She wasn't happy when she heard about Gagliano. I spent half the morning over at her office talking about it."

"If she's wound as tight as you said, who knows what this is doing to her? I'd keep my distance if I were you." Suddenly she smiled. "It sounds like Gagliano's lucky he's still got a unit on him. Did you hear where he was shot?"

Streeter hunched his shoulders in a shiver. "I can't even think about that." They practiced in silence for a while. "It's spooky how Swallow can get to Carol anytime he wants," he said. "Then he gets to Gagliano. The papers said that a lawyer's secretary called Steve yesterday asking him to go to that old factory. Probably the same woman who picked up Watts' ribs. I met Gagliano once. He's not too sharp."

"Or careful." She looked at his sweatshirt. "Western Michigan?"

"I went there for a couple of years, but I never finished." He glanced over the water and his voice lowered. "On a football scholarship. But there was an accident and I stopped playing." He debated whether to tell her the whole story but then decided he'd wait until he knew her better. Or until never. Letting people know that he'd killed a teammate in a drunken frat-party fight was no small matter. Only his closest friends knew about it. Streeter was a junior linebacker when he drove a huge forearm into the guy's chin, breaking his neck on the spot.

"What kind of accident?" Linda stared closely at him.

"A football-injury thing." He took a short swing and shanked the ball wildly off to the left. "Haney have any ideas where Kevin is?"

"Not really." She waited a few seconds. "What's your strategy?"

"Let the cops catch him and then take credit for it. Actually, I'm doing a lot of what they are. I must have talked to forty people in the last few days. Ones who should have spotted Swallow by now. I'll just keep nosing around and see where it takes me. Either Swallow or this mystery woman'll to screw up sooner or later. That's how these butt-heads usually get caught. The pattern's clear. Carol gets a note, then Watts is killed. Another note, then Gagliano. I just hope his next move is a note instead of an attack on her. Haney say anything else?"

"Streeter, I'm off work now. All day long, I was looking forward to seeing you and, silly me, I thought maybe you felt the same. I don't need a damned interrogation." Linda paused. "Are you really that worried about Carol?"

He shrugged. "Listen, I was looking forward to seeing you, too. Really. No more questions. By the way, Carol asked if she could move into the church for now. It's safe, and that way she'd have the cops and me looking out for her around the clock."

"Are you going to do it?" Linda now stepped back and leaned in to her club.

"Who knows?" Streeter smiled. "Would you be jealous?"

Her face flushed but she ignored the question. "I just wonder how you'd like having her around all the time. You seem like a private person, Streeter. Do you really want to get directly in the line of fire? I'd give it serious thought before you decide."

He nodded. "That I will."

They finished their bucket and Linda said she had to get going. They kissed briefly at the car, and then Streeter headed back to the church. Rush-hour traffic was picking up, so he had time to think about Carol.

"This is fucked, Street," she had told him that morning. "Kevin got past the cops already without any problem. He can get to me whenever he wants. He can get to anyone. Look at Gagliano."

Streeter made the mistake of asking what would make her feel better.

She looked hard at him for a long time and then threw him a cryptic smile, like they had a personal joke going. Stepping toward him, she lowered her voice. "I have an idea," she said in a husky, confidential tone. "If you don't like it, I'll understand. Your place is solid. Secure. Like you, Street. I'd feel protected there. Kevin doesn't know about it and I wouldn't really be around all that much. I'm usually at work or at the courthouse. I just need a place to crash at night and relax and feel safe."

Streeter focused on her eyes as she spoke. She had the most exotic dark eyes. Long and narrow. Model's eyes, world-class. Here she was talking about moving into his place, and in a tone that made it sound almost personal. "This isn't some kind of step to get us back together, is it?" he had asked her. "I mean, I'm sure it's not, but I have to be sure." Slick choice of words.

She gave him the weird smile again and just said, "What are you so afraid of? Lighten up."

It wasn't much of an answer. "I'll get back to you on it," he told her.

"If it makes your decision any easier, I've talked it over with the police in charge of my protection and they're all for it," she concluded.

Now, as he drove north, he had to admit that luring Kevin to his home turf appealed to him. *Mano a mano,* and all that kind of thing. But Carol in his home? Maybe she was different now. Not so demanding. People change. Despite her obvious anxiousness, she had a very un-Carol-like attitude. Almost composed. But what was with all that smiling and whispering? He'd have to think about it.

8

Kenny Chapel actually thanked Streeter when he slapped the handcuffs on him. He seemed to mean it, too. In all the years Streeter had been a bounty hunter, he found that bail jumpers thanked him or apologized more often than not. Still, it always surprised him.

"It's cool, man," Kenny muttered as the metal clamped around his tiny wrists. "Thanks. Really. And not too tight, man. Thanks, man."

With his palms practically touching each other in front of him just below his waist, Kenny's bare arms looked white and stringy. Almost delicate, like they belonged to a scrawny child. Only an extensive web of crude tattoos on both indicated that these were the arms of a man in his early twenties. Streeter almost felt like uncuffing the bony little guy and letting him go.

Kenny had been sitting on the floor of his teenage girlfriend's living room, focused like a heart surgeon on a plastic water pipe, when Streeter saw him through the window. He'd brought Kenny—a house burglar who favored one-stories—back to court twice before. Both times the thief was unarmed and docile. Like now, particularly after he took a few monster tokes of hash. Streeter knocked and entered. Then he brushed past the perpetually pregnant and aggressively sullen girlfriend.

Frank had taught him long ago that, when looking for bail jumpers, he should "always check the girlfriend's pad. Two things they need when they're on the run," Frank had said. "Money and poontang. They always go right for both."

The apartment smelled of smoldering tobacco and hash, combined with a flicker of soiled diapers. A baby cried from the back bedroom. Streeter went to Kenny and stood over him. The burglar looked like a kid playing with his toys on the floor.

"Time to go, son," Streeter said softly. "The judge is waiting and we don't want Frank to lose any money because of you, do we now?"

Kenny pushed several filthy strands of long, tangled hair from his eyes and looked up with an abstract smile. He didn't recognize Streeter at first. Then he saw the handcuffs and remembered where he'd seen the big man before.

"Damn," he whispered, his smile fading. He looked to his hash pipe and then back up. "Want some, man?" he asked hopefully.

Streeter said nothing but merely jingled the cuffs. Kenny nodded and got up. His scraggly girlfriend, looking like a grungy anorexic who'd swallowed a bowling ball, began to whine. "Just what the hell are we supposed to do if he goes to jail?" Wearing a T-shirt that implored one to "Party Naked," she took a long, intense puff from her cigarette. She spoke again, the words coming out in thick blasts of smoke: "What about his family? You ever think of that? Did ja?"

Streeter looked at her and then glanced around. The "living-room set" consisted of two brown beanbag chairs and a Formica coffee table. Plus a twenty-seven-inch color TV and a stereo system in the corner. There was a bright-yellow price tag dangling from the tape deck. On the walls, four aging posters of rock groups stared down defiantly. A pizza box and several empty beer cans cluttered the top of a wooden picnic table in the dining area.

"I don't think you really want to blame me for all this, lady," he responded.

"You bastard," she shrieked with a finality indicating that she'd won the debate. She turned and stomped off to the bedroom where the baby smell originated. Streeter had his back to her and was ushering Kenny out when she reappeared, holding an aluminum baseball bat. She pulled it to her right side and stepped toward the bounty hunter. Then she let out a scream and swung at his head. Because of her advanced condition and Streeter's being a foot taller, the best she could do was hit him feebly on the shoulder. But the blow startled him and he turned around to face her.

"Hell, lady," he said evenly. "Be cool."

Grunting "Bastard," she again drew the weapon back. She swung once more, but Streeter easily caught the end of the bat in his right hand. He yanked it from her and shook his head.

"Knock it off or I'll take you in, too," he said.

Kenny, in a flash of drug-induced optimism, ran out the door. He was down the stairs at the end of the outdoor walkway before Streeter realized he'd bolted. Bat in hand, he took off after the burglar. By the time he saw Chapel again, the smaller man was getting seriously winded. Kenny hurtled forward from the stairs into the parking lot. With his hands cuffed and his long hair flapping angrily from side to side, he had the stuttery waddle of a penguin. Streeter caught him well before he got to the road.

"What do you have to be such a goof for?" he asked as he

grabbed Kenny's arm. "You know you're not going anywhere. And tell that loony girlfriend of yours, if she ever pulls that crap again, she'll be joining you in a cell downtown."

Kenny looked up at him like he'd just seen him for the first time that day. "It's cool, man. Really. I mean thanks, man."

Streeter dropped the bat into his car trunk and put Kenny in the front seat, and they headed downtown. Chapel's girlfriend lived in the western suburb of Lakewood, so they had about ten miles of city driving time. "You got yourself one screwed-up life going on here, Kenny," Streeter said as he drove. "Your damn head's jammed so far up your rear end it doesn't look like it's ever coming out. I don't want to lecture you, but what the hell's going on?" He turned to look at his passenger. "Dope, kids, squalor. And you with all those felony B-and-E's. Then there's your lady. Jesus! Where'd you find her? You've got things wired so bad you may never straighten it all out."

"I hear you, man," Kenny said with pained sincerity. He shook his head sadly and looked down at his feet. "Life's a real bitch."

"That's horseshit and you know it. Life's just life. You're making it a bitch." Streeter was quiet. When he spoke again his voice was more relaxed. "I hate to see you throw it away. Anyone who can open up houses like you certainly can learn a skill. Welding, auto repair. Become a locksmith, for crying out loud. Make something out of yourself. You've sure got the smarts."

Kenny shook his head again. "I hear you, man." He sounded like he couldn't possibly agree more with what was coming his way. "I plan on getting it together. It's just that life's such a real bitch. It gets oudda hand real fast for me. Always has."

"Right! You've just got to change the way you operate. You know Frank's . . ."

"I thought you said you didn't want to lecture me," Chapel interrupted, turning to face Streeter. He sounded irritated for the first time. Frank had been his bondsman since he started crossing the line as a teenager. "It sounds like that's just what you're doing here, man. I get the picture. Okay?"

Streeter shook his head. "It's your life."

They stopped for a red light on East Colfax. Denver's skyline loomed neatly in front of them. From certain angles, it looked like a mini–New York. The light changed, and as they pulled away from the corner, Kenny spoke. "You still looking for that jerkoff Kevin Swallow?" He threw it out there without facing the driver.

Streeter couldn't hide his surprise. He shot a long glance at Kenny. "What do you know about him?"

Chapel eased down in the seat. A grin yawned across his face. With his hands still cuffed in front of him, he pulled a cigarette from his shirt pocket.

Streeter reached over with his right hand and deftly grabbed it from Kenny's mouth. "No smoking in here and I asked you a question, son. How did you find out about me and Swallow?" There wasn't a hint of patience in his voice.

Kenny sat up and looked pained again. "You promise to tell Frank that I'm still good people? I can't have that guy all pissed off at me, you know."

Streeter didn't answer right away. Then, "Kevin Swallow. Come on."

"Ramos, the fence. Edgar Ramos told me. Jesus, Streeter, lotta people heard what's going on. Everyone but the goddamned CNN. You been all over town asking about him. The cops, too." Then he answered the unasked. "No one's seen him, I know of. He don't have many friends but a lotta people know the guy. No one's seen him, and Ramos would know if they did."

Streeter stayed quiet and Kenny started to fidget.

"But it might could be that I heard something that'll help you out," the burglar finally said.

Streeter shot him another long glance. "I'm listening."

"You promise to talk to Frank for me?"

"Maybe. It depends. What did you hear?"

Kenny shrugged and shook his head. "I know this bartender. Weird guy. Makes a little book, too. Lives out in Aurora. Gino Gallo. You mighta dealt with him. Anyhow, I was having a beer one night a few weeks ago at this place he works and he's telling me about his sister. Gina. Ain't that a pisser? Brother and sister named Gina and Gino. Anyhow, Gino was talking to her earlier that day and she was bragging about her squeeze. The guy's supposed to be a regular boner who's done serious state time. Gino said she calls him Kev. No full name, but I'm thinking Kev, like in Kevin. As in Swallow. This all stuck with me because Gino musta gone on about the situation for half an hour. Jesus, the guy gets off on something, he don't shut up about it."

"Do you actually know Kevin Swallow?"

"What's the difference? Anyhow, Gina's saying Kev lives with her and they're doing all kinds of shit together. Seems Gina inherited their old lady's place out past Evergreen. Something like that. I gather Gina's some kind of con groupie that only goes out with total maniacs, which would fit Kevin's description. She says that what the two of them's doing is heavy-duty. Gino's going on about how his sister's this lost soul and how he's praying for her every couple of hours. It was like listening to a sermon." He paused. "Sort of like listening to you."

Streeter ignored the crack. "Where does Gino work?"

"He don't anymore. Got fired."

"Do you know where he lives?"

"Out in Aurora. He has a place on Horse Turd Lane or one of them screwy street names they got out there."

"What makes you think he's leveling with you?"

"Why would he lie? To impress me?" Then, in a rare moment of candid self-reflection, Kenny added, "Never no one tries to impress me. That oughta be obvious." He looked straight ahead again. "Will you smooth things out with Frank?"

Streeter didn't answer at first. Finally, "I'll talk to him when I get back tonight."

After he got Kenny situated at the jail, Streeter headed home. Frank had dozed off at his desk, and was leaning back with his mouth wide open when Streeter walked into the office. He sat across from the bondsman, thinking about what Kenny had said. It made sense, Kevin living in the mountains. No wonder he hadn't been spotted in town. Gallo might be a coconut, but what he told Chapel added up. Suddenly, Frank made a loud, stuttered snore. He was silent for a second and then he lunged awake. When he saw Streeter he jolted forward in his chair.

"Godawmighty," he sputtered. "The hell you doing, Street? Watching me sleep? That's pretty weird." He frowned. "You get that little bum Chapel taken care of?"

"Yeah. I just got back here a couple minutes ago. Do you know anyone named Gino Gallo? A bookie, probably lives in Aurora."

Frank rolled his head carefully to each side and then stretched his arms out, yawning. "The name sounds familiar but I can't place it. What about him?"

Streeter told him Chapel's story. "Kenny's worried you're mad at him and won't write him up now. I'm supposed to put in a good word. Consider that done."

The bondsman waved his right hand casually. "I'm not so mad that I won't get over it. You gonna go visit Gallo?"

Streeter nodded. "First thing tomorrow."

"It's probably all crap, coming from Kenny. Even if it's not, it doesn't mean this Kev is necessarily Swallow."

"True, but what else do I have to go on? I'm glad for any lead."

Frank nodded. "That reminds me." He got up from his chair, moving stiffly. "You got a message on the voice mail from Irwin. You might want to have a listen."

Streeter frowned, reached across the desktop, and grabbed the phone. He punched in the numbers and waited. Carol's voice sounded agitated and scared.

"Street, call me as soon as you can. Kevin's starting to make phone calls to me. Three of them, two late last night and one this morning. All at my home. He says hello and dead air. Then he hangs up. I've got to get out of here. Hope I can move into the church. Let me know the minute you decide. If I can't go to your place, I'll get a motel room. Please call."

Fort God was safer than any motel, and Streeter felt saddened by the fear in her voice. Turning to Frank, he said, "Looks like we're getting a houseguest."

Frank frowned. "You sure about this? Carol can be a major pain."

"That's true. And, no, I'm not totally sure. But Swallow's going tear her down completely if he keeps this up. She won't be that much trouble and, besides, we'll be getting free police protection. You'd want someone to do it for you."

"I would at that. It's your call."

"It won't be for long. Someone'll get to Swallow soon, and if he tries anything here we'll get him for sure. Look, if you're really against it, I'll say no."

Frank shook his head and made a sour face. "Don't worry about it. I wouldn't mind taking a shot at this asshole myself. Like I said, it's your call."

"Then she moves. It's all for the best." Streeter almost sounded convinced.

9

Brian Cullen leaned back in his chair and shook his head. "It was just last week the cops told me Swallow's after my ass, but I'm wondering what Laurie'll make of it," he told his partner, Terry

Blue Nathan. "Hell, she could see it as another chance to get back at me. Might even try something on her own. To say the least, she wouldn't shed any tears if I go down. Laurie's one handsome, bright lady, but, hell, no woman's worth getting exploded over. End of discussion."

"You're kidding," Terry said, studiously opening a can of beer as he settled into the couch across from Brian's desk. He still wasn't sure how he felt about the Kevin Swallow business. Cullen getting killed would mean financial headaches. The two men had run a private-investigations firm together for almost sixteen years, and Brian brought in most of the clients. Still, there were times when Terry wanted to smack the surly Irishman himself. "Look, I know it's hard to figure out any woman, much less a pistol like Laurie. But this is strictly between you and that car bomber. You're being paranoid as hell."

"Just 'cause I'm paranoid don't mean everyone's not out to get me." Cullen's eyebrows shot up and he smiled.

It was true that, following their separation a year earlier, Laurie Cullen had caused Brian serious emotional grief. She'd slid into a payback mode against her selfish and at times sadistic husband. Determined to make him miserable, she'd dated many of his single colleagues and friends. She never followed through and actually slept with any of them, but she enjoyed making sure he heard about each flirtation. A shade over forty, she still had the tight body of a woman much younger, and there was no shortage of male volunteers. She'd even toyed with the idea of including Terry.

"I'd love to see the look on his face if he thought there was something between us," she had told Nathan once. "Especially with you being black. Brian may have lost some of that legendary racism of his over in Vietnam, but I think if you scratch him hard enough, you'll still find a regular Bubba under there."

"Well, let's just not scratch the man too hard, then," Terry responded. "You and me are just friends."

Brian now spoke again to Terry Blue. "Don't be so sure about her. I know how much she's been trying to give me a healthy taste of hell. Just look at all her fooling around. And I got to hear about most of it right from her, no less. You wouldn't believe who-all she's gone out with." He shook his head. "A woman her age."

Terry didn't know what to say, so he just looked around the room. Brian's office was done up in a deep cowboy motif. There were framed Remington prints on all the walls. Men on horses shooting and roping. Highly detailed statues of horses sat on the shelves. Ornate brass-and-green-glass banker's lamps provided the subdued lighting. The furniture was all white oak and the chairs were rockers with wicker backs. Even the couch Terry sat on had an Old West feel to it, stiff with thin cushions. The big man himself favored cowboy boots and bolo ties, although Terry knew he'd probably never been within six blocks of a horse in his life.

"Don't put it past her that she might try to come after me herself, knowing this shit bird Swallow'll get the blame," Brian said as he reached into his top desk drawer and pulled out a cigar half the size of a Dura-Log. He shook his head and then fired a wooden match to it.

Terry thought he detected a hint of admiration in his partner's voice. He knew Brian might be perverse enough to actually appreciate Laurie's venom. If it takes one to know one, then it certainly takes one to marry one. He'd first met Cullen in early 1969, when they landed in Saigon for a twelve-month stint in country. Brian seemed like your typical dime-store greaser. But after a month out in the bush, a black grunt named LaMont Plummer saved his life. LaMont pulled the marginally wounded but wildly indignant Cullen from a crossfire. Brian made the rescue a racial thing: "All blacks are my brothers." He was determined to save at least one African-American life as karmic repayment. Soon after that, Terry became the subject of his redemption. Brian carried him for four miles back to the fire base, where he received treatment for small amounts of shrapnel in one leg. And the Irishman visited him in the hospital religiously before Terry was shipped back to the States.

The two didn't meet again until ten years later, when they ran into each other in Denver. It was Brian's hometown and Terry was traveling through for a magazine sales job he hated. They had dinner and Brian told him that he ran a small private-investigative agency specializing in insurance surveillances and process serving. He talked Terry Blue into working for him. Over the years, the job blossomed into a full partnership as Terry proved to be resourceful and innovative. For his part, Brian was a generous if moody associate, increasingly prone to day drinking and arbitrary hostility as his marriage deteriorated.

"What makes you think Laurie wants to see you hurting?" Terry took a sip from his Budweiser and then fingered his chin. He wore his hair short and parted severely. With his black-rimmed glasses and white shirts, he looked like either Malcolm X or a middle-aged appliance salesman. "Dating people you know's one thing. But you're talking about a whole new ballgame here. Why put it on Laurie like that?"

Brian studied his cigar for a long time. "Gut feeling," he finally sighed. "I been in this business so long, Terry Blue, I got a sixth sense for this kind of thing. Besides, who else would want to hurt me?"

Terry raised his eyebrows. Is he kidding? Cullen had a way about him that could make enemies just by standing in line at the movies. That mean face, getting puffy and more rumpled every year. And that never-back-down attitude. Not to mention his habit of lying when the truth was even remotely inconvenient. Terry knew Laurie had lived with it for years, but Brian didn't reserve it exclusively for her. "You can be a virtual pain in the neck as often as not, Cullen," he told the man, contemplating his cigar. "There's more than a few guys out there wouldn't mind capping your ass."

Brian shrugged. "You're probably right, but just the same, I might go have me a little talk with that lady. Let her know I'm keeping my eye on her."

Suddenly, Nathan could see why Brian felt comfort wallowing in his exotic theory. Cullen wanted to believe he was important enough to Laurie that she'd put in the effort to come after him. His saying he'd go talk to her let Terry know the Irishman was using Swallow's threat as a way to stay in contact with his ex. More important, it was a way to let her know that he was in danger and he could stand for a little soothing and comfort. Brian still thought Laurie hung the moon and he missed the hell out of her every day. Personally, Terry knew she'd never physically hurt him, but if Cullen felt better thinking so, that was his business. Being stubborn came as natural to Brian as pouring a drink.

Six days earlier, the police had warned them about Swallow and his initial note to Carol Irwin. The big Irishman had trouble remembering the case. His recollection of Carol was more clear, her being so attractive. But he barely flinched when the sergeant told him about the possible danger.

"If he comes after me, he better pack a lunch," was what he told Haney. "It might just be an all-day job trying to kill old Brian Cullen."

"Whatever you say, Superman," Haney responded. "But Swallow's no idiot. You see or hear anything unusual, you give me a call right away. Apparently, this guy thinks you fucked up his case. Did you?"

"Now, that's not incredibly true," Brian had responded. "Swallow was as guilty as O.J., and he's just trying to put it on me and Gagliano and the lady lawyer. Besides, if he's so damned smart, how'd he end up in prison?"

Haney shrugged. "What you really might want to be asking yourself is, how'd he manage to get out?"

10

It was a beautiful piano. Red mahogany polished hard as marble. Keys white enough to blind you and sharps glossy as tiny tuxedos. Streeter loved just looking at it. About two months earlier, he'd acquired the shiny baby grand when a cocaine dealer Frank wrote up decided that disappearing was better than taking his chances in federal court. His collateral, the piano, got left behind. It was less than a year old, and even though Kohler & Campbell wasn't a top-of-the-line make, it retailed for eighty-five hundred dollars. At nearly six feet long by six feet wide, it took up a good chunk of the church loft's main room, giving the place a pronounced dignity.

Streeter even committed himself to taking lessons, which was a novelty for him. After a few days of pounding the keys senselessly on his own, he'd caved in and signed up for weekly sessions with a music teacher. For years, he'd thought about getting a piano so he could play classical and jazz. Those were the only types of music he enjoyed. As a teenager he'd taken lessons for a few months, but then quit when football practice started. This time he was determined to learn to play, and he made himself practice for at least an hour a day. He'd recently rented the video of *Five Easy Pieces* and he went nuts seeing Jack Nicholson's soulful playing of Chopin's Prelude No. 4 in E minor, Op. 28. So he bought some classical and jazz tapes for inspiration, and the more he worked, the more determined he became to master the instrument.

Now, with his practice hour over, he carefully closed the keyboard cover and got up from the bench. He always felt relaxed when he finished. Then he walked over to the couch, grabbed the newspaper, and sat down. Turning to the sports page, he checked the latest line for this Saturday's college-football games. He'd made a few bucks already off Northwestern and Alabama, so he'd ride them for another week if the point spread felt right.

But before he could read the numbers, he heard footsteps coming up the stairs. It sounded like more than one person. Stairs from the first-floor hallway emptied into the loft just a few feet from the piano. With Frank constantly popping up, Streeter never locked the downstairs door. He assumed this was his partner escorting Carol, but he didn't recognize the first head that came up over the low partition. The man attached to it looked to be in his late twenties and prematurely balding. He wore a police uniform and a constipated scowl, struggling to appear professional. Carol's bodyguard. No wonder she was nervous. He scanned the room.

"The can's over there." Streeter nodded to the far corner.

The guy shot him a hard glance. He didn't seem to know what to say and it looked like he was straining for a good comeback. Before he spoke, Carol's head rose next to him as she gently bumped him from behind. He stepped aside and looked down at her. As he did, his face brightened.

"Up you go, hero," she said to him. She glanced at Streeter and rolled her eyes. "And here I was worried about Kevin when I've got this guy on my side."

The cop looked at Streeter again and frowned. Clearly, her comment bothered him. He wasn't tall, maybe five seven, but he had thick shoulders. Streeter pegged him for a serious weightlifter trying to offset his height and retreating hairline. "Mind if I look around, sir?" the guy finally said. "I have to secure the floor."

Streeter shrugged, not sure he liked the tone of the "sir." "By all means. Nothing worse than an insecure floor." He turned to Carol, who by now was in the loft. She carried only a small gym bag. "Don't tell me that's all you brought. I don't remember you being a light traveler."

"The rest is in the car. When he's done securing, Officer Barrows'll get it. This is Jeff Barrows. He's on a special detail. Me." She paused. "Thanks for letting me come on such short notice, Street. Really. I couldn't have taken another night at my place. By the way, you don't mind if I smoke up here, do you?"

"Is that really a question?"

"I hope not. Certainly you don't believe all that media nonsense about secondhand smoke."

Streeter looked closely at her. She seemed harder than she used to be. He'd noticed that the other day at her office. There was an edge in her voice and a bite to her words that had never been there before. Less whiny. Maybe the years had toughened her. Maybe it was the strain of the threats. "If you have to smoke, it's all right with me." Then he turned to the cop. "If it's all right with you, Officer Barrows."

Jeff glanced at her and grinned. "Whatever she wants." Slowly, he began walking around the room. Although the loft had hardwood floors and brick walls, there was a certain warmth thanks to enormous throw rugs, a few overstuffed chairs and couches, and two walls of packed bookshelves. A trivia nut, Streeter had seventeen sets of encyclopedias and more than three hundred assorted reference books. He also had several hundred novels. The officer glanced at the framed movie posters—there were twenty of them—that hung throughout. An ancient stereo, sans CD player, sat in a corner. He stopped at each of three slot windows and ran his hand around the edges. When he finished, he went into the kitchen and checked out the pantry. "Are there any other exits up here, sir?" He looked back at the bounty hunter.

"No. And don't be so formal. Call me Streeter."

"Yes sir." He turned away and kept inspecting the kitchen.

Streeter frowned and looked at Carol.

"He's polite to the point of torture." She seemed amused. "You'll get used to it."

Barrows now walked into the large bedroom. He spent a couple of minutes in there as Carol went to the nearest couch and dropped her bag on it. Streeter noticed her jeans fit perfectly over her butt and the tight pink T-shirt strained across her chest in all the right places. Some things about her definitely hadn't changed.

Jeff came back out into the main room. "This is good," he said. "Small windows. Only one way in and out. Will you be staying in there, Ms. Irwin?" He jerked his head toward the bedroom.

She turned to her host, still smiling. "Will I, Street? Are we going to double up, like the old days?"

He glanced toward the bedroom, vaguely wondering if she was serious. "I didn't put those clean sheets on in there for Barrows, but I'll sleep in Frank's spare bedroom downstairs." Then he turned to the officer. "How do you work it from your end?"

Barrows cleared his throat. "We're assigned to come in three eight-hour shifts. I'm on from four P.M. until midnight. My relief works from then until eight A.M., and then someone else comes on until I get back at four. I'll need an extra set of keys. We'll set up a base down at the bottom of the stairs, if that's all right with you, sir."

Streeter now shot him a hard look. "I tell you what, you don't call me 'sir' and I won't call you 'Junior.' A deal?"

Barrows thought for a second and then nodded. With that, he headed back down the stairs to get the rest of the luggage.

"He tries, Street." Carol sat on the sofa next to her bag.

"It's pretty obvious what he'd like to try. That's one major case of puppy love hiding behind that cop's face. He's not doing a very good job of it, either."

"So I noticed. There's no harm in having a motivated body-guard. He was one of the officers who responded when I got the spider threat. He's decades younger than me, but that doesn't bother him any. I swear, he'd put his head into a blender if I told him to, and he asks me out about three times a day. He knows I'm not interested in dating cops, but he doesn't give up. Do you have an ashtray?"

"Looks like you still enjoy having men pant over you." He went to the kitchen, grabbed a saucer, and brought it to her. "I quit smoking about a year ago. You'll have to make do with this."

"That's fine." She lit her cigarette and put the match in the saucer. "And, yes, I like a little panting from time to time. Don't you?" Then she glanced at the baby grand. "Now, what's this?"

He looked at it, too. "I call it a piano. Touch it in the right places, it makes music."

Carol looked at him, smiled broadly, and nodded. "So I've heard. Imagine that, an artistic Streeter. Who would have thought? Perhaps an evolving Streeter. Next you'll start reading books without pictures, even. Or maybe you'll join a support group and start sharing your feelings. You better be careful or you might lose your reputation as the Lone Hard-On."

His eyes narrowed. "You've been here all of eight minutes and already I'd like to lose my reputation as a host."

She nodded again. "Truce. Let's start over."

"You seem to say that a lot. Don't worry, I can hold my own in an argument."

"As I remember. There always was a lot of arguing with us. A lot of blaming." Her face and tone both darkened. "Back then I was having a hard time with my new practice. You could have been more supportive, but I put way too much of it on you. Like my success was your responsibility. For a year or so after we broke up, I blamed you for my failures. Back then I hated you. Quitting criminal defense was a huge blow to me and I blamed you for most of it. You and Jack Nevers."

Streeter frowned. Jack and Carol's law partnership had dissolved about a year after the engagement blew up. Within two years, she'd switched to business law. "Jack Nevers. Now, there's a name from the past. I run into him around town from time to time. Do you ever see him anymore?"

Carol was silent for a moment. She crushed out her cigarette. "I really haven't talked to Jack since we terminated our partnership. Oh, I see him at the courthouse and we say hello. But there's still tension between us. He really was a terrible law partner. No sense of teamwork whatsoever. But that's all ancient history now."

"I guess." Streeter went to the kitchen and grabbed a beer from the refrigerator. "You want one?" He held up the bottle.

"Thank you, no. I'm fine."

He walked back to the couch and sat down next to her. "On a different note, I might have a lead on where Swallow is," he said.

Carol straightened up. "Really? A good lead?"

"Who knows? The guy who told me about it isn't even remotely reliable. But he had no reason to lie. I'm going to check it out tomorrow. I'm talking to someone in Aurora. Someone who may be connected to Kevin's girlfriend."

"Have you told the police yet?"

"It's too early for that. If I go to them with every little rumor, they'll be ignoring both of us before long. And I have my doubts about it. One thing for sure, Kevin's gone deep underground. People who should have seen him by now haven't. My hunch is he's not in town, and this lead works along those lines."

Carol grabbed another cigarette. "And you say the man you're going to see is connected to the woman?" she repeated. "Do you know her name?"

Streeter didn't speak for a moment. Usually, when he was working a case he would only confide in Frank. "I'm not sure about anything yet, Carol. When I find out more, I'll let you know."

"What's the connection between the Aurora man and Kevin's friend?" Carol leaned forward, obviously excited.

"Let's not get carried away here. This could easily be bullshit."

Before she could press on, they heard Barrows coming up the stairs. He walked into the loft carrying two large tan suitcases. Soft leather, obviously expensive. Carol smiled. "Good to have you back, Jeff. We thought you might have gotten lost."

Barrows set down the suitcases. "Some old guy downstairs almost talked my ear off. Frank, the bondsman." He turned to Streeter. "Your partner?"

"Yeah."

"That guy must have a million stories." Barrows shook his head and grinned. "I could listen to him all night."

Streeter suddenly felt better about the cop. "You might end up doing just that before this is over. Get him in the right mood, Frank'll talk a blue streak."

"Could you put those in the bedroom, please?" Carol asked the officer. "We're trying to figure out our strategy. We'll need your ideas, too. I want all the help I can get."

Barrows nodded. "My idea is simple. Stay close to me and the other cops, don't go out much, and try to relax. Just let the police do their job." Then he glanced at Streeter. "I hear you're trying to find Swallow, too."

"I'm asking around."

Barrows nodded and slowly looked back at Carol. "You'll be safe here. When you go out, one of us'll be with you." His eyes narrowed and his voice lowered. "As far as I'm concerned, Kevin Swallow's dead meat. We'll get him."

"I love it when you get so decisive on me like that," she said. Barrows didn't seem to know how to react, so he picked up the suitcases and walked into the bedroom. She turned to Streeter. "I'd appreciate you letting me know how you make out tomorrow."

"When I get something solid, you'll be the first to know." He could see Carol was getting her hopes up and he wished he hadn't mentioned the new lead. From now on he wouldn't tell her anything until he nailed the information down tight. Like Frank always advised him, "No point in telling me what you *almost* did."

11

Far-southeastern Aurora is an interminable sea of strip malls, cutesy townhouse enclaves, and winding streets. This pattern is interrupted periodically by nondescript squat office buildings, mostly for low-end professionals like chiropractors, accountants, and insurance agents. The suburb sits to the immediate east of Denver and runs the length of it from north to south. Gino Gallo lived in an area where the streets circle and twist in agonizing patterns. Their names tend to sound the same, and about every third one is a short cul-de-sac.

"You look on a map and it's like the whole place was designed by a bunch of honked-off winos in rehab trying to hide something," as Frank once described the area. Streeter always allowed himself extra time to find addresses there.

The homes on Gallo's street were built in the seventies, and featured small windows and long driveways. All were fairly well maintained and landscaped. Gino's place was kept up better than most. It was painted a pale blue, and the yard, containing only one tree and few shrubs, was groomed like a pool table. There was a sparse severity to it that Streeter didn't expect from a bartender-bookie.

The bounty hunter pulled his brown Buick Belvedere up behind an older gray Chrysler in the driveway. Gallo's car was as clean as the rest of the place. Streeter leaned forward in his seat, resting his elbows on the steering wheel with his hands together on the top. In the yard next door, an elderly woman was raking leaves. She stopped, nodded, and gave him a half-amused, half-perplexed look. He nodded back and got out. When he went to the front door, he could hear a mechanical, wheezing sound inside. It seemed to move. Unable to place it, he knew he'd heard it before. He pressed the doorbell. No answer. Then he pounded hard with the heel of his hand. It had been cool the past few days and the door felt stiff. From inside, the wheezing sound stopped.

"Hold on," came from within. "I'll be right there."

In another minute or so the door creaked open. A blast of what smelled like cleaning fluid belched out. Instinctively, Streeter pulled his head back.

"Yeah?" the man at the door asked. He was short and round, with a face to match. A sad, bandito mustache divided his features horizontally. There were puffy, bluish bags under each eye. The face looked older than the man behind it, who was in his late thirties. But his most striking feature was not really his own. He wore a slick paintbrush toupee the color of gas-station coffee. It was too large and it clashed with the graying sideburns of the man under it. Perhaps to keep it from sliding, Gino held his head so stiff it looked like he was balancing a book on it. He wore a green polyester shirt with a gold zipper running halfway down his chest. Faded navy sweat pants sagged under a potbelly.

"I'm looking for Gino Gallo," Streeter said.

"We're all looking for someone." The man's face pulled back as he spoke, his cheeks fattening briefly in a mild belch. For such a short, ugly man, he wore a confident smile. "Or something. It's just that most of us just don't know who or what."

Streeter frowned. "You could be right, but I'm one of the lucky ones. You are Gino, aren't you?"

The man looked past Streeter now, his face wincing in concentration, the smile still in place. "Before I answer, tell me who you are and what you want with Gino."

"My name's Streeter. I was talking to somebody who said he

knows you. Or should I say, knows Gino? He suggested I talk to Gino, that he could help me out with a little problem I'm having."

The man nodded graciously. "I am, in fact, Gino Gallo. What kind of problem?"

"I'm trying to locate someone. This guy who told me about you said the person I'm after might know your sister, Gina. Could be living with her."

Gino's smile faded and he pulled his head back a shade, still careful not to disturb his hairpiece. His eyes narrowed, but he didn't say anything.

Streeter took a half-step back. "Kevin's the name of the man I'm looking for. We used to call him Kev. You ever heard of anyone named Kev? Kevin Swallow?"

"I tell you, friend, you're opening up a whole new avenue of questions here. How do you know Gina?"

Gino's smile returned as he spoke. Evidently, Streeter reasoned, there was little connection between it and whatever the man was thinking or feeling. "I don't know her. But I'm a friend of Kev's. I haven't seen him in ages and I want to find him, so I'm here asking about Gina's friend Kev. This doesn't have anything to do with your sister, per se." He was losing patience but his voice remained even.

Gallo's eyebrows shot up and his head moved almost imperceptibly to the side, indicating the living room behind him. "I want to show you something." With that, he pushed the door open wider and stepped aside for the man on the porch to enter.

The invitation surprised Streeter. "Sure."

Gino shut the door behind him as he walked in. Once he was inside, the cleaning-fluid smell became stronger. At about fifteen feet by twenty-five feet, the living room was larger than one might expect from the outside. But it was barely furnished. Actually, there wasn't room for much furniture. Squarely in the middle was the biggest, most detailed model-train set Streeter had ever seen. He stared at it in silence.

His host seemed to read his mind. "Bet you never saw anything like that before, did you, brother?" Gino asked with obvious pride. "It's the old Burlington Northern line running outside of Vail."

Streeter nodded. So that was the wheezing sound he'd heard from the porch. The set rested on a huge L-shaped plywood table about three feet high and propped up by sawhorses. It depicted a mountain scene around a village. There was snow on the top of the hills and a small lake at one end. Two rail lines ran through numerous round tunnels in the largest mountains. The whole setup had remarkable detail; even the tiny people in the town wore hand-painted expressions. Whoever put this together definitely fell into the Get-a-Life category. Streeter glanced over at his host, who was also staring at the layout. Gino's grin had turned almost maniacal.

Suddenly, the smile faded and Gallo turned to his guest. "It was that little thief, the burglar, who sent you to me, right?" There was an evangelical tone and cadence to his words that gave them authority. "I tended bar over at The Gold Coins until they cut back the staff. But I remember talking to some people about Gina and her friend. One of them was that bozo who steals from people's homes and then brags about it in bars. I can't recall his full name, but 'Kenny' comes to mind."

Streeter didn't say anything. On the wall behind Gino's head was an ornately framed painting of a train scene. Next to that was an autographed black-and-white photo of Dean Martin.

"Gina." Gallo grunted the word, looked off to the side, and continued. "There's a lost soul. Poor girl was raised right but she fell hard to temptation. She smokes and she drinks and she fornicates." He looked back, and his expression had become sad. "And all in the house my mother left for her. But Gina's not alone. We're all sinners, Mr. Streeter. *Born* sinners. You put a pencil in front of a little baby and what happens? The baby'll steal the pencil. Now, that's a fact. We have to accept Jesus Christ. Do you accept Jesus Christ as your Lord and Saviour, Mr. Streeter?"

"Up to a point." He could see by Gino's pained expression that that was not a terrific answer. He changed his approach. "Actually, you can find me in a church every day of the week. I practically live there."

Much better. Gino's face softened again and he nodded sagely.

The bond forged, Streeter pressed on. "Am I on the right track? Is your sister living with old Kev?"

"All I know is," Gino said, glancing back at his train, "she said something to me about being with a Kev. At least it sounded like Kev. Then, later, she said his name was indeed Kevin. From what she described, he's a real prize. I believe he's spent time in our state-prison system."

"Can you tell me where they live?"

Suddenly, Gino looked back at his guest, his voice getting hard as he asked, "How is it that you know a man like Kevin?"

Careful, Streeter thought. Don't appear too close to Swallow. "We used to bowl together. I didn't know he got into trouble. It's been so long since I've seen him. All I wanted to do was say hello."

Evidently, it was not very convincing. Gino said nothing.

"I can look up your sister's name in the Jefferson County property-tax records and go find her myself," Streeter continued. "I know she lives near Evergreen."

Gino nodded as if to agree, but then replied, "The place isn't in her name. Not under 'Gallo,' I mean. It's still in our mother's maiden name. And you can check with the operator up there, too. Gina has no phone in her name."

True. Streeter had called directory assistance the day before. There were no Gallos in or near Evergreen. He had also called the Jefferson County real estate tax records office that morning. Again, nothing under Gallo. Gino was his best shot at finding the man named Kev and Streeter knew it. The time for talk was over. He pulled out his wallet and took three twenties from it.

"Will you accept a humble donation from one sinner to another?" he asked. "I'm sure you can do more good with it than I can. Losing your job must be a horrible blow, financially speaking."

Gino took the bills and studied them. "I haven't been up there in maybe twelve years. I'm not sure I can even recall how to get to the place. But the county records people should be able to get you the address and maybe even give you directions. Just ask for the paperwork on the Stewart place. Evie Stewart was our mother. That's the name the property's under."

"Is that S-T-U-A-R-T?"

"No, S-T-E-W, as in beef, with an A-R-T on the end. Got it?"

Streeter nodded. "Thanks. That should do it."

Gino turned his attention back to the railroad set and was silent. The smile was gone and he looked down to where a striped train-engineer's cap was lying on the tracks. He stuffed the twenties into his shirt pocket and grabbed the cap. "I expect so, brother. I wish you luck in your search."

"Amen to that, brother. I'll just show myself out." The bounty hunter was backing up as he spoke. Gino said nothing. When he opened the door, Streeter glanced back once more toward the trains. Gallo, the hat in his left hand, reached up to the top of his head with his right. Slowly, he pulled the ratty toupee off and replaced it with the engineer's hat.

Streeter closed the door quickly behind himself on the way out.

12

Terry Blue Nathan walked into the Cruise Room of the Oxford Hotel, squinted, and looked for Laurie Cullen. In the subdued Deco lighting, the cigarette smoke seemed almost tangible. It added to the elegant atmosphere. There was a row of high, pale booths against the left wall, with the long bar fronting most of the right. Laurie was sitting at the third booth in, smoking while running an index finger around the rim of her martini glass. That woman never could just sit still, Terry thought as he walked toward her. Probably even twitched in her sleep.

There were two reasons he chose the Cruise Room to meet Laurie.

First, he was sure Brian wouldn't show up. The drinks cost too much and, although it was in a remodeled turn-of-the-century hotel within a few blocks of their office, Brian hated the punker chic of the place.

"Forget it," was how he'd put it to Terry. "You got those snooty little broads with purple hair and nose rings. On top of that, you got a bunch of lawyers and investment guys trying to act like hot shit around them. No way I go back to that joint."

Second, Terry chose it because, with its more urbane clientele, he could have a drink there with a white woman and not feel like a child molester. Mixed-race couples still weren't the norm in Denver.

Laurie was wearing a sleeveless green top. Her hair was shorter than usual. Terry didn't like it as much that way, but he had to admit she was still attractive. Blond hair, body out of a gym ad. And she wore enough liner to set off her hazel eyes just about right.

"Mr. Nathan, I see you still dress like one of Farrakhan's body-guards," Laurie said when he got to her booth. "You are definitely the most anal-retentive-looking black man I've ever met." She smiled and thrust her hand out for him to shake.

Terry might dress a little uptight, but Laurie was kidding about the rest. With his rich, wood-colored skin and large, dark eyes, she thought he was handsome. There was an intensity to him that she admired. He always knew the score and what the righteous move was. Ever his own man, even if she couldn't figure him out. Like his being a registered Republican or his partnering with Brian.

"And what do we have here?" He studied her face as he took her hand. "A poor man's Madonna. A middle-aged poor man, that is."

"Touché," she said as he sat down. She looked at him and he returned the stare. "Enough chitchat and idle flattery, Terry. Let's get you a drink and then tell me the latest on Field Marshal Cullen."

He nodded. A waitress who barely looked old enough to drink legally herself appeared and asked for their order.

"I'll have another 'see through' "—Laurie pointed to her martini glass—"and my friend here will have a . . . a what?" She looked at Terry.

"Rémy, room temperature. In a large snifter, please." He looked calmly at them.

The waitress nodded, smiled with a poise well beyond her years, and left.

"I'll tell you all about him in a minute, Laurie," Terry said. "First off, how've you been? We talk on the phone, but I haven't seen you in a while."

"I can't complain. Life's been more than tolerable for me all these months. And you?"

Terry nodded. "Been good myself." The waitress rematerialized with their drinks, set these on the table, and again silently disappeared. "Speaking of Cullen, I've got to ask you something," Terry continued. "You're one special woman, Laurie. You're smart—master's degree in library sciences—and you're holding up nicely in the physical department, too. So tell me, how did you ever end up with a loose cannon like him? I'm not trying to pick a fight, but it doesn't make sense. He have a ton of money I don't know about or is he some big stud? What the hell's the draw?"

She flicked her cigarette in the general direction of the ashtray and shrugged like she was tired. "Don't forget, you ended up with him, too, my man. And you're no fool, either. Two years at Stanford and you ended up with him, too."

"I didn't have to sleep with him all those years. Besides, putting it back on me like that doesn't answer the question."

Her face softened and she looked beyond Terry. "True. How *did* I end up with Brian Patrick Cullen? I know he has all the sensitivity of a caveman on a steroid binge and he's not the most gorgeous thing. As far as his sexual prowess, forget it. But when I first met him, he had a terrific sense of humor and a nice, slow cockiness. His face didn't have all that anger it has now. And he had a way of making me feel safe. You know, protected. The man was so sure of himself. He'd take on the world for me. It was very appealing, and even though he wasn't the greatest lover, he made up for it with a ton of enthusiasm. He adored me." She glanced back at him. "How either of us got hooked up with Mr. Cullen isn't the point. What was it you wanted to tell me?"

"You remember that Kevin Swallow business I told you about. The car bomber. Well, Brian believes you might use that as an excuse to try and hurt him. Everyone's focused on Swallow, so you could see this as a free pass. I told him that's nonsense, but he thinks you're the only one around who really wants him to go down."

Laurie shook her head and grimaced. "That man is so delusional. Like he matters enough for me to want to hurt him. And what does he mean, I'm the only one? You know damned well we could fill half the convention center with people who'd like to see Cullen get horsewhipped."

Terry Nathan shrugged and took a sip of his drink. "There's no talking to him about it. My personal opinion is that he likes to think you still care enough about him to try something."

"*Care enough?* Good God, we must have been quite a pair. Talk about your basic dysfunctional couple." Laurie shook her head again. "He's got to know that Kevin Swallow's his real problem. I'm totally out of it."

"Yeah, well, he's got you on his mind and he won't listen to much else on the topic."

"I'll say this once and that's it." She leaned forward as she spoke. "I have *no* interest in hurting him. You tell Lard Ass there not to flatter himself on that score."

Terry nodded and finished his Rémy with one short gulp. He put down the snifter and adjusted his glasses. "All I know is Cullen's obsessing on you more than he's done in quite a while."

"Lucky me."

"Sure. But he's thinking about you, and when that Irishman gets to thinking about something for too long and too hard, he can come up with almost anything. I just wanted you to know that you'll be hearing from him soon. He told me he plans to have a chat with you and let you know his thoughts on the subject. I think he sees this threat as a reason to get back in touch with you."

She motioned to the waitress and waved her hand over the table to indicate they'd like another round. Then she looked back at Terry. "You don't have to warn me how his mind works. Or I should say, how it doesn't work. If you're his friend you'll keep him on a short leash. Swallow's probably coming after him, and Brian stomping around making stupid accusations won't help matters."

To Terry, having Brian on a short leash definitely was one fine idea. "I hear you."

She studied him for a while without saying anything. Finally, she spoke. "I know you told me that Brian's not afraid of Swallow and he's acting all macho about it. But this really is getting serious. Look at Watts and Gagliano. It sounds like Brian's turn could be coming up. I have a friend who's a police dispatcher, so I called her after you told me they'd contacted Brian last week. I was curious. She said everyone there's talking about it." Laurie watched as the waitress set another round on their table. "That lawyer Swallow's after is sure taking it serious. My friend said Irwin's even hired herself a skip tracer to look for him. Some guy named Streeter.

"You know how the cops like to gossip. Apparently, Irwin wasn't too popular with them, and they see it as a slap in the face that she hired him. This is getting to be a fairly high-profile case with the media. I saw in the papers today that they're finally linking the Watts and Gagliano attacks to the threats to Irwin."

Terry considered that. "Streeter. The name rings a bell. He's a bounty hunter working out of Lower Downtown. I think he did a skip trace or two for us a long time ago. I never met him personally." He paused. "Might be a good idea if I gave Mr. Streeter a call. Me and him could compare notes and swap information, seeing as how we're all after the same thing."

Laurie shifted in her seat. "That's probably not a bad idea. The worst he can do is tell you to get lost. But I'd suggest you talk to him by yourself. Let Brian keep playing with his stupid little theories. Don't even tell him about it. Not yet, at least."

"You got that right. I'll keep our boy on that short leash you mentioned. Let's just let him fixate on you for a while longer."

They'd been talking on the phone for a few minutes when Streeter glanced at his watch. It was almost ten-thirty on

Wednesday night. He didn't recognize the voice, but he had heard of Terry Nathan before. Brian Cullen's partner.

"It could be there's information we can exchange that'd be to our mutual benefit here," Terry was telling him. "We have a common interest in finding Mr. Swallow. How about meeting me at the clubhouse at City Park tomorrow? You know the place?"

"Sure do," Streeter responded. "Best barbecue in the state. I'll be sort of near there in the afternoon, anyhow."

"Fine," Terry said. "Four o'clock sound okay?"

Streeter remembered doing a few skip traces for Cullen maybe five years earlier. Although he'd never met Terry, if he was as gruff as Cullen, he'd be a pain in the ass. Still, Streeter could put up with a jerk if it got him any information on Kevin. Besides, Nathan sounded okay. Sure of himself but not cocky. Very unlike Brian Cullen.

"I'll be there."

13

City Park is one of Denver's few real parks. Other grassy areas may lay claim to the title. The yuppified Washington Park, for instance, is a wide figure-eight bike path where lumpy white people in spandex outfits walk their silly dogs. It has a couple of stagnant, goose-shit ponds, a boathouse, a community building, and tennis courts. Cheesman Park in Capitol Hill is basically an open-air gay spa where puzzled seniors waddle around a running track made from what appears to be hardened Play-Doh. Most of the rest of the city's so-called parks are little more than glorified picnic areas with softball diamonds, ranging in size from a couple of acres to an overblown living room.

But City Park, on the near North Side, lives shamelessly up to its full name. It's a true park boasting the full jangle of urban life: drive-by shootings, awkward racial tensions, idle city maintenance crews, and dismal ethnic festivals. It also has a golf course—nicknamed the Nairobi Country Club by mean-spirited WASPs—a zoo, a lake, running paths, European-looking statuary, numerous ball courts, a high-tech museum, gardens, and bike paths. It's the largest and most feared park in town. In short, it's the only one worth visiting. It's located in a fairly high-crime area that's being nervously integrated from three sides by adventurous white couples and sentimental gays. All of them have a keen eye for turn-of-the-century houses made affordable by their proximity to minority neighborhoods.

Terry was leaning against a low fence next to the practice green in front of the clubhouse when Streeter got there. It was twelve minutes to four. Usually the bounty hunter arrived first, a habit Frank had taught him. Get the lay of the land and avoid surprises. But here was Terry Blue Nathan, relaxed and watching people putting like he'd been hanging out in the warm autumn sun all afternoon. Streeter took an immediate liking to the man. He seemed alert yet detached, like there was a lot going on under the surface. In his forties but still with an athletic build. Short-sleeved white shirt, pleated pants, and expensive shoes. Probably Allen-Edmonds. Black-on-burgundy saddle shoes, rich-looking and soft as a puppy. Streeter always looked to the footwear to see what a man thought of himself. Terry was understated, unique, and he knew the score.

"Have you been here long?" he asked Nathan.

Terry straightened up a bit, studied Streeter, and then put out his hand out to be shaken. "A while," was all he said.

"Let's sit outside and watch these clowns knock themselves out while we talk." Streeter nodded to the practice green. "I had such a lousy long game I finally gave up. Do you play?"

"No. Can't see paying good money to chase a little white ball around all day. Who needs the frustration? Besides, where I grew up there wasn't much grass. Only golf I ever saw was on the tube."

"Where was that?"

"Back east." He paused. "D.C."

They took a table in the shade and Streeter went inside to grab a couple Miller Genuine Drafts. He came back with the beers and they watched the putting for several minutes in silence. Three young men were practicing wordlessly on the green. The soft tap of their clubs on the balls was interrupted by the growing rush-hour traffic on nearby York Street. Terry spoke first.

"I don't need a golf lesson and I suppose you have other things to do with yourself today, too. You having any luck finding Kevin Swallow?"

Streeter shrugged. "Some. I bet your pal Brian wouldn't mind getting his hands on him. Cullen's got to be on Kevin's short list, maybe even next. Does he have police protection?"

Terry shook his head and grinned. "No. Brian's not much for that kind of thing. Personally, I believe he'd rather get himself blown up than spend too much time with the police. I guess they're keeping an eye on him from time to time, but no one's assigned to stay with him. I wish they were. Swallow sounds like one serious motherfucker."

"As a human being, he's a total waste of groceries." Streeter sat up. "But he's not the kind of guy to give up. I only met Cullen a couple of times. He sure seemed to have enough of that Irish bravado, but he better watch his ass pretty close on this one. It's going to take more than swagger to deal with old Kevin."

Terry took a drink from his beer and flashed a grin. "Yeah, bravado's one name you can call it, I guess. Let's just say, if Brian were to enter a popularity contest, he'd get maybe one vote. His own."

Neither man spoke for a moment. Finally, Terry straightened in his chair and leaned in to the table. He looked closely at Streeter. "It seems that we both got a real interest in finding Swallow. Tell you what, why don't we pool our resources and work together? I hear a lot of good things about you, and from your end, it could be that a man like me'd be helpful. Two heads are better than one, like they say."

Streeter took a slow pull off his beer and looked out past the putting green for a moment. Then he turned back to Terry. "You, me, and your partner?"

"Forget Cullen. He don't know from Shinola on this whole mess. He's off on some personal tangent and right now he's too much of a hothead for us. I'm talking just you and me. Look, I'm not saying we should go to the prom together. Just keep each other posted and watch each other's backside. This is going to be one rough, ugly job and you know it."

Streeter grinned. He sensed Terry had the balls and the brains to make it worthwhile. Plus, he'd come in handy immediately. "Sounds like a plan, Mr. Terry Blue Nathan. One thing jumps out at me right now where I might like to have someone come along. You ever pack anything besides a lunch?"

"Got me a .38 that I carry from time to time, if the situation calls for it."

"Keep it handy. I have a line on where Swallow might be staying. Up near Evergreen. My information's flimsy as hell but it's worth a ride in the country. How's your schedule look for the next couple of days?"

"Not so busy I can't shake free."

Streeter drained his beer. "Then let's check out Evergreen. I'll give you a call tomorrow to nail down the details. Be ready to move first thing Saturday morning."

Terry nodded and they shook hands on it. They finished their beers, and then Streeter headed home. When he got back to the church, he went straight to Frank's office. The bondsman was just getting off the phone as he walked in.

"How'd it go with Cullen's partner?" he asked Streeter.

"Pretty well. He wants to team up with me looking for Swallow."

Frank frowned deeply. "Jesus, I don't know. That Cullen's not too easy to take, from what I hear. You sure you want to deal with him?"

"I'm not going to. Terry Nathan and I are pulling together for now and Brian Cullen's out of the picture. Even Terry doesn't want him working with us. Besides, I got a good feeling about Nathan and I don't mind having someone covering my butt."

"That sounds better."

Streeter glanced around. "Have you seen Carol today?"

"I saw her and the uniform go upstairs a while ago. But then they came down right after that. She said they were going over to her office and they wouldn't be back for a couple of hours."

"I'm heading up to my place," Streeter said. "See you later."

When he got to the loft, he looked around his room. Carol's suitcases were sitting in the corner and she'd put most of her clothes in a drawer he had cleared for her. The room smelled faintly like her new scent. He'd never had a woman live in the loft, so it seemed strange with Carol's clothes in his closet. Then he thought of how she was acting toward him lately. Like she was giving the signals of someone on the make. What the hell was she up to? Sarcastic, but never over the top with it. Always the hint of flirtation. He was getting mixed messages, and he was surprised at how it intrigued him. There had been a strong chemical bond between them, even though it had faded years ago.

Then he focused on Linda Parnell. He hadn't seen her in about a week, but he thought of her often. Missed her, too. Her dark hair flowing at the driving range. Their moments in her car.

Linda hadn't worn perfume. Just a fresh scent of her, the taste of her mouth. She seemed so much more up front than Carol. Not really predictable, but genuine.

He glanced around his room once more, not sure what he was looking for.

14

Officer Barrows hated the shift change. He didn't know why he was taken off four to midnight, but orders were orders. Jeff couldn't stand working midnight to eight under any circumstances, much less now. It meant that he'd see Carol for only a few minutes before she turned in at night and then briefly again when she came out in the morning. If that. Like now, Saturday morning. He'd check out the garage and the church grounds, and wait for his replacement. The next cop probably would arrive before Carol came down. She stayed up in the loft longer on weekends. And Barrows couldn't just hang around after his shift like a lovesick schoolboy, even though that's how he'd been feeling lately.

He'd spent most of the last eight hours reading magazines and drinking coffee in front of the door leading from the first-floor hallway to the loft. Snoozed off maybe twice, but just for a few minutes. He'd only seen Carol once the night before. Right after he went on duty she came down the stairs to put her gym bag in her car and grab her briefcase. On top of that, she was bitchy. Complained about work and how tired she was. She barely said good night on the way back upstairs. He chalked it up to being that time of the month and tried not to take it personally.

When he walked into the garage that morning, the first light of day was filtering through the tall stained-glass windows. It gave the place a crimson tint. He walked past Streeter's Buick and wondered if there was anything going on between its owner and Carol. Despite being increasingly jealous, he liked Streeter. Always loose and steady. Plus, he had that killer weight room. Behind the Buick was Carol's white Saab. The light from the stained glass hit her windshield like blood. Then Jeff looked closer and realized it wasn't the light he saw. It *was* blood. He froze. "Holy shit!" was the best he could do. He walked to the driver's door and leaned over the windshield. Red fluid—thick and syrupy—dribbled down the front of the pane. In the middle, a white paper was taped to the glass. At least mostly white, since some of the blood had spilled onto it. There was typing on the paper:

> Further we go, marching to your death,
> You have to know by now what to expect . . .

Those first two lines were enough. "Damnit!" the cop yelled. "How'd he get in here?" He hurried back through the garage door to the bottom of the stairs and radioed for assistance. Jeff knew that the man in charge would come down his throat with a meat cleaver for letting Swallow into the church. But for now, Barrows just kept asking himself, "How the hell did he get in here without me hearing him?"

Carol was surprised when she woke up to find Streeter shaking the bed. He had never come into the room while she was sleeping. But here he was, in his bathrobe, no less. She was puzzled. He couldn't be getting amorous. There wasn't a hint of lust on his face. He seldom betrayed anything when he was under stress, but now he looked more stern than usual.

"Carol." His voice was mild but firm. "Are you awake?"

"I am now." She sat up. "What is it? You look like they just took *Jeopardy* off the air."

"Throw something on and meet me out there." He nodded toward the door and then glanced at her blue nightgown, which showed several inches of soft cleavage. Actually, he more than glanced.

"I've got something on and you seem to like it." She half smiled, half frowned. "Maybe it's more than you're used to seeing me wear to bed, but it sure got your attention."

"Grab a robe, this is serious," he said and then walked out.

When Carol got to the main room, Streeter was working with the Mr. Coffee on the kitchen counter. Jeff Barrows was standing near the steps. Next to him was the day officer, an older Hispanic man. No one was even close to smiling.

"What's going on?" Carol pulled lightly on the belt of her pink terry-cloth robe. It was short but thick and it made her look almost plump. And sexy, especially to Barrows. "What is it?"

"When was the last time you went to your car, ma'am?" the Hispanic officer asked.

At first she blinked in confusion. "What happened?" Her voice rose. She blinked again like her eyes burned, but she didn't cry. "Late last night, I guess. Why?"

"Don't worry. Everything's under control," the cop said. His voice was even, soothing. "Officer Barrows said you went down there right after he came on duty. That would have been around midnight. Is that what you mean?"

"Yes." Now she started crying, but her voice was more calm than her face. "I took my gym bag down and brought up my briefcase. I worked very late. Well into the morning."

"Did you notice anything unusual about your car while you were down there?"

"No."

"Did you hear anything?"

"Of course not. What happened?"

The officer shot Streeter a glance and then looked back at Carol. "Apparently, someone got into the garage over the last few hours and left a note on your car. We found it on the windshield."

"Got in?" She took a step forward and looked at Barrows. Her tears stopped. "How could that possibly happen?"

"Honest, I have no idea," Jeff said quietly. "I was down there all night. Awake the whole time. There wasn't one sound. Carol, I'm sorry."

"Kevin Swallow got in here last night, into this building, and you didn't hear him?" She glanced at Streeter. "No one heard him. I'm in this *fortress* surrounded by all you big, brave guys and Swallow still comes and goes as he pleases. What a bunch of incompetent bimbos." She was shaking noticeably when she finished.

"I knew you'd take it like a trooper," Streeter stepped in. "Look, he didn't get to you, and calling us clever names isn't going to help anything."

"Wasn't the garage locked?" Carol sat down on the nearest couch. She wiped her face with her right hand and then pulled a crumpled tissue from her robe pocket.

"Mr. Streeter said he recalls locking the garage door," the day officer interjected. "He was the last one to come in."

"Except for Kevin." Carol looked at each of them and then blew her nose quietly.

"Evidently, although we're actually not sure who it was," the day cop offered. Then, after a pause, "The lab people will be here soon to dust for prints. I'm going to ask that you remain in the loft until we're done cleaning up down there."

Carol nodded and was quiet. Finally, she looked at the bounty hunter. "There's no place that's safe, is there? And now he knows where you live, Street."

"I thought of that myself," was all he said.

Carol went back to the bedroom to shower. Streeter headed downstairs to do the same, with Barrows following him to the first-floor hallway. The Hispanic officer stationed himself in the garage to drink coffee and to wait for the lab technicians.

When Streeter got out of the shower and finished dressing, he called Nathan. He had told him the night before that he'd pick him up about nine to go to Evergreen. "I'm running a little late, Terry," he said.

"No sweat. When do you think you'll get here?"

"Give me an extra hour or so."

"Why the wait?" Terry asked.

"We had a little break-in last night. Someone came by and put a note on Carol's car. Left a damned mess, too."

"Say what? I thought you had the mounties over there watching out for you. The cop get drunk or something?"

"Who knows? But I want to talk to Carol and then see what the police find. It had to be Swallow."

"The man knows where you're at now. Knows how to get inside your house. How's that sitting?" Terry asked.

"Not very well. That cop they had over here's no Eliot Ness but he's sharp enough. And this place gets locked up every night. I can't figure how he did it."

Terry was silent for a moment. "I talked to Cullen a little while ago. Apparently, he had a chat with Laurie, his ex, and she mentioned that you and me are working together. Now he wants to meet with both of us." There was another pause. "Wants Laurie in on it, too."

Streeter frowned. "I thought you told me they were mortal enemies. Didn't Cullen think she might even come after him?"

"I know. It doesn't figure. The two of them must have gotten together yesterday and hammered something out. Who knows? Neither one's got the common sense of a turkey. But he sure wants to meet us at the office around four. That okay with you?"

"Yeah. We should be done in Evergreen before then. I'll be by in an hour."

When he hung up, Streeter went back to the garage. The police had finished dusting the car and all the doors and windows for prints. They'd removed the note from the windshield and were packing up. One uniform was standing over at the small side garage door taking photos. Barrows was hanging near the Saab, just staring at it. His thick shoulders slumped like he was carrying a heavy dumbbell in each hand. Poor guy was half in shock. The bounty hunter walked over to him.

"Carol's safe, you know," he told the cop.

Barrows didn't seem to hear him at first and then he looked up. "What?" There was no color in his face, and even his beard looked pale.

"I said, basically, you did your job. Carol wasn't hurt. You were sent here to protect her, not the Saab."

"Right. You and me both know the only reason she's alive is because this prick wants her to squirm some more. If he can get to the car, he could have gotten to her, too. Everyone knows that. These guys"—he nodded toward the officers—"you, Carol. Most of all Swallow. Let's call it like it is, okay?"

"Look, you can sit here and beat the hell out of yourself or you can get back in the game. Carol's fine and your job is to help keep her that way. My suggestion is that you find out what happened here last night and then figure out how to make sure it doesn't happen again. You can't change what's already done."

Barrows looked closely at him. "This is pretty hard to keep down."

"You'll be fine," Streeter said. He looked at the Saab and then back at the cop. "They getting any good prints?"

"Not off the car." Barrows looked slowly around the garage. "It was wiped clean. They might get something from that side door." He looked back at Streeter. "But there was no sign of a forced entry. Are you sure you locked it when you came in?"

"Of course. I do it automatically every night. Swallow might be good, but I can't believe he got his hands on a key to the door."

Barrows shrugged. "There's no other way to get in here besides right past me in the hall. That's pretty unlikely, because I was there all night and the other first-floor doors were locked. Or else he'd have to come through the overhead doors, which would have made a ton of racket." He paused. "Carol was just down here before. Ruiz, the day man, let her look around. She wanted to read the note."

"Do you know what it said?"

Barrows shook his head. "No. The typical bullshit he always writes, I suppose."

Streeter nodded and headed upstairs to see how Carol was doing. When he got into the loft, she was sitting at the kitchen table thumbing through a legal pad. She seemed distracted, but calm.

"Feeling any better?" he asked.

"I'll live." She glanced up at him.

"They told me the side door wasn't tampered with," Streeter said. "Swallow just walked in, no problem. I always keep that door locked."

"Kevin probably knows all about locks. He knows about everything else that's mechanical. I swear, he could build a rocket launcher out of a cigar box and some firecrackers. I bet that lock didn't even slow him down. I'm sorry he found us, Street. Is Frank okay with all this?"

"I haven't seen him yet but I'm sure he'll manage. We knew this would happen eventually. He probably just followed you home."

"That Mexican officer told me he thinks it was animal blood smeared on the windshield. There's something else you should know. That note on the windshield." She looked down at her pad. "What he wrote. I think he was talking about you."

Streeter went to the table and stood over her. "Oh yeah?"

She looked up. "There's a lot of the usual crap about the list getting smaller. But he also wrote, 'Pain will be the end, a mutiny for the bounty. Death will come to the one who serves you daily.' You're a 'bounty' and you serve me daily."

"What did he mean by 'mutiny for the bounty'?"

"Who knows? But I'm sure the word 'bounty' can't be a coincidence. The cops serve me daily, but you're the bounty." She reached her right hand to his and squeezed it. "Be real careful, Street."

He glanced down at her hand. "We're all going to be more careful from now on. Look, be extra nice to poor old Barrows, okay? He blames himself for everything. He's not going to be any good to anyone if he's pouting like that."

"I'll be nice."

"I'm going to be gone for a few hours. There's something I'll want you to look at later. Ruiz'll be downstairs, and you should stay up here until I get back."

She nodded. "Where the hell can I go?"

As he walked down to his car, Streeter thought about the note. "Mutiny for the bounty." Did Swallow just get the name of the movie wrong or did he actually mean something specific by that? Swallow usually picked his words carefully in the stupid little poems. Why should this be different? It nagged Streeter as he drove to Terry's.

15

Nathan was waiting in front of his apartment building when Streeter pulled up. He lived in Brooks Towers, on 15th Street. It's a luxury forty-two-floor high-rise in a mostly office-and-commercial area not far from the city's huge performing-arts complex. The Towers is a prestigious address and Streeter could easily see Terry living there. Sporting a long-sleeved white Ralph Lauren polo shirt with the tails out, beige Dockers, and sandals, Nathan was leaning against a cement planter and reading *The Wall Street Journal* through prescription Vuarnets. He casually tucked the paper under one arm when Streeter honked from the curb. Then he moved toward the Buick, slow and cool, like maybe the entire Dallas Cowboys cheerleader squad was watching him.

"Hey, ace. You expecting Dan Quayle to meet us up there?" Streeter asked as Terry slid into the passenger seat.

Behind the shades, Terry lifted his brows. "Can't all of us look like white trash."

Streeter glanced down at himself. He was wearing a gray T-shirt, faded Levi's, and a pair of black Chuck Taylors. Work clothes and tightly fitted. He put the car in drive and pulled out into traffic. "I thought we decided that you were going to bring something in case there's trouble."

Terry looked over at him. "I'm wearing my holster in back. Don't need a suitcase for a .38 short-nose. Be cool, Streeter. We're not landing on the beach at Normandy up there. Just taking a little ride in the country, maybe snap a few pictures like we decided on the phone last night."

"It's not the trip that's got me wound up, Terry. I'm not afraid of running into Swallow. It's *not* running into him that makes me nervous. That crap at the church this morning's gnawing at me. I was sleeping twenty feet from the garage and I didn't hear a thing. The cop on duty was just on the other side of the door and he didn't hear anything, either. On top of that, Swallow's note sounds like he's after me. That definitely is no way to start your day."

Terry smiled. His teeth flashed as white and even as a row of reflectors. "The hunter's being hunted. No fun, is it?"

"You got that right. It's weird being on this side of things. I don't mind if someone comes in the front door looking for me. Take my chances with that any day. But this guy can be in a different state and still take you down."

"What makes you think he might come for you?"

"The note he left on her car. Another poem, about a bounty and someone who watches over Carol. It's mostly her notion that he means me, and she's been known to be off target from time to time over the years. But she may be right."

They drove south to Highway 285 and then headed west, toward the mountains. The foothills yawned dramatically in front of them. Both men were quiet as they started climbing toward Evergreen. The old Buick glided smooth as a spaceship. Although Streeter wasn't much of a mountain man—he seldom went there except to ski—he liked this part of the drive. The highway seemed to slide into the mountains, and the climb felt fluid and effortless. On both sides were huge stretches of rolling meadows, but housing developments were creeping in from the north, from the Denver suburbs.

"Where'd you first meet Cullen?" Streeter broke the silence.

"In Vietnam. A long time ago."

Streeter glanced at his passenger. "What was it like over there?"

Terry was quiet for a moment. "It was no picnic. I take it you didn't go."

"No one ever asked me to. I was in school at the time."

"College boy, huh?"

"That's me. I was going to take the NFL by storm."

"You played ball?" Terry turned to look at the driver. "What happened?"

Streeter shrugged. "What happened? Shit happened. I had problems with a teammate and ended up drifting away from the game."

Terry was still puzzled but he let it slide. He figured Streeter would explain more if he wanted to. They drove without talking for a while.

"I'm thinking," Streeter broke the silence again, "that, besides Carol, your partner might be the only other person left on Kevin's list. Is he aware of that?"

"Yes sir. The man told me this morning he's armed to the teeth and ready to shoot anything that gets close."

"That won't help much with Swallow. Watts could have had a bazooka and he still would have eaten those ribs. Still be just as dead, too."

"The guns make him feel better. Besides, I think Cullen digs all the attention. That man never gets rattled in what you'd call a normal way. He was born rattled and that's just about how he likes it."

"What do you make of him wanting his ex-wife to be there with us today?"

Terry didn't say anything for a while. He just watched the sheer mountainsides glide by his window as they wound up the road. There wasn't a cloud in the sky, but the higher they went, the more the temperature dropped. Less than an hour west of town, Evergreen is about thirty-five hundred feet higher than Denver. It's usually five to ten degrees cooler there in late September. Finally, he spoke. "No telling. Laurie's one sharp woman but Cullen might still be her fatal flaw. I never could see them together in the first place, so their hooking up now doesn't figure, either. All he told me was they got together yesterday. At least they're talking civilly to each other."

"But why does she actually have to be there when we get together?"

Terry shrugged. "Cullen always liked Laurie to get involved with whatever he was working on. She's an idea person. I've never been married, so I don't know what a husband thinks about along those lines. Might be he's more scared than he's letting on and Laurie comforts him. Or it might be he just wants her around for as long as they're not fighting."

"A fine-looking man like you's never been married? How'd that happen?"

"Some days I'd say I've just been lucky, other days I'd say I've been unlucky. Being married always seemed like more work than it's worth. Besides, if you don't want kids, and that would be me, I can't see any reason to get all tied up like that. You ever been hitched?"

"Let's just say that I've had my share of blood tests. You don't want children?"

Terry looked at the driver. "No thanks. Come from a childhood like mine, you're not all that interested in repeating the whole family thing. Once in a lifetime's enough."

Streeter nodded. "Amen to that." He thought of his own childhood, growing up with an alcoholic father, but he said nothing further.

Evergreen loomed ahead. It's a fast-growing but funky un-incorporated mountain village of a few thousand people surrounded by ever-encroaching custom-built homes. From the northeast, it was nondescript: generic strip malls surrounded by rolling hills freckled with houses. Like any suburb, only bumpy. But from the way they approached, the old part of town looked like something straight out of a TV Western. There was one street winding through town, with shops, restaurants, and taverns on both sides. Rustic, old Colorado. Mountain attitude from the locals, too. Willie Nelson used to have a spread near there, and people left him alone.

They drove past the legendary Little Bear Saloon on the right and then took a left at the old town's major intersection. The directions from the clerk at the assessor's office put the Stewart place about three miles to the west.

"You sure you did the right thing, not telling the police about this place?" Terry asked as they left town, heading into a narrow canyon. "Might be nice to arrest Swallow right this morning."

"True, but, based on the guy who told me about this, the chances of Kevin being here are slim. I want to chase down every lead, though."

"What's the plan once we get there?"

"I thought, if we can't see anyone outside from the road, one of us'll go in and do a pretense visit. You know, pretend to be looking for someone else or just asking directions. We have to make an ID on who's in there. But if we're real lucky, whoever's home might be outside. I brought a camera with a long-range lens either way."

Terry shifted in his seat. "So just exactly which one of us you plan on sending in with the pretense? That might get more than a little risky."

"I know." Streeter shot him a glance. "Which one of us do you think he'd be less likely to recognize?"

"I never saw the guy myself, and I don't think he ever saw me."

"Me either, but if Carol's right about that bounty garbage in the poem, Swallow knows who I am and he might know what I look like."

"So you're saying it's me most likely to go in?" Terry asked.

"We'll decide when we get there. We can always flip a coin."

"Yes sir, you got yourself a plan, all right." Terry rubbed his chin thoughtfully with his fingers and stared straight ahead. "Must have been half the night putting it together, too."

They turned right off the paved highway onto a dirt road, as the clerk had told him to do. Then they weaved slowly on the clay and sparse gravel for a half-mile before angling to the left again, onto another dirt road, which was no more smooth.

"Where the hell does this woman live, anyhow?" Terry asked, his hand gripping the dashboard. "We dealing with Grizzly Adams here?"

"It should be just up here, two or three more houses on the left. Set back a ways. What the hell were you expecting? Mountain people like their privacy. Not everyone can be Brooks Towers material. I guarantee you one thing, if we have to get out in the woods, my white-trash clothes won't look half bad."

Terry mumbled something and turned to look out his window. Then he said out loud, "How are we supposed to know which one is his? None of them seem to be numbered."

The houses sat on two- and three-acre lots. They were mostly A-frames or disoriented-looking triplexes built in the seventies. None were very well maintained, although they seemed to be holding up pretty well. The yards were wooded and otherwise overgrown with tall natural grasses and weeds.

"The clerk told me it should be the fourth house on the left, once we turned onto Peak View Road," Streeter explained. "Some of the mailboxes have names on them. Check those over there." He nodded to three metal boxes on a wobbly wooden T-frame on Terry's side of the road. They were about fifty feet before the next driveway. Streeter slowed the Buick down. "Can you read any names?"

"Not so fast," Terry responded. They slowed even more and Nathan stuck his head outside the car. "Nothing, nothing, and S-T-E-something." He pulled back inside and faced the driver. "That last one had to be Stewart."

Streeter nodded to his left. "Check it out when we go by."

The Stewart place was set off from the road about thirty yards. Its drive wound down to where the house was, a few feet below the actual road level. The lot was only dotted with aspens and scrawny pine trees, so they could see the front door from certain angles. Streeter crawled the Buick past the property. As he did, both men strained to see what they could. It took about half a minute to drive by the lot, and when they got a few hundred yards farther up the road, Streeter pulled over.

"Didn't see anyone outside," Terry said while looking straight ahead. "Guess that means we go to the pretense part of your master plan."

"Not necessarily. Did you notice anything right out in front of the deck?"

Terry turned to face him. "No car, if that's what you mean. Any idea what he might be driving?"

"Nothing in his name. I checked Motor Vehicles yesterday. Gina Gallo has a Ford van registered to her. No van out there, but I did see a motorcycle, and it looked like the gas tank was pulled off. My hunch is someone's working on it. I thought I spotted some tools lying on the ground next to it."

"How the hell did you see all that so fast?"

"It's easy when you're not wearing celebrity blackout shades. Damned Stevie Wonder had a better shot at seeing something than you did. I'll park here and we'll walk back to get a closer look. There's plenty of trees over to the north for cover."

The two got out of the car and Streeter grabbed his camera from the back seat. He gave it to Terry. Then he took a pair of high-powered binoculars out as well and carried them himself. They walked about fifty yards on the dirt road and then turned off to their right, onto what appeared to be open land just to the north of the Stewart place. Tall prairie grass and pine needles stabbed Terry's sandaled feet, but he didn't complain. They made it to a stand of about forty tall aspens which were close to the peak of their fall color. The leaves were such a bright orange it almost looked like the trees were on fire.

"Gotta love those aspens," Terry said as they squatted in the middle of the stand. The Stewart house was about forty yards to the south. "You were right about the bike. Looks like whoever it is plans to be working on it for a while."

They could hear the harsh sounds of rock music coming from a speaker set out on the front deck. An open bottle sat next to the speaker.

Streeter looked through the glasses. "They like Dr Pepper and Stevie Ray Vaughan. I bet it's Swallow. Stevie Ray was into all that hard-on blues they go for in prison. This could be your lucky day, Terry. You might not have to go in there after all."

They'd waited for about fifteen minutes when suddenly the front screen door swung open. A man who looked like the centerfold for *Iron Horse* magazine walked out. Bending down, he picked up his Dr Pepper, and he took a long swig. He was wearing oil-smeared blue jeans and one of those strapped white undershirts like Stallone wore in *Rocky*. It showcased his bloated muscles. He wore a full beard and a ratty baseball cap—backwards, of course. His dishwater-blond hair was pulled into a ponytail that was unraveling. Strands fell over both shoulders and he kept brushing them back. Unfortunately, he was wearing round, dark shades, like welder's glasses, that allowed no hint as to what his eyes looked like.

"So that's the guy who can kill you from the next state?" Terry whispered. "Man looks like he should be running a porno shop."

"You don't have to be a *GQ* coverboy to throw poison on barbecued ribs," the bounty hunter said quietly, adjusting his binoculars. "Those damned shades aren't going to make this any easier. I'll tell you one thing, from here he doesn't look like the mug shot. Give me the camera."

Streeter set his binoculars on the ground and took the Canon. He held it to his face and focused, his mouth opening a bit. Then he began to click off pictures. He shot an entire roll of film. When he was finished, the two sat there for another half-hour to see if they could spot a woman who might be Gina. The biker spent most of that time kneeling next to his machine with his back to them. Finally, Streeter signaled that they should leave. As they walked back to the car they could see clouds rolling in from the west. It was just after twelve when they got to the Buick. They put the equipment in the back seat. As they did, a green 1989

Ford van drove past them, heading toward where they'd just been.

Terry saw it first. "Turn away from the road." Both men quickly faced the woods to their right, so that by the time the van got to them the driver couldn't see their faces.

"Think that was Gina?" Terry asked when the van had moved on.

"Could be. Not much we can do about it now."

They got into the Buick. "Let's get these to a one-hour Moto-Foto," Streeter said as he turned the car around and headed south. "I want Carol to see them today."

Gina Gallo got out of the Ford and walked to Kevin, who stood up as she approached. She was wearing tight jeans and a sweatshirt, and she carried a six-pack of beer. "Kev, did you notice anyone snooping around here just a short while ago?" Her face was twisted in deep concern.

Swallow frowned. "No. What do you mean?"

"Well, sir, back on the road over there I just saw two guys putting stuff into a car. It was a big old American thing. And one of them was a colored dude dressed like a businessman. You don't think someone knows about you being here and all."

He shrugged. "I don't see how. Was either of them real fat and wearing thick glasses?"

"No." Gina put her right index finger into her mouth and started chewing the nail. "I wish this was all over. That's what I wish. This hurting people is getting me down, Kev. I'm not so sure I want to be involved with it anymore."

"Oh, man, let's not go over that again. I told you we'll have this other guy out of the way soon. I planted that thing at his house last night and I gotta believe he'll use it by today. Then we get to Irwin on Monday and it's all over. Don't worry, babe." He frowned and his voice got a mean edge. "And what's this 'don't want to be involved' shit? Like it or not, Gina, you're in up to your eyeballs."

"I just hope you're right about everything. That deal you rigged last night to get the other PI, that's neat and all, but what if it doesn't work?"

"It'll work just fine. We'll be done with everything by Monday."

"Good, 'cause all those hang-up calls we got yesterday make me nervous."

"Be cool." He glared at her. Kevin had his own theory on who was calling them, but he wouldn't share it with her. "Come Monday, all your worries'll be over."

16

The minute Laurie Cullen walked into her condo that Friday night, she knew someone had broken in. Instinctively, she reached into her purse, where she kept a tiny pearl-handled nine-millimeter. She looked around the living room. There was a trace of a musty odor in the air that she couldn't quite place. When she got to the kitchen, she solved that riddle. A pile of plump ashes littered the white tile floor. That explained the fat cigar butt near her stoop. It also meant that whoever'd been there was gone, throwing it down on their way out. She let go of the nine. As she walked into the dining room, she saw the reason for the visit. In a shiny pool of water on the table sat a tall glass with a dozen roses in it. There was a note propped up on the container, although it was wilted where it had been splashed. Laurie easily recognized Brian's handwriting. The man wrote like a ten-year-old riding in a cattle car.

"How could I ever have accused you?" the note asked. That

question was then answered with unintended clarity. "I must be nuts. Please forgive me." As if to add an absurd hint of mystery, it wasn't signed.

"How'd that slob get in here?" Laurie asked out loud.

She went and dialed Cullen's home number, and left a message for him to call her. "Do it fast or I'll have you picked up for breaking and entering," she informed his machine. She also dialed her number into his pager. Then she made a quick survey of the rest of the condo. Nothing else was disturbed. There was no sign of a forced entry. Brian must have made a copy of her key last Christmas, when he kept an eye on the place while she went to Mexico.

Within a few minutes, the phone rang. It was her ex, nearly gasping at the other end. "Laurie. I called as soon as I got the page." He tried to put sincerity in his voice, but he sounded moderately drunk. "Did you get my little peace offering?"

"I did." She paused. "What the hell gives you the right to come in here when I'm not at home? I've got half a mind to call the cops." Laurie could hear laughter and music over the line. "What bar are you at?"

Brian now went for an authoritative tone. "I'm out on a field surveillance."

"What bar?" she repeated flatly.

"Caldonias."

"Aren't you a little old for that? Look, it should take you about ten minutes to get here. If you can't drive, call a cab. We've got to talk."

"Right." Brian was back to shooting for sincerity, this time laced with a shade more concern. "I want you to know I'm there for you, baby."

He hadn't called her that in years. "Spare me, Brian. Just get over here."

Cullen arrived half an hour later. He'd stopped off at a convenience store for a coffee and was, if not sober, at least coherent and marginally focused. Laurie was waiting outside, pacing, and smoking a cigarette.

"I got here as fast as I could," he said as he walked up to her.

"My lucky day." She dropped her cigarette next to the cigar butt. "Look at this." She nodded to the cigar. "It's like what you'd find at the bottom of a gorilla cage."

"Here I make a good-faith attempt to say I'm sorry and you talk like this."

"Stuff it, Brian. This is my home and I want that key you made. You're never to come here again unless I invite you. Is that understood?"

As he looked at her—desirable in the thin, tan summer dress—an all-too-rare pulse of honesty swept through him. "Okay, I shouldn't have done it, but I just wanted to connect with you somehow. It wasn't breaking and entering, baby. It was a cry for help."

"Pull-eze, Brian. It's not a cry, it's a *whine*, for sympathy. I stomped your brittle Irish ego and now you want me back to show that you won." Her voice softened as she spoke. Despite herself, his 'fessing up got to her. So much of their marriage had been spent with him either ignoring or bullying her. His being even remotely vulnerable was a nice change.

Brian's head was tipped down slightly and there was a trace of moisture in his eyes. Laurie had seen him cry only twice during their entire marriage: once each when the Broncos lost their second and third Super Bowls in the late 1980s. She was stunned but quickly regained her composure. "If you were so miserable, why didn't you say something before? Maybe, if I ever once got a genuine response, we could have talked. I had nothing to work with. You'd just give orders and retreat."

"If I took a real whack at this opening-up stuff, could we have another shot?"

"Hold on there, sailor. What makes you think I even want another chance? You weren't the most passionate man around."

"And you weren't exactly putting off smoke yourself. Hell, the only reason you took up knitting was so you'd have something to do while we made love."

"Maybe if you would have even tried to take care of yourself. You must have put on three hundred pounds that last couple of years. Your idea of exercise equipment is the refrigerator and the remote."

"Arguing about this ain't getting us anywhere, Laurie." He seemed deeply sad. "I've got plenty on my mind with that crazy bastard Swallow running around killing people. By my calculations, he'll be coming after me soon."

She shook her head. "Why'd you tell Terry you thought I might use that as an excuse to hurt you? What a crock. Where do you get these ideas?"

"I know it was horseshit, but it made me feel better thinking you were still paying attention to me. Look, I'm really sorry I said those things. I won't bother you anymore."

She gave him a long look and then, in a softer voice, "You want some coffee?"

Brian nodded. They sat and talked for almost four hours. He spent much of the time copping to how badly he'd behaved or, more surprisingly, really listening. Laurie told of her meeting with Terry. They speculated on how Swallow might make his move. And they talked about how they had treated each other over the years. In the end, she was exhausted but touched by his newfound tenderness and amused at hints of his old sense of humor. She agreed to meet with him, Terry, and Streeter the next day.

Terry arrived at his office that Saturday afternoon a couple of hours after he and Streeter got back from Evergreen. Laurie and Brian were already there, talking over coffee. The two men shared a suite in an old building in LoDo. They rented out most of it and still had three thousand feet left over for themselves.

Brian had talked Nathan into going halves on the run-down structure back in 1985. Good move. They renovated it, and with the dramatic resurgence of the area, they could now practically retire if they sold the place. Terry was amazed at how gentle the Cullens were with each other. Laurie's attitude didn't fit in with how she had talked just a few days earlier, and Brian surprised him because he generally never acted that way toward anyone.

"The happy couple," Terry said. It was almost a question. "What's to it, Laurie?"

"Good to see you, Terry." She took a couple of steps toward him and opened her arms, careful of the coffee cup in her right hand. They hugged formally. "Bet you're surprised to see me here."

Terry's eyebrows shot up casually to indicate that nothing much surprised him.

"I hear you got a new partner." Brian stepped forward as he spoke. He tried to sound mad but he was in too good a mood to pull it off.

"The man should be here any minute." Terry liked seeing Brian upbeat, freshly shaved, clear-eyed, and horsing around like that. He even had on a pressed oxford shirt and pleated pants. "We had us quite a morning."

"What happened?" Brian asked. "You get anywhere looking for Swallow?"

"Might have actually found the man. Streeter took pictures of this biker we're looking into. Lives up in Evergreen. He's over showing them to Irwin now. If she makes the guy, the cops should take care of him today yet. That's the plan, anyhow."

"I sure as hell hope they do," Cullen said, getting serious.

"I bet you might at that, Brian. He's got to be getting around to you pretty soon."

Cullen looked at his coffee. "How'd I get so popular all of a sudden?"

Terry Nathan shrugged. "You're that kind of a guy, I guess."

Just then the door to the reception area opened and Streeter walked in. He was still wearing his work clothes from the morning. He looked grim as Terry introduced him to the Cullens.

"It's been a while, Streeter," Brian said.

Cullen seemed more relaxed than the bounty hunter remembered. Come to think of it, more relaxed than he should be, given who was after him. "Maybe five years," he responded.

"You want some coffee, Mr. Streeter?" Laurie asked.

"If it's no trouble. Some creamer, too, please."

Brian suggested they all go into his office and get comfortable. The room was just about the same way Streeter remembered it: a little cowboy shrine. He wondered if the PI lived that horse-rancher life-style outside of the office. Judging by the softness of Cullen's hand when they shook, he decided probably not. Terry took the couch while Laurie and Streeter each sat in a rocking chair and Brian poured Streeter a coffee.

"I gather we struck out with the pictures from Evergreen," Terry said to Streeter. "Your face doesn't exactly indicate good news."

"You got that right." He took the Styrofoam cup that Brian offered him. "Carol said the biker didn't look like Kevin. 'Course, she's never seen him with long hair and a beard and dressed like that before, so she's not positive. This guy was a lot bigger, she said. With those sunglasses on, there's no way she could make a decent ID, but she's sure that's not him. Sure enough not to go to the cops. Hell, we had the guy's mug shot and we couldn't come close to making him."

"Anyone can grow some hair and pile on the muscles," Brian said, sounding irritated. "That's all those shitheads do down in Cañon City."

Streeter nodded. "I mentioned that but she said even in the close-ups she didn't think it was him. I said, if he delivered those ribs to Watts without being recognized, he's changed a lot. She just said this isn't him."

"Bottom line, we're right back where we were yesterday," Terry said.

"Which isn't very far," Laurie added.

Streeter glanced at her. He could see why Brian wanted her around. The lady had a nice way about her, assertive but calm. She looked like she was always about to smile. It made her seem as though she knew something no one else in the room did. Nice fragrance, too. Streeter pegged it as Donna Karan. Exclusive. Only a half-dozen stores in Colorado carried the stuff.

"You got that right, baby," Cullen responded. He was clearly being deferential to his ex-wife. "Hit the nail on the head."

Streeter noticed that Terry looked surprised at how his partner was acting.

"Turning over a new leaf there, are you, Brian?" Nathan asked.

Cullen frowned at him for a second and Laurie looked amused. "Brian thinks he's on parole and I'm his PO," she explained.

Cullen walked to his desk and lowered himself into the wooden swivel chair behind it. "This Swallow's pretty sharp, from what I hear."

"His big thing is killing from a distance," Streeter said. "That's what makes him so dangerous. If he comes after you, look for a surprise: a bomb, a booby trap. You never know how he'll do it, but it most likely won't be him waving a gun in your face."

Laurie looked at her ex. "You should find a new place to stay until he's locked up. He might be good, but he can't keep track of ten people at once."

"Don't be so sure about that," Streeter said, thinking of the note at the church. "He seems to know what everyone does and where everyone lives. He's always a jump ahead of us. A regular mind reader."

"Well, let's at least make him work for it a little," Laurie responded. "You should find somewhere else to live for now, Brian. Maybe at Terry's."

Nathan sat up at that one. "That won't fool anyone. Be the first place the man looks if Cullen's not coming home at night." He knew that was true and, besides, the thought of Brian living with him indefinitely made him shudder.

Brian nodded and then focused on Laurie, his face brightening considerably. "How about your place? If he did his homework, he knows we're on the outs."

Laurie sat back in her chair. "Hold on. I didn't mean me."

"You've got tons of room, Laurie," Brian pressed. "I won't be no trouble, honest. And, hell," he added, his grin widening, "we already got an extra key."

Streeter studied her face. It surprised him when she agreed.

"We'll give it a try," she said slowly. "But we use separate cars at all times and you stay in the guest room. If you lose your way back to bed from the can just one night and end up in my room, you're out on the spot."

"You won't even know I'm there, baby." Brian sat back.

17

Before he left Cullen's, Streeter went to the conference room for privacy and called Linda Parnell. They hadn't seen each other since the driving range. But they'd talked the day before and made tentative plans for dinner that night.

"Howdy, stranger." She sounded reserved but not unfriendly. "So how's the vigilante business?"

"Not great," he answered. "Looks like we came up empty today. How does Marlowe's at seven-thirty sound?"

"Just fine."

"You sure you don't want me to pick you up?"

She hesitated, then, "Don't bother. I live at the other end of town. Plus, if I drive, we'll both have our getaway cars handy."

They hung up and Streeter drove back to the church to get ready. Carol wasn't there, so he showered and changed in the loft, rather than downstairs. He put on a light-blue shirt and tan dress slacks. When he finished, he went to Frank's office.

"Looks like you're stepping out there, Big Guy." Frank was sitting at his desk, reading a Tom Clancy paperback, and sipping a Johnnie Walker Red, neat. He was wearing a double-breasted navy sport coat, charcoal slacks, white shirt, and club tie. "Spending some time with your friend Linda tonight?"

Streeter nodded. "You're rather dapper yourself. All you need is a yacht and a martini."

"That's all any of us needs." Dazzler glanced at his clothes and set the book on the credenza behind him. "I'm seeing my lady from down the hall." Frank had been dating the owner of the Workout Space for several years. They were both about the same age and were content seeing each other once or twice a week. "You got a call from a lawyer a couple hours ago. Jack something-or-other. His number's right here. He said he's returning your call. He'll be at that number all night." Frank ripped the top page from a notepad and slid it across the desk.

Streeter picked up the paper. "Jack Nevers. I called him yesterday at his office." He glanced back at Frank. "He used to be Carol's law partner. You remember, way back when I was with her."

"What did you call him about?"

"I figure that he might have worked with her a little on the Swallow trial. I thought I'd see if he remembers anything helpful about the guy. It's a long shot, but I'm talking to anyone who knew Kevin. Maybe Jack knows something like where he used to work or who he hung out with."

Frank stood up. "Well, I'm heading out. The phone's all yours."

Streeter took his place behind the desk. He'd always liked Jack Nevers and thought he was good for Carol. Jack was coolheaded, competent, and patient. Plenty of courtroom experience and a good sense of humor, too. He was forty, with thinning red hair, pale, lightly freckled skin, and tortoiseshell glasses. Streeter dialed the number. "Hey, Jack. Thanks for getting back to me so fast. What's to it?"

"Streeter." Nevers sounded mildly preoccupied. "How's the bounty-hunting business? Man, it's been a while."

"A year or more, I guess."

Nevers nodded with the receiver to his ear. "You or Carol. Christ, I haven't seen her in ages. I don't suppose you have any idea how she's doing. I remember right after your breakup she wanted to kill you. 'Course, back in those days she wanted to kill a lot of people. That is no woman to have as an enemy."

"True. But she got over it. We declared a truce and we're actually friends these days. As a matter of fact, I'm doing some work for her."

Jack frowned. "What does she need you for? I thought she had some little corporate practice. Does this have to do with that threat business from her old client? I read about it in the paper today."

"You might say. I'm digging around trying to find the guy. It's a big mess and he's in deep hiding."

"The paper said there might be a link between threats to her and that cop being poisoned. When I saw Swallow's name, I remembered the case."

"That's what I wanted to ask you about," Streeter said, adjusting himself in the chair. "I was wondering if you worked with her on his trial."

"Not at all. That was totally her baby from start to finish. She'd barely talk about it to me."

Streeter frowned. "Well, that takes care of my second question. I wanted to see if you remembered anything about Swallow that might help me find him."

"Not a thing. All I knew was what I read in the papers. Carol was really jammed up about that case. She never told me a thing and I didn't meet the man myself." He paused. "Carol Irwin. Man, back when we closed the office, I didn't think she was going to make it. When she snaps, she snaps all the way. Did you ever hear what she did when I told her I was moving out of the office? Jesus Christ!"

"No, but she grumbled a little about you when we were together."

"That's no surprise. She'd come to me for advice once in a while, and if I so much as questioned what she was doing, she'd act like I stabbed her in the back. Anything but complete agreement she considered treason. Anyhow, I finally had enough and I told her I was history. She went crazy and fumed for days. Then, one night when I got home from work, I was walking up my driveway with the mail. Carol's car comes screeching down the block and turns in to my house. She revs her engine and heads right at me. Luckily, I dove out of the way. But my Blazer was still in the line of fire. The crazy broad rams into the back end of my new Blazer. After that, I told her to stay away or I'd get a restraining order. I mean, hell, if I hadn't jumped out of the way she might have killed me."

"You're kidding."

"I wish I was." Nevers' voice quavered at the recollection. "But that's not half as crazy as what she did when you two split. When she got her hand all cut up."

Streeter frowned. "Her accident with the disposal?"

Jack's voice lowered. "That was no accident, pal. It happened about a year before she tried to run me down. Carol was so rattled about your breakup that I'd drop by her place once in a while, just to make sure she was okay. This one night she was screaming about what a total asshole you are, then she'd turn around and contradict herself. First she's blaming you, and the next minute she's saying what a piece of shit she is and how she deserved what you did. All of a sudden, she stomped into the kitchen and shoved her hand down the sink. She put her other hand on the disposal switch and said something like, 'If he treats me like garbage, then I must be garbage.' I take one step toward her and she hits the fucking switch.

"Blam, the disposal kicks in. By the time I yanked her arm out, her hand was cut up and she was screaming. I got her to the hospital and they patched it up. But, Jesus Christ, Streeter. What if I hadn't been there? That woman's got real serious problems. I told her to see a shrink, but I don't know if she did."

"I had no idea that's how it happened." Streeter's mouth felt dry and he was queasy. "I know Carol's shaky, but I had no idea she could do something like that."

"Ms. Irwin has a ton of anger inside of her. When she gets worked up she has to turn it somewhere. On me, on herself, on anyone. I'm surprised she never came after you, screwing around on her and whatnot."

Streeter couldn't think of anything to say at first. Then, "Look, Jack, I have to get going. Thanks for the help." When they hung up he just stared at the desktop for a minute. Then he got up and poured himself a strong Scotch.

Marlowe's Downtown is a tall, upscale restaurant located on the city's 16th Street pedestrian-and-shuttle-bus mall, featuring dark wood accents and huge windows. High-strung professionals go there to see and be seen, and tonight was no exception. Streeter walked in a few minutes before seven-thirty. He ran a quick hand through his hair, straightened his shoulders, and headed for the bar.

"I'll have a house red. Anything dry," he told the bartender in the linen jacket.

The drink came, and in a couple of minutes, Linda appeared at the door. She wore dark gray pants, partially covered by a long white sweater that went almost to her knees. It gave her a casual, artsy look. Glasses on, she smiled warmly. They hugged hello and he was surprised at how tight she held him. Then they moved back to the bar and sat down.

"You look a little shaky, Street."

"It's been one very strange day, and I just heard something that made it even more bizarre. How about a drink and then I'll tell you about it?"

She nodded. "I could use a little fortification. White wine'll do it."

Streeter turned to the bartender and ordered. When it arrived, he filled her in on the trip to Evergreen, the unsuccessful photography, and Laurie and Brian Cullen's reunion. But he went into more detail when he related Jack's story.

"That's pretty serious stuff," she said when he'd finished. "Has Carol ever seen anyone professionally? A therapist?"

"She told me years ago she was getting counseling but I didn't ask why. A lot of people get therapy, so I didn't think much of it."

"Has she ever mentioned suicide?"

"Never. What do you think her problem is?"

"It could be any number of things. A personality or bipolar disorder, severe depression. I'd have to know a lot more. Let's just hope they catch Swallow fast. The stress she's under could trigger another episode. Self-mutilation generally recurs."

"What should I do?"

"Keep a close eye on her and be as reassuring as possible. She needs to feel safe. How's she been acting?"

"Surprisingly, she's holding up pretty well. She can be brittle at times, but usually she's calm. There is one thing that puzzles me. We've had a strictly platonic relationship for years, but in the last few days it's almost like she's coming on to me. Subtle, but it's there. Carol can be seductive without trying hard. Certain suggestions, looks, her tone of voice. And when I said there's no way we could ever rekindle what we had she just told me to lighten up."

"And is there no way it can be rekindled?"

He looked off. "I can't imagine it. Sure, she can look tempting, but all that's ancient history."

Linda studied him. "Just out of curiosity, what are the sleeping arrangements?"

"She's got my bed. Hell, she's taken over my loft."

"And you sleep where?"

"In my bed, too. Linda, when I take on an assignment, I go all the way. Carol's safety requires my complete attention. If anything happened to her in the middle of the night and I wasn't there, I'd never forgive myself." She didn't smile, so he continued. "Okay, I sleep downstairs at Frank's. You're not jealous, are you?"

"In your dreams." She paused. "Maybe a little, but that's not the point. Look, Street, you seem to be unresolved about Carol. That's not a terrific way for us to start our friendship." She shot him a grin. "Of course, her being psychotic and possibly suicidal makes me feel a whole lot better. But, seriously, you should consider what your real feelings for her are. You seem to have a history of letting Little Elvis make important decisions for you. It might be a good idea to rethink that strategy. And I say that regardless of whatever happens with you and me."

"Well, well. It looks like you've given my situation some serious thought. Aren't you wonderful?" He smiled.

She shook her head slightly. "And aren't you hopeless. It's a good thing you're so cute." She thought for a moment. "Last week you mentioned that being a bounty hunter was getting to you. I imagine this Irwin business makes you more concerned about your life-style."

"Just the opposite." He shook his head. "When I do the day-in, day-out stuff for Frank, I think a lot about trying something else.

Then I jump into the middle of a case like this. I get so caught up in it, I forget how restless and dissatisfied I usually am. The heat of the moment, the hunt, whatever it is. It becomes almost like a game: beat the other guy, find the bad man, save the girl. That must sound like kid stuff."

"It might be avoidance or it might mean you're in the right place, after all," she responded. "You should probably explore your feelings about that, too."

"There's the F-word again. You mention it a lot."

She shook her head. "You *are* hopeless. Look, I'm starving. Let's eat."

They shared a Cabernet over dinner and the talk stayed away from Carol Irwin. When they finished, Linda said she wanted to turn in early because she had to leave to go to Vail first thing in the morning for a wedding shower. Streeter didn't try to talk her into staying out. He was preoccupied with Jack Nevers' story, so he just walked Linda to her car. When they kissed good night, the wine smelled rich and organic on her breath. He kissed her again and told her he'd call her Monday.

18

As he combed his hair at the bathroom mirror, Brian was still amazed at his good luck with Laurie. He knew he was taking a chance of infuriating her by going into her house with flowers. She takes it the wrong way, she's gone forever. Judging by the look on her face when he first got to the condo, that almost happened. But crank up the old tear machine, humble yourself, and—bingo—you're moving in with her. He smiled at his reflection. Everything was going better than he could have hoped. But his smile faded as he thought of how he hadn't just cranked up the old tear machine. His crying was genuine. This last year without Laurie had been much harder than he'd ever imagined. She was his best friend, and his feelings for her ran deep. Since their breakup, his life had gone downhill. He'd been drinking heavily and, other than a few one-night stands, he hadn't dated.

No, the swinging-single life hadn't worked for Brian, and not just because his ladykiller days were behind him. It was Laurie. She was irreplaceable. She had a fire inside her and a way of making life seem interesting and important. A way of making *him* seem interesting and important. By the time he finished thinking about it, he was leaning forward, both hands on the sides of the sink, his head lowered. Spending the rest of his life without Laurie terrified him much more than Kevin Swallow could ever hope to. He shuddered and put his comb in his back pocket.

As they were leaving his office, shortly after five, he had told Laurie he'd go home, pick up his shaving kit and some clothes, and be at her condo by seven. He said he'd take her out for a nice dinner, somewhere dark and expensive. One of the big hotels in the Denver Tech Center, just south of town.

"That'll be nice, Brian," she had said cautiously.

Now he glanced at his reflection and smiled. He'd get back with Laurie and not screw it up this time. Plus, opening up and leveling with her the night before felt good. Made him feel lighter. Close to her, too. This sincerity hustle worked better than he'd ever imagined. He pondered whether or not to take a shower. It would be his second that day, a rarity, but why not? Maybe a little steak and wine, and Laurie might not mind so much if he ended up in her room later. He looked at his watch and realized he didn't have time to clean up again. Instead, he opted for what he referred to as a Polish shower: warm water on the face and a couple blasts under each arm with Right Guard.

Throw on a little cologne and God only knows where he'd actually end up sleeping that night.

Washing up, he whistled softly. As he returned the towel to a rack behind him, he studied his profile in the mirror. He was wearing just tan slacks, and his round white stomach reminded him of a vanilla ice-cream cone. Brian frowned and thought of what Laurie had said about his body. "Starting tomorrow," he whispered, "we cut back on the groceries." No doubt about that.

Then he opened the medicine cabinet and pulled out the Right Guard can. Fluorocarbons and the possibility of their poking a hole in the earth's ozone layer didn't concern Brian. He grew up using the spray cans and he wasn't about to change. It felt heavier than he recalled. Lifting his left elbow to get under that arm, he simultaneously pulled on the plastic top. Just as he started to pull, he heard a loud car horn out the window to his right. He turned his head to look in that direction, which almost certainly saved him from severe facial burns. It probably saved his life, too.

The pull wire connecting the top of the Right Guard can to the toggle switch Kevin had put where the nozzle used to be was about three inches long. A little longer than usual in a bomb like that. The extra length gave Brian's face time to turn fully away before the can blew up. The explosive charge inside wasn't quite as large as Kevin wanted, but he figured it would be enough to instantly kill whoever opened it. He figured wrong. For some unknown reason, the bulk of the blast went down and away from Brian. He saw a hard flash of light and heard the blast that would permanently reduce the hearing in his left ear to nearly nothing. Flames shot through his entire left armpit, up the arm, and along that side of his stomach, scorching hair and skin. His left hand felt like it had been slammed by a hot jackhammer. Brian was tossed to his right, straight into the bathtub. Tossed hard, but he didn't die.

Kevin was slumped against the backboard in bed when the 10:00 P.M. news began. Gina was in the bathroom, brushing her teeth for maybe the twelfth time that day. On television, a tentative but drop-dead Hispanic anchorwoman led off the night's stories with an item she didn't know quite how to handle. It was violent, but so offbeat and quirky that her face struggled not to smile. Kevin's own grainy mug shot was displayed behind her as she spoke.

"In Denver tonight, a forty-six-year-old man was severely burned when the aerosol deodorant can he was using—which was actually a crude homemade bomb—exploded into his armpit. Police believe the bombing is part of a series of attacks by a Kevin Swallow. Swallow had been convicted of the 1991 car-bombing murders of a Denver couple, but was later released when the convictions were overturned by the Colorado Court of Appeals. Brian Cullen, a longtime private investigator, is in serious condition at St. Joseph's Hospital tonight with second-degree burns and a severe concussion. The bomb went off in the bathroom of his home on South Ogden Street, near Washington Park, shortly after seven P.M. Cullen was alone at the time."

"The fuck does she mean, 'crude' bomb?" Kevin muttered. "Damned PIs. None of them want to go down like they should. Gina!" he yelled, his eyes still on the set. "Get in here, babe. You *have got* to see this."

The bathroom door opened and a flood of light swept into the room, outlining Gina's figure. She was wearing a sheer black baby-doll pajama top and a pink thong bottom which was smaller than her fading tan line. The toothbrush was shoved far into her mouth. As wet toothpaste dribbled down her chin she twisted maniacally on the brush. "Wah ist?" she asked, frowning and studying the TV as she walked.

Kevin looked up and said, "They had a story on Cullen getting blown up. Only he didn't die, either." He turned back to the set.

"How the hell did he live through that? I bet that can was no more than three inches from his stupid armpit when it went off."

He'd gone through Brian's house a week earlier, searching for the right vehicle for the bomb. When he saw the deodorant can, he thought he'd found the perfect thing. Putting the actual bomb together was child's play, and he slipped back into the house on Friday, the day before, to exchange it for the Right Guard in the bathroom.

For her part, Gina sat on the bed, her shoulders slumped. The toothbrush was in her balled fist and a small pool of wet white toothpaste had sloshed over her thigh. Secretly, she was glad that Cullen hadn't died. She didn't want another death on her increasingly guilty conscience. "Does this mean we have to wait around, Kev? You promised me that we'd leave town Monday, you know."

He stared at her without saying a word. At times like this, Gina looked like she just fell out of a comic book. Toothpaste mustache, mismatched lingerie, excessive eyeliner, and a self-absorbed pout. That once-pretty face that now appeared to be forty and strained to look twenty. "I know I did, babe," he said evenly. "And by Monday night we'll be headed north. You don't have to come back here until you're good and ready."

Gina smiled, her tongue shooting out like a poodle's to wipe the toothpaste from around her mouth. "Oh, Kev, you're the best. I always knew that."

"Yeah. Why wait? Besides, those two guys you saw out there today might be trouble. We nearly did what we were after with Cullen. He's hurting plenty. I give a shit if he actually dies or not."

Gina stared at him in admiration. "You can be a very kind man sometimes, Kev."

He looked closely at her to see if she was serious, but he couldn't tell. "Besides, that damned break-in this afternoon has me worried," he said. They had taken a long motorcycle ride a few hours earlier. When they got back, they found that someone had broken in and ransacked the place. They weren't sure if anything was missing, but it was obvious that whoever did it was looking for something specific. "Anyhow," he continued, "I've got my plans nailed down. We've got some serious work tomorrow, but we should be ready to make our move first thing Monday morning."

Gina frowned deeply and looked around the room. "Who would do such a terrible thing? I've never had a break-in up here before."

Kevin was pretty sure he knew who did and why, but he didn't want to think about that now. Had to be the same guy who made the hang-up calls the day before. The man was getting close, Swallow reasoned, but he probably wouldn't be back for a while. And Kevin didn't want Gina any more spooked than she already was. Just keep her focused on completing the plan and then hit the road Monday. "I'm sure it was just some Mexicans. Your standard break-in. Crime in this country's getting out of hand. It's enough to make you wanna puke."

She nodded knowingly. "What happens Monday?"

Kevin walked to the television set and turned it off. Then he glanced at Gina on the bed. "We're going to bomb Irwin and you get to deliver it yourself."

Gina's eyes widened in fear and confusion. "Me? That's cool, Kev, but it don't sound all that safe." She put the toothbrush back in her mouth and idly worked it, her mind focusing on what he had just told her.

Kevin walked to the bed and looked squarely into her eyes. "Do you think for a minute I'd have you do something that was dangerous? I'd never take any chances with your personal safety."

She pulled the toothbrush out for a second. "I surely hope so, Kev."

"You'll be fine." He kept steady eye contact as he spoke, his words coming in warm tones. "Just deliver the thing and leave. That's all there is to it."

Out came the toothbrush again. "What thing?"

"The dynamite, babe. Just a few sticks of dynamite with a little old timer and triggering device. Let me worry about all that."

The word "dynamite" sent her forehead into frown spasms. "Dynamite? Now, sir, I know for a fact that's dangerous."

"Not the way I'll have it set up." Pacing in front of her, he explained, "The way I figure, between what happened to Cullen and that note I left Irwin this morning, they're going to tighten security. Don't worry yourself about the details, but she's got to be in court most of the week, so we'll nail her as she heads out Monday morning. We'll need a shopping cart and some old ratty clothes for you."

"I don't get what you're saying." Terror was obvious in her voice. She frowned and seemed about to cry.

Kevin spent the next ten minutes patiently laying out the broad strokes of his plan and how Gina would be the star of the show. She studied him as he paced and talked, but the frown never left her face.

"That's a lot for me to remember," she said when he'd finished. "What if something goes wrong?"

Kevin wanted to slap her. "Gina, quit getting all chicken on me." Then he knelt down in front of her again. "You were so gung ho on this plan when we started. I swear, if you wimp out on me now, you'll fuckin' wish that dynamite was for you." Suddenly, his voice lightened. "Don't worry, babe. We'll go over it so much tomorrow you'll be able to do it in your sleep. Think of how well you handled that call when we nailed Gagliano?"

A weak smile trickled across her mouth and she nodded. "I did good that time."

"Damned straight you did. And you'll be perfect this time, too. Just imagine how excited you'll be, walking down the street with all that dynamite in your cart. It'll be one major rush. That much power under your control."

"Cool," Gina concurred, nodding her head, but still confused. "I never thought of it like that. Just you make sure it's safe for me."

He reached up and carefully pulled her head onto his shoulder. "I wouldn't let nothing in the world happen to you. That's a promise."

19

When Streeter got home from Marlowe's, Frank gave him the message from Nathan about Brian. He immediately drove to St. Joseph's Hospital. Traffic on 17th was light, so he got there fast. It was shortly after eleven when he found Terry alone in the fourth-floor waiting room. Cullen had just gotten out of surgery, and Laurie was down the hall by the intensive-care unit, pacing and having a nicotine fit. Brian's upper left side and arm were badly burned, he was temporarily deaf in his left ear, and he'd have a bitching headache for a couple of days. But he was stable and out of mortal danger.

"What the hell's going on, Terry?" Streeter asked. There was a TV flickering *Saturday Night Live* in the corner, but the volume was off. "Brian decides to move in with Laurie and then this happens. All he had to do was make it to her place and he probably would have been okay."

"Go figure." Terry's voice was calm, but there was pain in his eyes and his hands seemed unsteady. "They tell me he's going to pull through, but who knows how you come out of something like this?"

"How long do you think he'll be laid up?"

Terry shrugged. "Looks like I'll be running the business for the next couple of months, at least."

"What do the cops say?"

"Some cracker police sergeant by the name of Haney was running around here before. I didn't talk to him much. The bomb was in a damned deodorant can. You believe that?"

"You're kidding. I didn't even know you could do that."

"It's possible. He put it in a can of Right Guard. All you need for a booby-trap bomb are explosives and a way to detonate them. I've heard about bombs in all sorts of things. Radios, flashlights, floor mats. Some guy out in New York City even sent a bottle of champagne with a bomb inside."

"Pop the cork, huh? What'll they think of next?"

"Better still, what'll Kevin Swallow think of next?"

Streeter shook his head.

"All I know is I wouldn't mind getting my hands on him for about half an hour," Nathan continued. "Wouldn't mind that at all right about now."

"You'd have to get in line for that one, Terry."

"Does Carol know about this, Streeter?"

"I didn't tell her before I left and she didn't see the news. She can find out in the morning. It wouldn't be a good idea for her to be running around tonight more upset than she already is. Swallow might be counting on that."

Terry looked off, deep in thought. Then he turned back to Streeter. "I expect she should know soon. The lady's got to be next. No one left but her."

"That's what I figure," Streeter said. "And that'll be what she figures, too, once she learns about Cullen. Even with the doubled security and everyone trying to keep her under wraps, she's in the box and I'm sure she knows it."

Ironically, just then Carol herself swept into the waiting room, accompanied by two uniformed officers. One was Ruiz, normally the day guy, and the other was a chubby female Streeter hadn't seen before. Carol was wearing a long London Fog trench coat with baggy black sweatpants extending below it. She was pale and looked thin in the oversized clothes.

"My God, Streeter!" She stopped when she spotted him. "Why didn't you tell me about this? Didn't you think I'd be interested?"

The bounty hunter walked up to her and looked closely at her face. "You shouldn't have come here, Carol. Swallow probably anticipated that you would. You could be opening yourself up for trouble. How'd you find out about Cullen?"

"Frank told me. I went downstairs looking for you and he told me all he knew was that Cullen was hurt and that you went to the hospital."

Streeter looked at Ruiz. "Why'd you let her leave the church?"

The cop's face tightened. "Because she wanted to. She's under police protection, not house arrest. I told her it's best not to, but I can't force her to stay home."

Streeter turned back to Carol. "Brian's going to make it," he told her. "But he's in intensive care and he can't have visitors. Let's you and I and your entourage head back home and lay low. Okay?" He glanced at her left hand and flashed on what Jack Nevers had told him. He also thought of what Linda had said about avoiding stress.

Carol slowly shook her head. "I want to talk to his wife. She must feel terrible. A bomb in a deodorant can. We're not even safe in the bathroom anymore."

Her words troubled him but he couldn't figure out why. "Cullen didn't have police protection," he told her. "You'll be safe if you just stay close to the church from now on and let the police do their job. I guarantee nothing'll happen to you."

"You know you can't make that kind of promise. Just remember what happened this morning. And I have to be in court most of next week as well as going to the office from time to time. I can't stop living just because someone's trying to kill me." That last thought didn't come out right, so she added weakly, "You know what I mean."

Suddenly, Laurie Cullen walked in. She moved more slowly and less confidently than usual. Coincidentally, she was wearing the same kind of long raincoat that Carol wore, only she filled it out more. Her face was lined with concern, but she looked composed.

"Hello," she said squarely to Carol, extending her hand to be shaken. Her voice was serious but hardly desperate. "I'm Laurie Cullen."

"Laurie," Streeter interjected, realizing he hadn't even introduced Carol to Terry yet. "Laurie, this is Carol Irwin." Then he turned to Nathan. "And, Carol, this is Terry Nathan, Brian's partner." As he moved closer to the two women, he got a whiff of the fading Donna Karan on Laurie. Carol smelled mostly of cigarette smoke.

"This must be very difficult for you, Ms. Irwin," Laurie said with genuine sympathy. "I imagine those threats are a great strain."

"I'd hardly recommend it," Carol responded in a snide tone. "It's a nightmare, but that's not why I'm here. Laurie, I'm so sorry for what happened to your husband." She emphasized the "your husband." "I feel responsible. After all, I was the one who hired Brian to work on Kevin's case."

"Ex-husband," Laurie corrected her, less friendly than before.

"*Ex*-husband," Carol repeated. "That's right, Streeter told me. At any rate, I'm sorry. If there's anything I can do, let me know. When will he be able to have visitors?"

"I'm not sure." Laurie shifted her weight to the other foot and threw her head back casually. "Maybe next week. I just hope there's something they can do for his pain. Nothing hurts worse than burns."

"Cullen's too ornery to be hurting for long," Terry said quietly. "My guess is it'll be the nurses who'll need medicating before that man walks out of here."

Carol was about to say something when Sergeant Haney entered the room. He was a beefy, elderly cop who had a smoker's rasp and a boxer's blocky build. Given his green police-union windbreaker and checkered pants, it was obvious that fashion was of little concern to him. He glanced around and nodded at Streeter and Terry. He knew Streeter from a past case. When he saw Carol and the two uniforms he winced hard.

"You shouldn't be here, Miss Irwin," he said. He turned to Ruiz, his tone deepening. "And just exactly why is she?"

The uniform shrugged. "I thought about shooting her in the leg to keep her at home, but I doubt if you'd approve of that."

Haney glared at him for a second and then turned back to Carol, his voice mellowing. "I'm asking you nice if you'd let these officers take you back to Streeter's place. You'll be safe there."

"Yeah, sure. Unless Kevin drops by to leave me another note." She shot Streeter a glance. "Are you coming, too? We need to talk."

"I'll be along in a minute," he told her.

Carol said goodbye to everyone and left. When she was gone, Streeter turned to Haney. "Anything new on where Swallow is?"

The sergeant stared back at him, his face dark. "Nothing yet. How 'bout you?"

"Terry and I had a lead up in Evergreen, but when I showed Carol the guy's picture she said no. You find anything interesting at Cullen's tonight?"

"A blown-up bomb made out of a can of deodorant. I'd call that pretty damned interesting. We dusted the bathroom for prints but I won't be holding my breath on that one." He took a step toward Streeter. "Keep a sharp eye on that guest of yours, okay? And another thing, I'd watch my own ass pretty close, too.

I read the note he put in your garage, and my guess is that crack about a 'bounty' means you." With this, Haney left.

"Charming man," Laurie said. "I hope you'll be all right, Mr. Streeter. This is turning into a much bigger risk than you bargained for."

Streeter nodded. "I usually try to avoid this kind of thing. We have an unofficial slogan at Dazzler's Bail Bonds: 'If it's difficult or dangerous, we don't do it.' " Then he looked at Terry. "I'll give you a holler tomorrow. Try and take it easy."

"That I will." Terry seemed steadier now.

On his way back to the church, Streeter was preoccupied with Haney's warning. So much so that he couldn't remember exactly what Carol had said that bothered him. When he got home, the officers were at their downstairs station and Carol was in the loft, sitting at the baby grand, tapping idly on the keys. She stood up when he arrived.

"When do you give your first concert?" She nodded back toward the piano.

"The way I'm going, about eight years from Thursday."

"I'll mark it in my calendar. Actually, I listened to you practice yesterday and you didn't sound half bad." They were standing in the middle of the loft and she moved closer. "I'm glad that Brian Cullen's going to make it. According to my calculations, there shouldn't be anyone else on Kevin's list. Except for me, of course."

"You don't know that for sure. There's still the judge, for instance. Maybe others who were involved with the case."

"He's retired and lives in San Diego now. Kevin won't go out there first and then come back for me. Everyone knows what's coming next. And soon."

Streeter gave a small nod. "We'll be ready for him. Haney knows the score."

"Yeah, right. The only score that stooge knows is his bowling average. If my safety depended solely on that dipshit, I'd blow my brains out right now and save everyone the trouble." She moved closer and stared into his eyes. Her voice suddenly got soft. "Street, would you give me a hug? I need some serious comfort tonight."

He looked down at her for a moment and then slowly opened his arms. It was like he was moving on autopilot. Not resisting, but not really participating, either. She slid easily in to him, the top of her head settling just below his chin. He noticed that she'd put on perfume since the hospital. She smelled good and felt good. And her body seemed familiar.

"This remind you of anything?" she said into his chest. He didn't answer, so she continued. "Feels like the old days to me."

Streeter almost drew her up for a kiss. It seemed natural, somehow. He again recalled Nevers' story. Almost imperceptibly, he shuddered and pulled back. "Carol, what are you doing?"

She looked like she was just waking up. "Getting some comfort from an old friend." Then she glanced down to just below his belt and smiled. "Actually, it feels like two old friends. What's wrong?"

Now he stepped back completely. "That's not what we're about here, and you know it."

" 'That's not what we're about here,' " she repeated with an edge in her voice. "What kind of crap is that? We're about whatever we want to be about."

"And what is that, Carol?" His voice stayed even. "What *are* you about?"

She smiled again and stepped back toward the bedroom, keeping close eye contact the whole time. "Come in there with me and I'll tell you."

"Jesus, after all we've been through with each other, I'd have to be a real hog for punishment to start up something like that again."

Her smile widened. "Punishment? That can be arranged. I'm

sure you've got handcuffs around here somewhere. Just lighten up for once, Street. Are you afraid your little shrink lady'll find out you've been a naughty boy?"

He shook his head. "It's not about her."

Suddenly her voice turned cold and mean. "I won't tell. You can have your cake and eat it, too." With a sharp lift of one eyebrow she added, "Like you tried to do way back when we were together."

Her stunning shift made him gulp. "That was a long time ago," he said, frowning.

"Big fucking deal. There's no statute of limitations on that kind of low-rent move, Streeter. Always remember that." Carol gave a quick nod and added, lowering her voice, "Good night." With that she walked into the bedroom and slammed the door.

He stood there for a while, looking at where she'd gone and thinking how he hoped Swallow would make his move soon: Catch the man and get Carol out of here fast. That is one disturbed woman.

20

"They have you here twenty-four hours a day now?" Streeter asked Barrows late on Sunday morning. Jeff was on duty with a new male officer. "It seems like every time I turn around there you are."

"They switched me again." Barrows had thick, dark rings under his eyes and he looked paler than usual. But his voice was steady, determined. "Better days than that damned graveyard shift."

"I suppose you're right about that." Streeter nodded and then headed up to his loft. As he got near the top of the stairs he yelled out, "It's just me."

Carol was sitting at the kitchen table, making notes on a legal pad. A cup of coffee was in front of her. So was a full ashtray, which explained why the loft smelled like the waiting room for a midnight shuttle flight to Vegas. But, surprisingly, Carol looked rested and in control. Wearing blue jeans and a red Indiana sweatshirt, she seemed as relaxed as her clothes.

"Morning, Street," she said as she put down the pen and legal pad.

"What do you use for oxygen in here?"

She ignored the question. "I slept like a baby and I feel a hundred percent better." Then, after a pause, "I'm sorry about the way I behaved last night. Truce, okay? Let's start over."

He walked to the table and sat down. "There you go again."

"I know, I know. It's just that everything's coming to a head. When I'm upset like that, I tend to lash out at the people closest to me. I didn't mean to put you on the spot and then dredge up all that old crap."

He was tired of her mood swings but he just said, "We've got too much else to think about today."

She nodded and her face relaxed. "I spoke to Haney earlier. He's coming over any minute now to talk to us. If Swallow's going to make his move soon, Haney wants us all to be on the same page."

Just then, Barrows came up the stairs. "Carol? Streeter?" he yelled as he got near the top. "Sergeant Haney's here," he added when he got to the loft. "You want to have him come up?"

Streeter shook his head. "No. Let's meet in Frank's place."

The three of them went downstairs. Haney and Ruiz were in the hallway, and they all walked into the office together. Frank was behind his desk, drinking coffee and reading the paper. He spent at least part of every day in that room. Sundays, holidays, his birthday. It didn't matter. He looked up and smiled broadly. "What's this, a raid?"

"Mind if we meet in here, Frank?" Streeter answered with a question. "You have enough chairs and I'd like to get your thoughts, too."

"Fine by me." He waved his hand in front of him to indicate they should sit down.

"Do you know everyone?" Streeter asked.

Frank nodded. "Basically. Me and Haney go way back."

The sergeant spoke first. "I won't take up much time. I talked to my captain last night and we kicked around a few ideas. There's not much doubt that this freak's coming after Miss Irwin next. The case is getting more press and he's got to be feeling the heat. Plus, there doesn't seem to be anyone left except her." He looked quickly at Carol. "I understand you have to be over in district court this week."

"At least through Thursday. Maybe Friday."

"My bet is Swallow knows that. He knows everything else about what we're doing. Our thinking is that he's either going to make his move when you're walking from the car to court or he'll put something in the car itself while you're inside the building. He'd have to be nuts to make his move right in the courthouse. All the metal detectors and guards. We also don't think he'll pull anything near the church again. As far as the drive to and from court, that's not likely, either. Swallow's MO isn't moving targets. His best chance is to either get to the car while she's in court, or try it right in front of the courthouse. There's a lot of activity and people out there. It'd be easy for him to get lost in the shuffle and pull it off. That's where we're going to concentrate our efforts. We'll have plainclothes all over the outside. Not much we can do along the way except drive fast and take different routes. You going with her, Streeter?"

"Maybe, but there doesn't seem to be much I can do sitting in court all day."

Carol sat forward and looked at him. "Street, I'd really like you to be there with me. At least tomorrow."

"We'll see." He turned to Haney. "I'm not sure I agree that the church is all that safe. Kevin knows the layout around here. Look how easily he got in the other night."

Haney shifted slightly in his seat and looked annoyed. "You got a pretty quiet neighborhood. The courthouse gives Swallow cover. No offense there, Streeter, but you haven't had much luck tracking this guy up to now. Might be you want to leave the detective work to us. What do you say?"

Streeter stared hard at the sergeant but remained silent. Then he glanced at Frank, who was frowning. He didn't want to look at Carol. Barrows was unnerved by the exchange, but Officer Ruiz was flirting with a grin under his mustache. Finally, Streeter answered. "Whatever you say, Sergeant Haney. What the hell do I know, right?"

Haney sat up and was about to say something when Carol spoke. "No need to get defensive, Street."

He turned to her and she shrugged innocently. Streeter just flashed a grin. "You're right."

Now Frank got into the act. "You might want to listen to what he's saying, Haney. The way you come in and out of this place all the time, could be Swallow makes his move nearby."

Haney turned to the man behind the desk. "We'll look into it, Frank. We'll look into everything." He stood up. "If there's nothing else, I'm sure we've all got better things to do with our Sunday. Unless you have questions, I'm going home."

As everyone moved out, there was a nervous tension in the room. Streeter felt as though little had been accomplished, but he knew that arguing with Haney would do no good. Carol grabbed his arm when they got to the hall.

"I didn't mean anything by that defensive crack," she whispered. "Please come with me to court tomorrow. Just for the first day, okay?"

He nodded. "All right. Look, I need to use Frank's phone." Then he turned and headed back to the office. The bondsman was again studying his newspaper. Streeter closed the door behind him, walked to the desk, and called Terry Nathan.

"What's up, Streeter?" Terry's voice sounded tired.

"You want to stop by the church?"

"When did you have in mind?"

"How about now? I'll throw on a pot of coffee and we can kick around a few ideas. Haney just left and I have a bad feeling about his strategy."

"Give me about twenty minutes."

When they hung up, Streeter looked at Frank. "What do you make of all this?"

Frank shook his head. "Haney's in charge. It'll be all right, Big Guy. And stick with Carol for a day or two. What else you got to do? But I'll tell you one thing, when this is all over, I'd lose that woman like a bad smell. There's something crazy about her. She's different than she used to be, and I'm not saying it's for the better."

"You noticed that, too, huh?" He filled Frank in on what Jack Nevers had told him the night before. "She's got real problems. Until this is over, I think we should do all we can to make her feel safe and calm. That and talk to her as little as possible."

"I hear you," Frank responded.

Streeter went to put on the coffee. Shortly before one, Terry knocked on the front door of the church. They went back to the office, which was now empty. The bounty hunter grabbed the big chair behind the desk.

"You have a problem with the sergeant's plan?" Terry asked.

"I'm not thrilled with the approach he's taking. By the way, you look like shit. Didn't you get much sleep last night?"

"Much, hell. Didn't get any, really."

"Well, try to get a little tonight. You're going to need to be sharp for the next few days. My money's on tomorrow for Swallow making his move. By Tuesday for sure. And I think the cops are off base focusing on the courthouse. It leaves us exposed here. I want to pay attention to that. Can you be out front first thing in the morning?"

Terry nodded.

"I'd like you to park down the street and then follow us to the courthouse. Do you have a cellular phone?"

"Back at the office."

"Get it and keep it with you. In the afternoon, when she's about to leave court, I'll give you a call. I'd like you to follow us back to the church again. It's asking a lot, but I'd like you to do that for a couple of days."

Terry rubbed his chin. "No problem. After what he did to Cullen, I'll stay with you all day if that's what you want."

"Good. Also, I'll give you my piece before you leave. Keep it under your seat for the next few days."

"No need for that. I'll bring my own hardware."

"It's not for you. I can't carry while I'm riding with the cops or sitting in court, but I want to know my .38's nearby just in case."

"Makes sense."

"Haney and I had a run-in before. I don't like his attitude or his ideas. And he sure as hell doesn't like mine. My gut feeling tells me Kevin's going to make his move within a few blocks of the church. Coming or going. No way I'm taking any chances right out here."

21

Carol packed light for court. That surprised Streeter when he came up to the loft to get her on Monday morning. He wasn't sure what to expect, but he thought she'd have more than just the thin, dark briefcase and her purse.

"Are you sure you have everything you need?" he asked as she sat at the table finishing her coffee. "That doesn't look like much paperwork for a trial."

She stared up at him. "It's not a trial, Street. Just a long, boring arbitration where they'll need some tax-law advice. Besides, I'm working with an in-house counsel and we've got it covered."

"Okay." He grabbed the briefcase and stood there waiting.

She got up and put her cup in the sink. "Do you know who's driving us?"

"Your friend Jeff Barrows was warming up his Honda before. Haney wants us to use Jeff's car, to confuse Swallow. Like a guy who can put a bomb in a deodorant can or slip unnoticed into my garage can't figure out which car we're in."

Carol frowned. "Are you sure it has to be Jeff? Why not that big Mexican? Ruiz."

"What difference does it make? Besides, Ruiz isn't on duty today. I'm sure Jeff's a fabulous driver, and he really likes staying close to you. He wants to be your savior. Nothing in the world would please him more than to capture Kevin Swallow single-handedly and deliver him to you on a platter."

Her voice went flat. "It doesn't matter who drives."

They walked down the stairs, past the police lookout station. The woman officer from the other night was there. She nodded without saying a word. When they went into the garage, Barrows was sitting in his Honda Prelude with the engine running. He saw Carol and jumped out to get the door for her.

"I hope my little car is okay with you, Carol," he said as he reached for the passenger door. "We'll use a different car every day. Swallow probably doesn't know my Honda on sight. It won't help much, but why make it too easy to spot us?"

"That's fine with me, Jeff," she said with a definite chill in her voice. "Just so we get going sometime today yet."

Streeter and Barrows both chalked up her attitude to nerves, although the young cop looked disappointed. "It's only a couple minutes after eight, Carol. Don't worry, you'll be in court with plenty of time to spare."

He opened the door. She was to sit behind him, with Streeter next to her.

"Isn't anyone else coming with us?" Streeter asked after they all got into the white Prelude. "I thought you'd have a uniform riding shotgun up front."

"Haney said this is enough. I asked him the same thing and he reminded me in his usual hard-ass way that the department has other concerns: 'She ain't the only citizen entitled to police attention.' He also reminded me how many people he has down at the courthouse. I told him that you and I have everything under control."

He glanced at Carol in the rearview mirror as he strapped on his seat belt. She was looking out the side, apparently not listening. His grin fell. "Time to roll," he announced without looking back again.

He pressed the remote opener he'd taken from Streeter's car, and the double-wide door lifted. A bright autumn morning yawned in front of the church. Streeter spotted the gray portable Dumpster at the end of the driveway. Squinting to get a closer look, he saw someone leaning over the edge of it looking inside. An old woman. There was a loaded shopping cart next to her, sticking out into the driveway.

"Nice neighborhood," Barrows said as they rolled slowly out of the garage. "One of your regulars?" He nodded toward the bag lady.

"We get a lot of that down here," Streeter answered. "On summer mornings, with my windows open, they usually wake me up. I can hear those carts banging down the street at sunup. You wouldn't believe the noise they make."

Barrows stopped when they got outside, turned and aimed

the remote at the door, and pressed it. Streeter looked to his right and saw Nathan's dark Ford Bronco parked almost a block to the east, facing away from them. Terry knew their car would come from behind him, and he was positioned so he could follow it downtown.

Gina had no idea what she was looking at as she bent over the edge of the Dumpster. In fact, the entire walk from her van, parked around the corner, to the front of the church was one long, terrifying blur. All the way in from Evergreen, Kevin had assured her she was safe. That he had it rigged so well a child could deliver the bomb. And that what she was doing was for the best. But she was too scared and confused to take much of it in. She'd felt okay when she dressed in the street clothes and wiped shoe polish on her face. Still, once she got in the van and saw the loaded shopping cart, once it registered what she'd be pushing down the street and that she would be killing someone, she turned rigid with fear and guilt. She even told Kevin that she couldn't go through with it. Slick move on her part.

"Damnit, Gina," he'd screamed, his hand balling into a hard fist. "You don't do this and I'll rip your head off. That's no shit, either. I've come too far to let you ruin it by crapping out on me now." He glared at her as he started the van, his body quivering in rage. "Fuck this up and you'll wish you were blown up with the cart. I don't want to hear any more of this 'I can't' shit. You can and you sure as hell will."

She knew he would do what he said, so she spent the entire ride staring straight ahead and going over the sequence for detonating the bomb and getting away. Put cart in driveway—kick wheels out—look in Dumpster—when car stops, trigger bomb with wire on cart handle—walk, don't run away. It trotted through her mind over and over again. Especially the last part. She barely heard a word Kevin said. Her terror was so severe that it seemed to detach her mind from her body. She couldn't even feel her feet touching the pavement when she got out of the van and began pushing the cart. And she certainly didn't recognize the black man sitting in the parked Bronco studying her as she walked past him on her way to the church.

Now, as she looked inside the garbage bin, she became aware of the Honda approaching her. Suddenly, she jolted straight up. Damn! She forgot part of the sequence: she hadn't pushed the back wheels out to make sure the cart wouldn't move. Kevin had loosened them to where she could easily kick them out to the side. She shot a glance at the approaching white Honda. Then she threw her right foot out, striking the wheel on that side. It pushed through the rubber outer washer and fell off its little axle. She did the same to the left wheel and the cart sank in the rear, immobile.

"What the hell's she doing?" Barrows asked as they got about halfway down the drive. He instinctively slowed the car to watch. "Did you see that, Streeter? She's kicking at her own shopping cart. Gotta be nuts."

The bounty hunter had been looking up and down the street, not paying much attention to the woman. Now he studied her. She looked like a generic street person. At least she looked normal until they got closer. That's when he noticed she was wrong. What was it? The earrings. She had on a pair of bright-orange hoop earrings. Big thick ones. He also noticed that she was wearing black eyeliner, heavily but carefully applied. And this woman was young. Younger than him. Streeter sat up farther in his seat and leaned forward.

"I don't know about that, but she's sure overdressed for her line of work," he told the driver. "That's one classy bag lady. Check her out when we get there."

Gina turned away from the cart and watched the car coming toward her. She struggled to get back into the sequence, but forgetting about the wheels had thrown her off. Trip wheels out. Did that. Look in Dumpster. She started to turn back to the garbage bin, then realized she'd done that, too. Then the part she liked the best flashed into her mind. Walk, don't run, away. She turned to face the road, her back to the car, and started walking.

Barrows stopped about three feet from where the shopping cart blocked his exit. "The hell is she doing now?" He leaned out his window and yelled. "Lady! You'll have to move the thing! We need to get out. Hey, get back here!"

Gina was maybe ten feet away when Barrows' voice hit her. What did Kevin say to do when they yelled at her? Start at the top. Trip wheels out, look in Dumpster, trigger bomb . . . Shit! Trigger the bomb! I didn't do that yet. Kevin'll kill me dead for sure this time. She froze and then turned to face the church again. The cop got out of the car, looking mad. Gina studied his face. He looked so young, she thought. So earnest. She started to walk back to the shopping cart, her mind struggling to recall where the trigger wire was located. Glancing at the rear wheels, she frowned. No, did that. Kicked wheels out. Where's the damned trigger?

"Come on, lady." Barrows' voice softened when he saw her coming back. "Move it, okay? We wanna get outta here."

Carol watched them and then suddenly slapped the front seat. "Damnit. I forgot three files. They're up in the loft. Tell Jeff I'll be right back." She quickly turned and got out of the car through the driver's door. Once outside, she almost trotted toward the church.

Streeter had been watching Barrows and the bag lady so closely, he didn't hear precisely what Carol had said. Something about files. He wasn't even aware she had left the Honda until she was outside and a few feet behind the car. She was heading for the small side door next to the overhead. This isn't right, shot through his mind. Bag lady dressed like a hooker. The cart in the way. A hooker. This is Kevin! He jumped out of the car and yelled, "Wait right there, Carol!"

When she ignored him, he glanced back at the street, where the woman had now returned to the cart. Barrows was only a couple feet away, talking to her. Then Streeter looked again at Carol, who was reaching for the door handle on the side door. "Stand still, Carol! Don't touch anything!" He started moving toward her.

By the time Gina got back to the cart, she remembered that the trigger wire was on the left side of the handle. The cop was just a few feet away, and he kept talking to her. She tried not to listen, like Kevin had told her. Instead, she focused on the wire. She reached for the cart handle and found it dangling about three inches down. Pull hard, but don't jerk at it. Kevin had been very clear on that point. She took the wire and gave it a firm pull, as she'd practiced the day before. Somewhere in the cart, the detonator timer clicked into action. Six sticks of dynamite waited. She knew she'd done it right and a smile shot across her face.

"What the hell's your problem?" Barrows' voice sounded hoarse. "Move that thing and then stand over there. I want to talk to you." He couldn't understand why she pulled on the handle or why she was smiling and staring at the cart like an idiot. Then she looked up at him and her smile broadened. Although he was mad, Jeff smiled back and, instinctively, he winked at her.

Gina's pride was soon overtaken by confusion. What now? As she looked up at the cop, who was grinning at her, she felt a sharp hit of guilt: This nice man will die in a few seconds. He winked at me. He's just trying to be friendly and I'm going to kill him.

Barrows grabbed the handle and tried to pull the cart toward the side of the driveway where the Dumpster was. It wouldn't budge. He frowned. "What's the matter with this thing?" He stared closely at Gina and noticed what Streeter had seen earlier. Big earrings and the eyes all made up. This bag lady's sort of a babe, flashed through his mind. Both he and Gina stood there for a few seconds, studying each other.

Carol reached for the door handle when she got within a foot or two of the building. She heard Streeter's voice, but she wasn't sure what he had yelled. Then she grabbed the handle, turned it, and gave a hard pull. It swung open and she walked into the garage.

Streeter watched. When Carol was safely inside, he stopped and turned to look back out at Barrows. The cop was about a foot away from the cart lady and they were just looking at each other. "Barrows! Get the hell away from her! Now! Jeff, get away!" He began to sprint toward the Dumpster.

The officer heard the hollering and turned around to see where it came from. Streeter was running toward him, maybe thirty feet away. For her part, Gina felt she had to do something, and when the cop turned to look at the other man, it came to her. "He's right," she yelled. All thought of the bomb sequence was forgotten. Barrows turned back to face her.

"What?" Barrows asked. But Gina was again silent, immobile with fear.

By now, Streeter had reached them, and it was clear what he was yelling. He grabbed Gina by the shoulder with one hand and moved quickly toward Barrows, who was backpedaling away from the cart. Streeter grabbed Jeff's arm with his free hand and pushed everyone past the Dumpster. Each step got them closer to safety. When the bomb actually went off, all three of them had turned and were running full-bore away from it. They had made it almost twenty-five yards by then. The force of the explosion lifted them off the ground and threw them several feet. Luckily they landed on soft grass, although Gina hit her head particularly hard. But they were all alive.

The shock wave was enormous. Barrows' Prelude was flaming like a stove; the blast had lifted the front of it nearly four feet in the air. The noises were deafening: both the initial bomb and then the car slamming back to the ground. Windows up and down the street, including many on the church front, shattered loudly. In the wake of the explosion, the car and the Dumpster burned for a long time.

Streeter was mildly dazed. But he knew Carol and Barrows were alive. He pulled himself to his feet and heard a yell from down the street. Turning to the east, he saw Terry standing just behind his Bronco, waving his arms. Streeter shook his head to clear it and then started toward Nathan. As he moved, he saw Barrows kneeling on all fours, shaking his head. The bag lady was moving, too. Streeter's legs felt flimsy at first, but the more he ran, the more control he got. As he neared the Bronco, he could make out what his friend was yelling.

"He's getting away! Come on! It's a green van!" Terry turned and pointed east, to the next block, running north and south, perpendicular to their street. Then he looked back at Streeter. "Right over there. It's got to be him in the van!"

Streeter could see the vehicle making a U-turn about a third of the way into the next block. "Swallow?" He was gulping for air, so the word came out jumbled.

"Has to be," Terry said as he opened the passenger door for Streeter. "He must have sent the woman with the bomb and he was waiting for her. She looked strange when she walked by me, but I didn't know why. Come on! He's getting away."

Streeter got into the car and Terry ran around to the driver's side. He hopped in and shifted into first gear. As he pulled away from the curb, he anticipated Streeter's next question: "Your piece is under the seat." The Bronco turned the corner onto 34th Street, heading northwest. "Is Carol all right back there?"

"She was in the church when the cart blew." Streeter's breath was coming back but he was still gulping for air. He felt like he might be sick, but his adrenaline kept him focused. "There's a cop in there to take care of her."

The green van was almost two blocks ahead of them. Swallow must have seen them coming, because he made a hard left, tires crying loudly, at the next corner. When Terry got to that corner, he turned as well. The van was still within sight. Two blocks south, with Terry gaining on it, the van again tried to make a sharp left. This time Swallow wasn't as lucky. He turned too hard, causing the back end to skid wildly and fishtail to the side. Kevin slammed on his brakes and it looked for a second like he might roll. Instead he wrestled it under control, but the right rear tire couldn't take all the excitement. When it slid into the curb, it smashed against the concrete and blew out. Sparks flew from under the right rear as the van scraped the pavement, producing a long, loud howl as it went.

"Fuck me!" Kevin screamed at the windshield when he realized what had happened. He hit the brakes, knowing that the Bronco would catch him within a block if he kept driving. The van stopped with one harsh, low moan in front of a construction site for what appeared to be a convenience store and gas station. Kevin grabbed the small .38 from the seat next to him. It was Gina's. He never had much use for guns. Looking over his shoulder, he couldn't see the Bronco yet. Then he opened his door, jumped out, and ran toward the building to the west.

About twenty seconds later, Terry came around the last corner. To his surprise, the green van was just sitting there, mostly in the right lane. He hit the brakes and stopped behind it. "He's on foot!"

"Over there!" Streeter yelled pointing to the construction site. Swallow had already made it through the parking lot and past the gas-pump islands. He was running toward the side when they spotted him. By the time Streeter and Terry got out, he had turned the corner and was running along the far side. Several confused workers came out of the store and strained to see where the man from the green van was going.

"Move back!" Streeter yelled. Seeing two men coming toward them, both waving handguns, convinced the workers to get inside again.

Kevin tripped and almost fell as he ran along the side of the building. He could hear someone hollering and the voice was gaining on him. To his right was a four-story apartment building, to his left was the store. Straight ahead was a high wooden fence. When he got to the back corner, he took another left, behind the store. It was a dead end. The privacy fence ran the entire width of the building. There was about six feet of space between it and the back wall. Swallow stopped for a second and looked at his gun. Then he ran to the far end of the building and climbed the fence. He'd take his chances with whatever was on the other side. Not a good idea. When he got to the top and looked over, he saw two large dogs snarling up at him. One was a narrow Doberman with what looked like watery shaving cream around its mouth. The other was a German shepherd about the size of a circus pony. Kevin set his butt down on the fence and straddled it.

When Streeter got to the rear corner of the building, he stopped and pressed his back against its cinder-block wall. He could see the wooden fence and guessed that it ran along the back of the store, which must have slowed Kevin. Terry caught up and leaned against the wall next to him. They could hear the dogs howling insanely around the corner.

"The hell's back there?" Terry asked, his breathing choppy from running.

Streeter just shook his head and inched toward the corner. When he got right to the tip of the corner he rocked slightly, like he was gaining momentum to make the turn. Suddenly, he spun around the edge of the building, holding his gun out in front of him at chest level with both hands. His eyes were huge with anticipation.

Kevin had no idea what to do next. He had this bizarre notion that killing dogs was deeply wrong. After all he'd done in his life, Kevin couldn't bring himself to shoot a couple of vicious mutts. He looked back to the other end of the building. That's when he saw the man in a white shirt jumping into view, holding something in front of him. Instantly, he knew the man was Streeter and the something was a gun.

"Hold it right there! Now!" Streeter yelled. His voice was hoarse but deep.

Kevin frowned and looked back at the dogs. Both were jumping up and trying to bite his dangling leg.

"Drop the gun!" Streeter yelled and took a step forward.

Kevin's face hardened and he raised the .38. Streeter saw the motion. Luckily, it was slow enough to allow him to squeeze off two rounds before Kevin's gun was in position. One of the slugs hit the man on the fence in the right shoulder, causing him to spin in that direction. He lost his balance and fell back into the little alleyway. The gun bounced from his hand when he landed. Apparently, Streeter had hit an artery. Blood was pumping out of the shoulder in thick spurts.

The bounty hunter ran toward Kevin, his own gun raised. By now Terry was around the corner and he had his gun in firing position, too. When they got to Swallow, they lowered their pieces. Clearly, he wasn't going to give them trouble. Streeter kicked the .38 away from him as a precaution. Kevin lay on his right side, his legs moving slowly up to his chest like he was curling into one final fetal position. By now the ground in front of him was covered with blood. He was looking straight ahead, at about ankle level, and it sounded like he was choking.

"Go call for an ambulance," Streeter said, his eyes on Swallow. Terry nodded and left. Streeter knelt down over the man on the ground. "Don't move. Just lie still."

Swallow looked up. His eyes were crossed and he was pale. He opened his mouth slowly, like it hurt him a lot to do so.

"Just lie still," Streeter repeated, leaning farther forward. His face was now only a foot or so away from Kevin's. Without sunglasses and up this close, Kevin looked much more like his mug shot.

The dying man opened his mouth. "We'll get you. Gina . . ." His voice trailed off and his features froze. The sentence would never get finished.

The bounty hunter looked closely at Kevin. He knew he was dead but he moved his fingers around Swallow's throat to see if he could find a pulse anyway. Then he studied this man, who had killed at least three people. The man who'd terrorized Carol and threatened Streeter himself. Lying there with his prison-hippie beard and long hair, Kevin looked mad. Charlie Manson mad. He'd lived his whole life that way. Might as well go off to the next stop like that.

Terry returned about five minutes later. Streeter was sitting on the ground, leaning his back against the building. Swallow's body was in front of him, a few feet away. Their guns were on the ground between them. The dead man looked so bright to Terry, lying there with all that thick red blood on his white T-shirt.

"An ambulance won't help this man," Terry said as he looked down.

Neither of them spoke. Finally, Terry asked, "He say anything at all?"

Streeter looked up. "Nothing that made sense, but he was a hard guy to the end. Even threatened me again. He mentioned Gina. Said she'll get me. That lady won't be getting anything but jail time. It's finally over."

22

Much of the rest of Monday was a noisy blur to Streeter. He and Terry were allowed to return to the church about an hour after the ambulance and cops arrived at the scene. But first they answered police questions as the attendants put the body on the gurney. Then they answered more questions at the church. Finally, they were driven to the downtown police headquarters to make formal statements and answer still more questions. Terry was finished by two, but Streeter wasn't allowed to go home until well after five.

Earlier, when the bounty hunter and the PI first got back from the shooting scene, the front of the church was littered with television news trucks, police and fire vehicles, and other official cars. Sidewalks on both sides were lined with pushing spectators struggling with the orange crime-scene tape. A news helicopter even swirled overhead for part of the afternoon. It would take all day to clean up the mess. Frank was inside his office talking to a couple of the older officers.

"Too bad about Jeff getting banged up like that," Frank told Streeter and Terry. He nodded goodbye to the officers who were leaving the room. Barrows had a concussion, along with assorted bruises, and he'd be in the hospital in a day or two. "Jeff's a good kid and I hate to see him hurting. But, overall, I'd say we made out all right this morning. Swallow's history, Carol's alive, and there's one less rice-burner cluttering the American highway," he said, referring to the Honda. "End of story, and when you total it all up, I'd say the good guys won."

For his part, Sergeant Haney was torn between anger and guilt—anger about making the wrong call on Swallow's move, and grief over an injured officer. Streeter had a smooth path to do some serious "I told you so"–ing, but he didn't take it. Besides, Haney was too busy giving orders and downplaying the damage to the press to allow much hassling.

After the immediate shock wore off, Terry slid back into his usual detached cool. His thoughts quickly returned to running the business with Brian in the hospital.

Carol had the most perplexing reaction. Streeter thought she'd be relieved and delighted. Finally safe, she could go home, which she did that afternoon. She should have been downright giddy, yet all she expressed was anger. "Damnit, Street," she'd told him in the church garage just before he left to go down-town. "This isn't right at all. I hate to see someone killed. You and your stupid guns. You didn't have to shoot him."

"What the hell does right have to do with anything?" he snapped back. "You're alive and Kevin's on ice. That works for me and you should be glad, too. Of course we all feel bad for Jeff. *That* wasn't right. But why take it out on me?"

She shook her head. "It must look like I'm ungrateful. But af-ter watching the explosion, watching it happen right out here—to see poor Jeff hurt like that."

"He's a cop and he knew he was getting in the line of fire every time he put on the uniform. Besides, you never showed concern for 'poor Jeff' when he was falling all over himself to be near you. And that piece of shit Swallow got what he deserved."

She glared at him. "Calling a dead person names doesn't make you noble. Maybe you could have taken Kevin alive, or just let him go for the police to arrest later. But no, you had to come on like Wyatt Fucking Earp. Always the big macho man." She paused, shuddering in anger. "You know I'm opposed to capital punishment."

"Give me a break, okay? If you hadn't run back to get those files, they'd be scraping you off the back seat. Seems Kevin wasn't opposed to capital punishment where *you* were concerned." Streeter didn't say anything for a moment. "We're both really wound up. Let's just drop it. The cops'll take you home."

She nodded. "Look, I know I shouldn't have yelled at you for what happened." It was as close as she came to a thank-you.

As he was being driven to headquarters, Streeter wondered if he'd done the right thing shooting Swallow. Killing a man didn't sit well with him. Maybe he should have just tried to keep him contained in the alley until the police came. To hell with it, he fi-nally decided. He did what he did on reflex and in self-defense. The result was that one very bad man was out of circulation for-ever. Frank was right: the good guys won. When Streeter finally got back to the church, he was exhausted but still wired. There was a message on his voice mail from Linda Parnell, so he called her.

"What a morning you had." She sounded anxious. "Are you okay, Street?"

"I've had good days and I've had bad days, but this was both. Yeah, I'm okay."

"Would you like some company?"

He could use the comfort and he wanted to see her, but he really needed sleep. "It's tempting, but I just want a shower and then hit the sack. Maybe tomorrow."

"Fine."

"Haney told me that Gina Gallo, Swallow's girlfriend, made a full confession," Streeter said. "That should end this whole business."

"Let's hope so. I can't stop thinking about Carol. Many psychotic illnesses share the same symptoms, and I certainly don't know enough about her to make a diagnosis. It could be any one of a number of problems. But I keep thinking of one in particular. It's called 'borderline personality disorder.' Look at her mood shifts, how impulsive she is. All that misguided, deep anger. And don't forget what she did to her hand with the disposal. Plus, borderline personality sufferers are extremists. Everything comes down to black or white. They're oversensitive to what they perceive as abandonment or disloyalty. Does that sound like anyone you know, Street?"

"Sounds like most of the people I know."

She ignored the crack. "Self-mutilation. Uncontrolled anger. Oversensitive to abandonment. Look what she tried to do to her ex-partner. And then her hand. She deserved to be mad at you, but she went beyond that. And remember her blaming you for her law practice going south. That was pretty extreme. People with this disorder can function normally and yet they're incredibly manipulative."

He thought of Carol's weird pass at him in the loft Saturday. "So?"

"So, Swallow's dead. I'd put some real distance between myself and Carol if I was you. She's seriously disturbed, probably suicidal. And if she is borderline, there's not much chance of her being helped, even in therapy."

"You're right, and that's just what I'm going to do. Carol already moved out and I don't plan to see her anymore, even as a friend. Sometime I'll tell you what she tried to pull on me here Saturday night."

When he hung up, he was too jazzed to go right to sleep. He changed into his workout clothes and went to the basement gym. As he walked down the stairs from his loft, he half expected to see Barrows at his usual station. For an unfocused half-hour, he lifted. Then he went up to read in bed. But he couldn't concentrate on that, either. He kept thinking of Carol's curious reaction earlier that day and how she'd acted the past couple of weeks. What she'd told him about Kevin. The symptoms Linda mentioned stuck with him, too. As he tossed around in bed, a sickening thought kept whipping through his mind. He didn't want to believe it even though he'd flashed on the idea over the past week. But he couldn't chase it away. Finally, he slipped into a jangled sleep at about three.

He awoke at seven, and the thought was harder to ignore. It festered, pushing on the wall of denial he tried to maintain. Then, shortly after ten o'clock, he found solid proof to back up his suspicion. As he went through a makeup bag that Carol had forgotten, he found the link that confirmed his worst fear. He made one phone call and got a recorded message. It stated that the person wasn't home. However, she would be "ever so happy" to return the call "if you'd just be so kind as to leave your name and number. Really." Streeter stared at the phone after he'd hung up from listening for the third time. Then he called Nathan at his office.

"Terry, can you come over here right now? Yeah, the church. We have to talk. You, me, and Frank. It's really important."

"I'll be over as soon as I can."

Streeter went to Frank's office. He was disappointed to see the room empty, but then he remembered that Frank would be gone until late morning. He sat in the big desk chair for over an hour, thinking about Carol. Shortly before eleven, he heard the front door open. The bondsman's voice, along with Terry's, echoed in the hall.

"Look what I found hanging around outside," Frank said as they walked in. He studied his partner. "Jeez, it looks like someone smacked you with a three-wood, Big Guy."

"What's up?" Terry asked.

Streeter nodded to the chairs across the desk from him. "You might want to be sitting down when you hear what I have to say."

Both men sat. "About what?" Frank asked.

"About everything that's happened and about the lovely Carol Irwin." He looked at Frank. "You mentioned to me more than once over the last few days that you thought there was something off target about her."

"Yeah, I did. 'Course, I never thought much of that lady. But now she seems more in control and loose in the head, all at the same time."

"That thought hit me, too," Streeter said. "She's got an underlying edge that she never had before. Then, yesterday, I noticed how really weird it was. Here she's finally out of the woods and she acts like she just got a speeding ticket. Mad as hell. She even implied that I didn't have to drop Swallow. It actually upset her that he was dead, almost like there was an emotional connection between them." He paused and looked closely at the two men. "I believe that she and Kevin were working together all along on this hit-list bullshit. Carol's a killer or, at the very least, an accomplice. I had questions about her almost from the start, but I should have figured this out sooner. It was just hard for me to believe she was that far over the top. As I told you way back, Frank, I had a blind spot for her."

Terry and Frank looked at each other.

"Hey, come on," Frank said as he stared back across the desk. "Just because she needs a little Prozac now and then, don't put her in with the killer."

"I know." Streeter stood up and leaned in to the desk, his palms pressed on the top. "That's what I was telling myself last night while the rest of the country slept. But I put it all together this morning and there's not much doubt about it anymore."

"What's your proof, Street?" Terry asked.

"Well, first, there's Kevin himself. Carol always talked about how sharp he is. His long reach for killing. It was an oversell from the word go, but when he did things like getting to the other PIs, I started believing it myself. Then there was that break-in here at the church. That was too far over the top to be just Kevin. He had to have help from the inside. True, he had Gina. But from what the cops told me, she was the type that gets in over her head reading the funny pages. Plus, Gina didn't have the access Carol did. Didn't we say it seemed like Swallow could read our minds? Maybe he didn't have to." Streeter thought for a moment. "Then there was Saturday night at the hospital. Carol said something that bugged me but I couldn't figure out why. Not until last night. Right when she first got to St. Joe's, she mentioned the bomb in the deodorant can. That caught my attention."

"Big surprise. That's how Swallow operated," Frank said.

"True, but how did she know specifically about the deodorant can? I didn't tell her and you didn't give her any details. You just told her Cullen was hurt and at St. Joe's. And she told me later that she didn't hear anything from the media until she read about it in the *Rocky Mountain News* the next day. The only way she would have known about the deodorant can was if someone actually told her. That would have to be either Kevin or Gina.

"And I've got one more little item here that takes it from speculation to fact. This morning I was getting her things together. She went home in a hurry yesterday and left some personal stuff. Her makeup bag. She's only got maybe eight or ten of them, so she probably didn't even notice it. Anyhow, I'm in a suspicious mood, so I go through it. Inside, I found a small notebook with telephone numbers arranged in alphabetical order. One of the entries really grabbed me. It was 'G.G.' The number had an Evergreen exchange."

He reached into his front shirt pocket, pulled out a piece of paper, and unfolded it. Then he tossed it on the desk. "Terry, call 'G.G.' and tell me what you think."

Terry nodded. He grabbed the paper and picked up the phone. "Hi, hi," the recorded voice of a woman came bubbling through. "This is Gina. I'm not home right now, or maybe I'm busy. Like in the can." A forced childish tee-hee came on next. "But I'd be ever so happy to get back to you if you'd be just so kind as to leave your name and number. Really. So long from Casa de Gallo." It was followed by a starting beep.

Nathan put the phone down and looked at Streeter. "Gina Gallo? The hell's Carol doing with her number?"

"Good question," Streeter responded. "What's she doing even knowing about Gina before yesterday? We didn't have the number and I never told her Gina's name. I just gave her the broad strokes about our trip up to Evergreen. When she didn't recognize Kevin from the picture I dropped it."

"That would explain why she didn't make him from that picture," Frank said.

"Right. Of course she wouldn't make him. It was the perfect way to throw us off the track. There's no good explanation for her having that number. And there's only one reason she'd want it: to keep in touch with Swallow. Gina didn't even know about the two of them, or she would have told the cops by now. One other thing. Remember yesterday morning, right after you came back from calling for the ambulance?"

Nathan nodded. "What about it?"

"You asked if Kevin said anything before he died. I told you he threatened me again and he even mentioned Gina. In bed last night I kept thinking about it. What he said exactly—or as best as I can remember—was 'We'll get you.' Then he mentioned Gina. I just assumed he meant she would get me. He had to be talking about Gina, I thought."

"Instead he was talking about Carol getting you," Frank shot in.

"Exactly. She'll *still* get me. Like she's been after me for a while and she's not giving up. Let's assume I'm right about Carol working with Kevin. Everything made sense right up until yesterday morning. All the other attacks, the way they went down. But that mess yesterday was nonsense. If she's working with Kevin, why would he bomb the car she was in? Gina was expendable, or else Kevin wouldn't have rigged the bomb to go off with her that close. But that doesn't answer why Carol wanted him to attack Barrows' car. Now, conveniently forgetting those files got her out and made her safe, but that still leaves me looking for a motive for the attack. If they're in it together, why attack yourself?"

"Maybe she wanted to nail Barrows," Frank offered.

Streeter shook his head. "What for? Besides, she didn't even know he'd be in the car until that morning. But she made sure *I* was in the car. She absolutely insisted on it. My bet is she and Kevin were after me."

"Why?" Terry asked.

"She always blamed me for ruining her criminal-defense career. Plus we had that bloody breakup and my affair. Keep in mind, this is a woman who tried to run over her law partner when he said he was moving out. I told you guys about what Jack Nevers said. This is also a woman who put her own hand in a disposal and turned it on. My friend Linda mentioned a borderline disorder thing that seems to fit Carol pretty closely. Vindictive, mood swings, uncontrolled rage at themselves and others. Look, I'm not saying she's totally like that, but I'm in the right ballpark with this. Carol and Kevin had to be working together."

"You better tell Haney and let him handle it." Frank said.

"What I've got isn't solid enough yet, even with the phone number. Besides, Haney's no fan of mine. He'd probably believe Carol before he'd believe me. For now, I'm going to talk to a detective friend of mine at the department. Bob Carey. I'll run it by him and see what he thinks. He gets back from vacation tomorrow. I know that he'll give me a good listen and he might have some thoughts on it. And, Terry, I want to visit Carol soon. I'd like you to come with me as a witness. Maybe we can shake her loose a little."

"What if she comes after you on her own?" Terry asked.

"I'll be careful. She'll probably need some time to reorganize herself anyhow."

"What if she drops by to get the rest of her stuff?" Frank asked.

"I'll bring everything down for you. Give it to her, and if she feels chatty, act like you don't know anything." He smiled. "That shouldn't be much of a stretch."

Frank shook his head. "There's a certain way about you, Street. Makes a guy want to run through a brick wall for you."

23

Carol thought constantly about the two men for almost twenty-four hours. Streeter and Kevin. Kevin and Streeter. Rage and pain. Chain-smoking and gulping coffee, she paced her apartment almost nonstop from when the police brought her home Monday afternoon until the middle of the next day. She managed only a couple jumpy bursts of sleep just before sunup Tuesday. Later, she cried until she got sick in long, dry convulsions. Then she beat her sofa pillows in a white fury. The wrong man won. Streeter lived, and Carol wasn't sure she wanted to do the same herself. Thoughts of suicide flared. Her arms and chest ached in grief.

In her mind, she rehashed all the plans she'd made with Kevin. Everything had gone the way it was supposed to right up to the minute Streeter played hero at the church. Years of careful work and catching the right breaks were destroyed when he pulled Barrows and Gina to safety. If he'd stayed in the car, he would have died the way they'd planned. If he'd died, that black guy with the cocky attitude—Terry Nathan—wouldn't have noticed Kevin leaving the neighborhood. If he hadn't noticed, no one would have followed Kevin and he wouldn't have been killed. But Streeter did get out of the car, and the warped chain of events started. Now there was still work left for Carol. Hands-on, dirty work.

She thought of when she first met Kevin. A court-appointed homicide case. High profile, lots of press. Her first murderer. Two counts. Her client was perfect for what she had in mind. Kevin, with his great looks, his street-honed patter, and his kiss-my-ass sneer. Like he could chew through concrete. Bravado and desperation, combined with an utter lack of conscience. Perfect qualities for what she needed. Plus he adored her. Within a few days, Carol was reciprocating that feeling. In love with the bad man who would kill for her. Practically from their first interview, the maniac and the attorney went for each other like a pair of sun-crazed lizards.

But beyond lust, each of them had something to gain from the other. Kevin needed a lawyer who'd cross the line and do anything to spring him. No way he'd cop a plea for twenty-five years plus, and a jury trial would put him away for longer than that. Maybe put him to death. He had to get back on the street, back in the game. Also, he had to get himself some big-league revenge on the flabby detective who brought him down. Cleveland Watts. What the hell kind of name was that? The old man was almost retired, for chrissakes. Why was he after Kevin so long and hard? Watts had to go down, and Kevin definitely couldn't do a long stretch in Cañon City.

Carol, too, ached for revenge. Her criminal practice was terminal, and that son of a bitch Streeter not only watched without helping, but he'd cheated on her while they were engaged. Cheated openly, like a low-life pimp. With a close friend of hers, no less. Nothing like that had ever happened to her before. He was far worse than that pompous Jack Nevers, in her mind. Streeter had to pay. Carol could think of little else, back then or since.

So the lawyer and her client jumped off the deep end within days of their initial meeting. First came the primal hit: muffled sex in holding cells with their clothes mostly on, or in conference rooms at the courthouse. Then came the legal plan. Create enough strongly appealable issues to get Kevin a new trial not too far down the road. They couldn't have anticipated that the technical problems over his taking the stand would play out the way they did. Hell, Carol was mucking it up bad enough on her own to generate a solid motion based on incompetent counsel.

Neither could believe their good luck. Kevin had a new trial and Carol could claim she'd done the right thing. Cap it all off with the DA's refusal to retry and they were home free.

Along the way, they picked up Gagliano and Cullen as additional targets. Both investigators treated Carol like a professional joke and a personal plaything when they were appointed to work Kevin's case. Cullen, a wet-brain leach, and Gagliano, a smarmy gigolo wannabe. Each salivating over the girl lawyer with the nice tits. It still made her cringe to think of them. All Carol had to do was tell Swallow how the two had come on to her and they instantly made the hit list. Getting to Watts, Gagliano, and Cullen was easy and fun for Kevin, even though the last two hadn't died. He came close enough, and their master plan was still working.

"Everything's falling into place for us, babe," Kevin reminded her over the phone just the day before he was killed. "Always has. The trial, the appeal, even Gina. If there ever was a perfect chump, it's her. Smart enough to help, yet she doesn't have a clue. To Gina, this is all one big gangster movie." He paused. "Only one hitch on the horizon. I think our friend from down south is closing in on me."

"What makes you say that?" Carol hadn't thought about him in a long time.

"Had to be him that broke into Gina's yesterday. And he made all those hang-up calls the day before, too. How could he get to me so fast? I didn't think that jerkoff was smart enough to butter bread by himself."

"What should we do?"

"We'll do what we planned with Streeter and then split. As far as our friend, we'll be out of here soon enough. He'll never find us in Mexico."

But all that had changed now. Carol sat in her living room and thought back. She had visited Swallow daily before his sentencing. The visits continued once he went to prison, although that took some major doing. Then, when he got out, they'd hooked up again to fine-tune the plan. They'd argued a little about his elaborate methods, but in the end, she told him to do it the way he wanted.

"Forget it, babe," he had told her months ago. "Any goof can shoot someone down. You want that, get yourself another boy. I don't just make them dead, I create death. I have so many ways to do it, I could take care of all four of these guys about a hundred times each and still not run out of ideas."

"What about all the attention you'll get?" she'd asked. "How do we handle that if you're running around leaving threats and announcing that you're the killer?"

He shook his head and grinned. "Who cares? We'll be long gone when it's over. I got friends down in Mexico, and with that money you got tucked away, we can live on the beach forever."

Seeing how pumped up he got excited her. What excited her more was the thought of Streeter dead and her in Mexico. No more courtrooms, ever.

But Swallow's death changed everything. She felt destroyed, like she no longer existed. Her main target was alive and being treated like a hero. Swaggering. In her misery, only Carol knew how evil Streeter really was. He had to die. Pacing her living room, she created a plan. When Kevin got out of Cañon City, he'd spent many hours explaining in detail how easy it was to rig booby traps. One method was so simple and foolproof, it grabbed her. Kevin had put the few materials needed in a storage locker she kept on East Evans Avenue. Carol had to empty the locker before she left town, anyhow. She grabbed a pad and pen and quickly scrawled some notes to herself. Kill Streeter as soon as possible and then take off for Mexico. Alone. Everything was in place down there.

It was close to three in the afternoon when she finished. Then she picked up the phone and called the church. Her makeup bag was still over there. Carol didn't really need it, but she didn't want to leave any connections with the bounty hunter. She was disappointed when Frank answered.

"Hi, it's Carol."

"Hello."

"Are you getting used to your place without a woman hanging around?"

A pause and then, "Yeah."

Carol thought he sounded more distant than usual. "Say, I left a makeup bag up in Streeter's room. Did he mention it?"

"Yeah."

"I'd like to stop by later and get it. Will he be there?"

"He's running around town and I doubt if he'll be in much. But I'll be here all day. Just come by and get it."

She wanted to talk to Streeter. "I'll try to do that today. If not, tomorrow morning'll be fine."

When they hung up, Carol felt nauseous again. She went to the bathroom and was sick for quite a while.

24

Streeter called Detective Bob Carey on Wednesday afternoon. With twenty-four years on the DPD, there wasn't much Carey hadn't seen. They agreed to meet at Nallen's bar downtown right after Carey's shift ended at five.

"I don't know, Streeter," the detective said as he eased himself onto the barstool. At six foot seven, he looked down at the man next to him. "I leave town for a few days and you shoot the place up." He nodded to the bartender, who was holding an empty mug over the beer taps. "Everyone's still talking about it at work. I even saw it in a short wire story back east yesterday morning."

The bounty hunter studied Carey. The detective had played poker with Streeter and a few guys once a month for the last eleven years. "How was New Hampshire?"

"Vermont."

"Whatever."

"My wife drags me out there every fall to 'see the colors' and stay with her folks. Fly two thousand miles to watch leaves fall off a tree and eat maple syrup. How the hell do you think it was?" Carey shook his head. "I actually looked forward to getting back to work today. That oughta tell you my opinion of Vermont."

"You work hard, you play hard."

The cop looked closely at him. "My hunch is you didn't call me to hear about life in the fast lane with Cookie and Robert Carey. What's going on?"

Streeter glanced around the room. Nallen's was a Lower Downtown bar featuring solid pub food and a heavy Irish motif. It was starting to get crowded and noisy. Turning back, he said, "I need your opinion. Supposedly, all the violence should end now that Swallow's dead. But I'm not so sure." He then proceeded to lay out his suspicions about Carol.

"Jesus, Streeter," Carey said when he'd finished. "I always thought Irwin was kind of a bitch, but you're making a serious charge there. Is she really capable of all that?"

Streeter nodded. "Anyone who'd stick their hand in a disposal or try to run down a friend is capable of damned near anything. It fits, her having the motive and Gina's phone number and all. You've seen worse on the job."

"Yeah, I have." He sipped his beer. "You never know what people'll do under the right circumstances. So what's your move?"

"I'd like to talk to Haney, but he and I aren't on good terms. I was wondering if you might act as a middleman. Sit down with me and him tomorrow. That would give me more credibility. But first I'm thinking of confronting Irwin. At least ask her why she has Gina's number. Either she'll have a good reason or maybe she'll unravel. I'm meeting a PI in here soon. Terry Nathan. We're going to Carol's to talk to her, if she's home. I've called all day and she never answers. Even tried her office and they haven't seen her." Streeter shook his head. "She told Frank yesterday that she'd come by the church to pick up her things but she never showed. That's just like her, to get weirded out and disappear. She always tries to run and hide from her problems."

"I was you, I'd want to know exactly where she is at all times. If your hunch is right, you want to keep her in plain view."

"I have to find her first."

Carey said nothing for a moment. "Go have your talk and then call me in the morning. Depending on what she tells you, maybe we can see Haney together. I'm not promising nothing. Look, it's been a slice, but I gotta run. And don't forget, a week from Friday. The game's at your house, so you can't leave early."

"If you're there, why would I want to? I swear, Carey, if I could get you to a poker table a couple days a week, I'd never have to work again."

The cop just nodded, grunted goodbye, and left. Streeter went to the bathroom. By the time he returned to his seat, Terry Nathan had arrived. "What did Carey say about your theory?" he asked, leaning against the bar.

"He seemed underwhelmed, but he might work with me on Haney. We'll see what Carol says first."

"You ever get a hold of her?"

Streeter shook his head. "She's not at her office, either. My hunch is she's hiding out at home and not picking up the phone. That's her style. Let's head over there."

They took Terry's Bronco to Carol's. She lived in central Denver in an elegant, older apartment building on Pearl Street, just south of the six-lane diagonal Speer Boulevard. It was getting dark when they got there at six-thirty. Carol lived on the first floor, in a corner unit in the rear. They didn't hit the lobby buzzer, because they wanted to come up unannounced. To get through the locked door, they stood there, acting casual, until someone came out. Then, without appearing anxious, they grabbed the door before it closed. It's a trick all process servers learn fast.

When they got to Carol's door, Streeter leaned his head right up against it. He listened for a moment and then turned to Terry. "Sounds like her radio's on back in her room," he whispered. "She's not moving around, though."

"Give the door a pound and see if she bites," Terry said quietly.

"No. Wait here and keep listening. I'll go out back and look through the window."

Terry nodded. Streeter went to the door just down the hall. He walked out into the rear parking lot, propping the door open with a rock. Carol's was the first set of windows as he turned right, just past a clump of tall shrubs. The windows were high enough so that he had to stand on his tiptoes just to see in the bottom edge of them. That wouldn't do. It was almost completely dark now, and her living-room light was on and the drapes were drawn. Glancing around, he spotted a large cinder block near the wall, by a water faucet. He grabbed the block and placed it, the tall way, next to the wall. When he climbed up, he strained to find an opening. There was a two-inch crack where the drapes hadn't been pulled completely together. He leaned slightly to his left and looked through it.

Her living room was every bit as messy as he recalled. Worse than her office. It was lit, dimly, by one bulb in a track-lighting scheme shining off the far wall. The other two bulbs were burned out. Just like Carol, he thought, not to replace them until all three went. Streeter squinted hard. Given the angle of the drapes, he could only see about two-thirds of the room. His eyes worked their way slowly from right to left, toward the wall with the brick fireplace. When he'd gone almost as far as he could, he spotted something that nearly knocked him off the brick.

Terry was still next to the door when Streeter walked back into the building. His head jolted when he saw the expression on the bounty hunter's face. "Damn, Street. You look like pure dog shit. What's wrong?"

Streeter stopped about five feet from him and leaned against the wall, his eyes looking down. "You still got your cell phone?"

"In the car."

He glanced up. "Go call 911. Carol's inside there dead as all hell. The whole place is torn apart."

25

"Sort of ironic, wouldn't you say?" Haney asked, standing in front of Carol's door, talking to Streeter. It was just after nine o'clock. "I mean, you drive all the way down here thinking she wants to kill you, and then *she* turns up dead. Ironic. Be real ironic if they find your prints inside, huh?"

The bounty hunter stepped closer. "Moronic is more like it. You saying I killed her, trashed the place, and then called the cops on the way out the door? Now, there's some top-flight police work."

Haney grinned. "I ain't saying nothing other than it's all kind of funny, in a ironic sort of way."

"A good vocabulary's a terrible thing to waste." Streeter's voice was even. "When can I go in there and look around?"

"Oh, probably never." Haney seemed pleased with his answer. "That's what we call a crime scene. You got no business in there.

Not ever. Besides, you got a feel for the place when you snooped in the window." He paused. "I *can* tell you that every room was tossed. Looks like a burglary. There's been a string of them around here lately and she's not the first victim to get tied up like that. First one to die, though. A lot of the usual stuff was taken, and Irwin had bruises on her face and shoulders and arms. The perp was some kind of sadistic son of a bitch. A burglary with a sick twist."

Streeter rolled his eyes. "A burglary? Doesn't that seem a little *ironic* to you? Carol's just been in the middle of a mess that left bodies all over town, and suddenly, a couple of days later, her house gets burglarized and she's executed. This is one hell of a coincidence, Haney."

"So what are you saying? Swallow came back from the grave to kill her?" His voice rose in anger. "Give me a break. It's a burglary, that much is clear. Plus, like I said, it matches the MO of those other home invasions. As far as an execution, that's bullshit. Looks like the perp didn't even mean to kill her. In fact, she may have done that herself."

"You're calling this a burglary-suicide? That's a stretch, even for you."

Haney frowned and shook his head like he was in pain. "No. That's not what I'm saying. But one of the coroner's guys told me it looked like she died accidentally. She was bound to the chair with her ankles tied to the legs, her hands tied behind her, and a rope around her stomach and the chair. The perp put masking tape over her mouth. It looks like what happened is that during all the excitement she couldn't breathe right so she started thrashing around. She fell backward, smacking her head on the brick fireplace mantel. Nasty gash in her head back there. We're not sure if she suffocated from the gag or if cracking her skull did it. Either way, it don't look like that's what the prowler had in mind. Like I said, with those other burglaries, none of the victims were killed."

Streeter stared at the door for a moment, then turned back to Haney. "If I can't go inside, am I done here? I'd like to head out."

The sergeant nodded. "I know how to get in touch if I need to."

Terry Nathan was waiting behind the wheel of the Bronco when Streeter got there. He had come out shortly after the police took his statement.

"You mind going over to Rodney's?" Streeter asked as he got in. "Frank went there for dinner, and he usually likes to hang out and work the room when he's done. You know him and a crowded bar."

Terry nodded and started the engine. "Fine with me. What'd they say in there?"

"They think it was a burglary and that Carol died unintentionally. It's a long story, but they wouldn't let me go inside to look around."

"Be kind of ironic, wouldn't it, Street? Her dying like that in a burglary right after all she went through with Swallow."

Streeter shot him a glance. "What's with that word all of a sudden? I don't hear anyone say 'ironic' for years and suddenly tonight everything's so incredibly ironic."

Terry frowned. "Chill out a little. I only meant that it's weird, you know, the way it all went down."

"Weird or not, that burglary crap seems too convenient. That's what I want to talk to Frank about."

They took Speer southeast a couple of miles to the trendy Cherry Creek area. Rodney's is a landmark watering hole for aging professionals who like meat specials, dim lighting, and martinis with an attitude. Though smoking isn't actually mandatory, it's certainly not discouraged. As he walked in, Streeter was tempted to buy a pack of Marlboros, but he didn't. He spotted Frank talking to his accountant and having coffee and a brandy in a tall booth to the left of the front door.

"Hey, Street, Terry," he yelled, waving them over. The bondsman smiled and slid closer to the wall to let them sit down. As he did, his accountant stood up.

"You don't have to leave because of us," Streeter said.

"We're all finished up, anyhow," Frank responded. "He was just heading out, weren't you, Arthur?"

The accountant merely nodded and then left without a word. Frank rolled his eyes as the two men sat down. "Artie's got all the personality of a broken toaster, but he's a magician with numbers. So how's things with little Carol Irwin? You manage to beat a confession out of her?"

Terry and Streeter glanced at each other, and then the PI spoke. "You don't want to be joking about that, Frank. We went over to her place tonight and found her dead."

The booth fell silent, and the buzz of conversation from the crowded bar took over. Frank's lower jaw dropped and his eyes narrowed. "What the hell's going on?" His voice trailed off.

"Your pal Haney said it looks like a burglary that got out of hand," Streeter explained. "She was tied up and gagged, and she may have died accidentally."

Just then the waitress appeared. Terry and Streeter each ordered a Beck's.

"How can that be?" Frank stroked absently at his chin with his linen napkin. "I mean, come on. She just puts you through all that with her old boyfriend and then she turns up dead. Very strange, not to mention very unlikely."

"That's just what I was thinking. And thanks for not calling it very ironic." Streeter paused. "Burglary, my ass. I'll tell you this, I'm not going to leave it up to a second-rate moron like Haney to figure out."

"What are you driving at?" Terry asked.

"Carol's dead, and I don't give a damn if the perp meant to kill her or not. If he hadn't tied her up she'd still be alive. That's murder one, last time I checked. Now, I don't feel any loyalty to her, given what I think she and Swallow had in mind for me. But this is just a continuation of that mess on Monday and those attacks on Gagliano and Watts and Cullen. And I'd bet my Buick that whoever did it was involved with Irwin and Swallow somehow. Had to be. After talking to Haney, it's clear the cops won't be working along those lines. They see it as just a string of burglaries." The waitress came back with their beers, put them on the table, and left. Streeter waited a moment and then added, "I'm going after this guy myself. The one who did Carol."

Terry winced and leaned forward. "Come on. What do you give a damn about all that for? The woman wanted you dead. Why work yourself up for her?"

Streeter shook his head. "I'm not doing it for her. Look, I'm into this thing way too deep to drop out now. Besides, if I'm right about this burglar being connected to her and Swallow, he might just decide to come after me."

"Why would he?" Nathan asked and took a sip from his beer.

"How do I know? But that's what I intend to find out. This whole thing hasn't made any sense right from the beginning. It's about time we figure it out. About time it all ended, too."

"I wouldn't try to talk him out of it," Frank said to Nathan. "He gets a hold of an idea like this, he don't let up."

The bounty hunter spoke again. "I know you got your hands full, Terry, running the business until Brian gets back. I don't expect you to keep going with me."

"I just won't have the time, Street."

Frank spoke to his partner. "So where do you look?"

"Right where it all began," Streeter said. "There's no reason to believe that Irwin and Swallow knew each other before his arrest, so that looks like the starting point. I'll read all there is about the bombing. Newspaper clips, court files, everything."

"What'll that tell you?" Frank asked.

"I won't know until I do it. There's got to be a common denominator, someone they both knew. Maybe Gagliano or Brian can remember someone hanging out at the trial. And I'll want to talk to what's-her-name. That bimbo Kevin was living with."

"Gina Gallo," Dazzler said. "I'm sure that Phi Beta Kappa'll be a lot of help."

"She might at that. Hell, she's my only connection to Swallow. When you get into something like this, all you can do is grab as much information as you can and see where it leads you."

26

Normally, Streeter would rather have taken polka lessons than study court records. But doing it without knowing what he was looking for was beyond agony. There must have been a foot and a half of transcripts, motions, and rulings. Still, he stuck with it for nearly two days. It wasn't until Friday afternoon that he finally left the courthouse, with a stiff back and a more complete appreciation of what a lousy trial lawyer Carol was. Neither of which helped. He couldn't face another piece of paper, so he headed over to St. Joseph's Hospital to talk to Brian Cullen.

"I tell you what, podner," Brian said over the food tray on his stomach. "I'm not all that inclined to want to see the guy that whacked Carol Irwin get caught. Hell, he should get a medal. Seems to me you'd be feeling pretty much the same way."

Streeter gave a quick shrug and waited.

Cullen looked off to the side. "I'll have to give it some thought, but offhand I can't think of anyone from the trial who was close to those two." He turned back. "Tell you one thing, Irwin and that little hunk of manure Swallow didn't seem to even like each other back then. If they were carrying on, they did a good job of hiding it. I was there every day for both trials, too. If I can think of anyone, I'll let you know." Then his face brightened. "And, Streeter, thanks for taking care of business last Monday. Made me feel a might better to see Swallow go down like that."

When he got back to the church, Streeter called Steve Gagliano and got pretty much the same response.

"Neither one of them seemed to have any friends. Period." Steve was adamant. "I don't think anyone visited Swallow the whole time, and Irwin never talked to people socially. Not that I didn't try. That lady was one edible commodity. But, then, you know all about that. You were banging her pretty good back then, weren't you?"

Streeter glanced at the receiver. "So, tell me, Steve, how's your crotch doing?" The phone at the other end slammed down hard.

The next morning, Streeter decided to interview Gina Gallo. He called the jail and was told that she had bonded out two days earlier. She'd been charged with conspiracy, aiding and abetting, and several lesser counts. But because of her clean record and ties to the community, and because Officer Barrows had testified at her bond hearing that she'd tried to warn him, her bail was manageable. Gino put up his house as collateral, and his sister temporarily moved in with him. When Streeter called, Gino sounded glad to hear from him.

"Gina told me how you pulled her bacon out of the fire there, Mr. Streeter," Gino said. "You want to talk to her, just come on out anytime. She's taking a shower now, so give her an hour or so."

The bounty hunter arrived shortly before noon. Gino, still moving stiffly under the same cheap toupee, invited him in and then yelled toward the rear of the house, "Gina, he's here!" He turned back to his guest. "Let's go talk in the kitchen. I've got coffee on and there's more chairs in there. These trains take up a lot of space." He nodded toward the elaborate setup.

They walked to the kitchen, which was as orderly as the rest of the place. Gino had a set of fifties-looking vinyl and Formica table and chairs, all in faded salmon. Streeter sat down as Gina walked into the room. With no makeup and wearing khakis and a white blouse, she was barely recognizable. Subdued, but she seemed content.

"Oh, Mr. Streeter," she said, extending her hand to be shaken. "I want to tell you how truly grateful I am for you helping me, sir. If you didn't push me and Jeff away, we both woulda died for sure." She paused. "Gino said you wanted to ask me about Kev. I don't know if I should talk about him, seeing as how we were so close. I don't want to show any disrespect for the dead, you know."

Streeter noticed how round and plain her face looked without cosmetics. This was a major transformation in both body and spirit. "Have you heard about Carol Irwin?" he asked her. "About her being killed on Wednesday?"

"Read it in the paper yesterday," Gino interrupted. "Makes you stop and think about how frail life is. Here her place gets broken into and she's killed just like that."

"Life's pretty frail, all right," Streeter responded. "Pretty bizarre, too." He looked back at Gina. "Did you know that she had your phone number in her address book last week?"

She frowned severely. "Get on out of here! How did she ever know about me?"

"My hunch is that she and Kevin were in on the killings together right from the start. Probably from way back at his trial. No offense intended here, Gina, but I think he just dragged you into it because he needed help and a place to stay." He hesitated. "Plus, good old Kev had that charge rigged short enough to kill you. That's why I'd like you to tell me all about your time together with him. He doesn't deserve your respect."

"Why are you interested?" Gina pulled back. "I don't want to get into any more trouble. You know, my lawyer says I shouldn't talk about the case."

"I think that whoever broke into Carol's was connected with

her and Swallow. Gina, whatever you tell me won't go beyond this room. But if I'm going to find out who killed Carol, I need to know everything about Kevin. I need to know if he was mixed up with anyone else."

She looked at her brother, her eyes wide in confusion. Gino reached up and carefully adjusted his rug before speaking. "This man did save your life, Gina," he told her. "If he says he'll keep it under his hat, I think you should trust him."

Slowly she nodded and turned back to Streeter. "Well, sir, I don't know that there's much to tell. Kev never did have any visitors the whole time. It was just him and me. We were so very much in love. He did all the planning and gave the orders." She then walked him through a jumbled recap of how they'd met and set up the attacks.

"Everything was going okeydokey right up to Monday morning." Gina glanced off for a second. "He told me that I'd be safe with all that dynamite, and then look at what happened. I coulda been killed. Jeff, too. Kevin said he loved me and then he turned out to be such a liar." Her face was pinched in anger when she finished.

"And you say no one came out to the house or called for him?"

Gina shook her head no, frowning to focus. Suddenly, her face opened wide in recognition. "Wait a minute, sir. There was something else that happened right near the end. It woulda been late last week. Maybe Thursday or Friday. We got a bunch of hang-up calls. Then, last Saturday, we went out for a ride on his Harley and when we came back someone had broke into my house and trashed it real good. Like they were looking for something. Kevin said it was probably just some Mexicans and not to worry about it. But he didn't seem none too sure, now that I think about it."

"Was anything taken?" Streeter asked.

"Maybe stuff from my drawers."

"Did you tell the police?"

She shook her head again. "It didn't seem important, given all the other stuff that happened on Monday. Why?"

"That means two break-ins in five days. Carol's apartment was burglarized and both places were trashed."

"I see what you're driving at, sir. Maybe the same person, huh?" Gina's eyes narrowed.

"Seems possible. You say the hang-up calls were first and then the break-in? Did Kevin ever mention any names?"

"No sir. But maybe that's why he was so agreeable about us leaving town on Monday. All along, he acted like we could just take our sweet time doing what we had to do. Then, suddenly, last Saturday night, he was ready to move out fast. There was one other thing."

"What's that?"

"Last Saturday, I saw two men in a car out near our place. One black guy and one white guy. It seemed strange to me that they were out there nosing around."

Streeter put one of Frank's business cards on the table and stood up. "If you think of anything else, give me a call at that number. Okay?"

When he left, he drove downtown to the *Rocky Mountain News* building. He had a friend who worked weekends in the paper's clip morgue. Streeter'd arranged to spend the afternoon reading all the stories on Swallow. It being Saturday, there was only a skeleton crew in the newsroom, so he could read undisturbed. As with the court file, there didn't seem to be anything of value in the clips. Swallow was arrested three days after the car bombing. The police searched his apartment and car. They found dynamite and tools to make a bomb. But no money. Watts speculated to reporters that he hadn't yet been paid for the Mallory contract.

"If he got anything for the job, he sure ain't telling us where it is," Cleveland was quoted as saying. In court, Kevin's demeanor usually was described as "calm, cold, and defiant," although he "seemed visibly shaken and agitated" at his sentencing.

Streeter sat in the library for a long time after he'd finished reading. He jotted a few notes to himself and then he thought about Carol. He tried to imagine what she was feeling when she made the murder plans with Swallow. Or when she was with him romantically. And what the hell passed through her mind when she thought of Streeter? Then he got up to find a phone.

27

The assistant city editor sent Streeter to a desk near the north wall of windows. He sat down and dialed Linda Parnell's number. They had talked on Thursday and he'd sketched out his theory regarding Carol's burglary. She was silent about it. Then he asked her out for Saturday night. She said yes and even proposed an official date. He'd actually drive to her house to pick her up, and they'd go to dinner.

"Hey, cowboy. I was hoping it was you." She now sounded genuinely glad to hear from him.

Streeter smiled. "Your prayers are answered. Listen, I have to go clean up for our big, for-real date. I'm so excited that I'm going to take a shower, even though it's not the end of the month."

"How flattering."

"Really. It's just before five now. Give me a couple of hours. Say sevenish?"

"Sevenish." She paused. "Any luck yet with Carol's murder?"

"I'm not sure yet." He tried to picture what she was wearing right then. "I found a couple of things that might help, but it's hard to tell. We'll talk about it tonight."

Pulling up to her curb at seven-twenty, Streeter felt a shiver of nervousness. He didn't want to be too prompt and seem eager, so he drove around for fifteen minutes, killing time. Since the week's excitement had died down, he'd been thinking about Linda more and more. Caring at all about a woman always made him anxious. She lived in a modest brick bungalow a mile or so south of Washington Park. Although it was early October, it was still warm out, and she was waiting on her wooden front-porch swing. As he parked, she got up and moved casually down the sidewalk toward him.

"Quite a chariot you got there." Her voice was soft, but she wasn't smiling. "I can't imagine a guy with a car like that ever having to sleep alone." She paused, then added, frowning, "Brown?"

He came around to her side, glancing back at his car. "It's good to see you appreciate vintage automobiles. Aren't you going to give me a tour of your house?"

"Maybe later. We'll see how much you spend on dinner." She was wearing a short white pleated skirt that accentuated her legs, and a ruffled black silk blouse. Open low. More makeup than usual, too.

"Well, I've got a pocket full of coupons and I'm in the mood for dead cow. Maybe the Sizzler," he said, opening the door. "If that doesn't get me inside, nothing will." As she moved past him, she smelled freshly washed, no perfume. He thought she'd never looked better. "Being with you has a definite high-school quality to it, Linda. Necking in the car, and now this shyness. I almost expect your mother to yell out for me to have you home early."

"Is that right?" She stopped and looked closely at him. Then she reached up and kissed his cheek lightly. "I'll try to behave like an adult tonight."

He drove them to Chives, on 6th Avenue in central Denver—a stylish, Deco restaurant featuring subdued lighting, soft jazz tapes, and a vaguely Southwestern menu. It had a good wine list, and Streeter ordered a bottle of Cabernet shortly after they sat down. When it came, he filled their glasses.

"You were going to tell me about Carol," Linda said after they'd settled in.

Streeter studied his wine. "Can't say I found anything too spectacular. Gagliano and Cullen were useless." He looked up at her. "I read the trial transcript. The whole court file, for that matter. Nothing. But there's a couple little items that caught my attention. First, I talked to Gina Gallo today and she said that someone broke into her house last week and tossed the place. Just like with Carol. Plus, the day before, she got some hang-up calls. Apparently, Swallow tried to downplay it, but he was upset. So much so he wanted to get out of Colorado fast.

"The second thing I noticed was in the newspaper clips. When he was arrested, there was a lot of speculation about what Kevin did with the money he got from Mallory's wife. But no one ever found any. He was even ruled indigent, which is how he got a court-appointed attorney."

"So?"

"So, if whoever broke into Gina's is the same person who did Carol, they were looking for something. Probably money. Could have been the money from the contract killing."

Linda sat back. "I suppose it's possible, if, if, if . . . That's pretty thin, Street."

"Tell me about it." He shook his head. "It's the only thing that makes any sense so far. Money's always a good motive."

"That may be true, but why would the burglar go to Carol's? Breaking into Gina's makes sense, but why go after Irwin once Swallow's dead?"

"Because whoever did it knew the two of them were so tight that the money or whatever it is would be joint property. Look, I know I'm reaching here, but there has to be a common motive for both burglaries."

He took a long pull from his wine. "One more thing. Swallow

was shaken up by the break-in, and the papers said that at his sentencing he fell apart. He was Joe Cool right up until he heard his sentence. Kevin had this rep for being a total hard-on, but he was capable of fear. Carol told me he'd never done prison time, so maybe the prospect of going to Cañon City got to him. My hunch is that whoever I'm looking for was someone he met after his trial. Down in prison. I bet he hooked up with some maniac and then he got in over his head. Maybe a prison gang. The Dirty White Boys or those Aryan Nation assholes. Whoever it was had some reason to come after him when they got out. And they were getting close. That's why Swallow was suddenly so antsy to leave town."

Linda shook her head. "It still sounds like a stretch. But let's say you're right. How can you possibly find them?"

"I'll talk to Frank tomorrow. He's got friends who work in the system. Maybe he can turn up something for me."

"You're really going after this. Seeing her dead must have gotten to you."

"Maybe." He looked down at his wineglass again. "But it's more than that. This seems like one huge loose end just hanging out there. It's driving me nuts. Besides, I haven't gone through half the money Carol gave me. What I'm doing now is just finishing up the job." He leaned back and studied her. "Old Carol was a wacko right up to the end. I almost feel sorry for her."

"Almost?"

"Well, she *did* want to kill me." He paused and shifted toward her. "Plus you should have seen how she acted last week. The night Cullen got his armpit blown up. We were in the loft and all of a sudden she came on to me. Made a real heavy pass. I told her to forget it and she turned real mean, real fast. She even sort of threatened me, although I didn't think much of it at the time. Then she informed me that there's no statute of limitations on my infidelity. Carol could be so vicious, and she never forgot. But it's the way she could shift gears so fast that was really scary.

One minute hot as a grill and the next minute ready to pounce."

Linda leaned toward him, too. "So you told her no. Why was that?"

"Probably because I didn't want to spend half the night digging her hand out of the disposal and feeling responsible for it."

She smiled. "Why not just admit you didn't want her because you're crazy about me?" Her eyes got that dreamy look he remembered from their first time together.

"Speaking of shifting gears, what prompted that?"

Linda lowered her voice. "I don't know, cowboy. Maybe it's the wine, maybe it's that herringbone sports jacket." She shrugged. "Probably not the jacket. But maybe it's those double-wide shoulders of yours. Whatever it is, all of a sudden I'm not very hungry. For food, anyhow."

"I thought you said I was trouble."

"I did and you are." She sipped her wine. "But it's Saturday night and I'm in the mood for a little trouble. I've been such a good girl all week."

Streeter thought he'd pass out. Instead, he reached for her hand. "So let's finish this Cabernet and then you can give me that tour of your place."

He didn't remember much about Linda's house other than that it was done heavily in antiques and that she was out of orange juice for breakfast. Most of the night they just stayed in her bedroom and made intense trouble for each other.

28

Driving home the day after sleeping with a woman for the first time always made Streeter feel kind of sad. Sure, there was a giddiness to it, particularly with someone as exciting as Linda. But there also was a sense of loss he couldn't shake. Anxiety, too. He figured that came from expectations they each might have over what would come next. The feeling of loss was more perplexing. As he headed north on Downing that Sunday, his best theory was that a slice of mystery was gone forever. There's only one first time. The excitement he felt as Linda undressed the night before. Initially touching her in all those warm little places. Enjoying her pleasure. He hoped they'd be together again, but it would never be quite the same. Did they do it too soon? Did she get as much pleasure? He wondered if Linda was going through the same emotional drill back at her place.

The other thing he felt was tired, and there was no mystery to that. They'd slept a total of maybe five of the twelve-plus hours they'd spent in bed. When he got back to the church, he practiced his piano for a long time. The routine of methodically tapping the keys comforted him. Then he had dinner, read some, and went to bed. He wanted to pump iron but he was too beat for that. Frank was playing cards and wouldn't get home until late. It wasn't until almost noon Monday that Streeter saw him again.

"Well, well," the bondsman said. He was sitting behind his desk when his partner walked in. "I take it you and your shrink hit it off pretty good the other night. You still weren't home when I left yesterday afternoon. Didja get lucky?"

"We both did, but let's not make a locker-room joke out of it, okay?"

He nodded. "I didn't mean anything by that crack. You must really like this lady."

"Yeah, I do." He sat down and put his feet on the desk. "She and I have real possibilities together. We'll see what happens." He was silent for a moment. "I just got off the phone with Carey. Seems that Carol swallowed her tongue and suffocated. They placed the time of death at about two o'clock Wednesday after-

noon. They're looking at first-degree murder, first-degree burglary, and kidnapping. He said they're convinced it's the same
prowler who did the other break-ins." He paused. "Swallowed
her own damned tongue," he repeated, shaking his head.

Frank shrugged. "I've heard of that happening. Look, Irwin
always was a talker. You know what they say. Live by the tongue,
die by the tongue."

"Jesus, that's pretty cynical. No one says that."

"Carol was bad news all the way, so pardon me if I'm not too
broken up. Get down with characters like Kevin and you gotta
take whatever comes your way. She was a grown-up and she
should have known that."

"I suppose, but she must have been scared shitless that day."

"No doubt. You having any luck finding the perp?"

Streeter filled Frank in on what he'd discovered. "Right now
I'm looking toward Cañon City," he said when he'd finished.
"That's where you come in."

"How's that?"

"Didn't you have an old pal who worked for the Department
of Corrections? Someone you knew from your days at the Sheriff's Department?"

"Mitch. From Korea. Seems like he was at DOC for most of
this century, but he's retired now. You know him, too. He's the
one you served the papers for a couple weeks ago. Remember?
Aunt Clara and her problem with that butt-head contractor."

"Yeah, yeah. Sure, I remember. Then he owes us one. Can you
hook me up with him? I'll pay for his troubles."

"Won't hurt to call. Hell, you buy Mitch a case of bourbon
and he'll find the perp himself. I have to go downtown now, but
I'll get to him later. He'll probably want to talk to you directly."

Shortly after seven that night, Frank yelled up to the loft for
Streeter to come down and take a call. "It's Mitch," he explained
as he handed the receiver to him in the office. "I told him what
you need and it sounds like he'll give you a hand."

Streeter dropped into Frank's chair. "Hey, Mitch. How you doing?"

"Still able to sit up and take in solid food, thank you. Dazzler tells me you want a little information from the department."

"If you can do it. I need to know all about an ex-con named Kevin Swallow. He was down at Cañon from late '91 to sometime in '95. Who visited him, who he bunked with, and especially anyone he might have gotten tight with. He probably got in with one of those scum-bag gangs like the Aryans or the White Boys. And I need it pretty fast."

"Swallow was the guy you shot last week, right?"

"Right."

"I read about it." Mitch paused. "It'll take some doing, but I know a lot of the guys down there. Guards and everyone else. There should be a record of his visitors, but it'll be tough finding out who he hung with. It'd help if I could buy some of the boys a beer or two."

"Whatever it takes. And buy a few for yourself while you're at it."

"Give me a couple of days and I'll see what I can come up with."

It was about the same time Wednesday night that Mitch called back.

"I got most of what you want and I think I can save you a trip down there," he told Streeter. "Talked to half the people I ever worked with and I found this one ex-guard who was there all the while Swallow was. He's moved up to Denver. I talked to him this afternoon and told him what you're after. He said he might sit down with you but I gather it'll take a little grease to get him going. His name's Cal Bosco. All of maybe twenty-five and he looks like he's just out of high school. Lives over on South Broadway, sort of above one of those dump bars down there just south of First. His number's 555-3781. He was fired a few months ago for fighting with another guard. Again. Guy's a real pain in the ass at times. Thinks he's Chuck Norris. Worked at the Colorado State Penitentiary—that's where your boy was held—the whole time, and, believe it or not, you can generally take what he says to the bank.

"Regarding visitors, Swallow didn't have any except for a lady named Kelly Spears. But not too often. Other than her, no one. No family, no friends. Now, as to who he hung out with, the way I hear it, the man was a total loner. No gang involvement. Hell, he barely even talked to his cellmate. And the funny thing is, people left him alone. Usually a first-timer like that has to make a lot of serious friends or he's getting the shit kicked out of him every couple of days. But Swallow just skated through like he was on a weekend retreat."

"The cellmate still down there?" Streeter asked, frowning.

"Only for about the next couple of lifetimes. The state pen is maximum-security, and Swallow's bunk partner did the Hat Trick. Triple homicide. Anyhow, talk to Cal. He'll steer you right if you're willing to pay."

"Thanks, Mitch. How many drinks do I owe you for?"

"The boys were pretty thirsty. Send me four hundred bucks and it should about cover everything. That sound all right?"

"No problem. Frank'll get it to you."

"Figure something like that for Bosco, too, but it should be worth it. And, Streeter, thanks for nailing Hinckley. Clara sends her best, too."

Streeter went up to the loft and changed into his workout clothes. When he got to his basement gym, he started doing push-ups to warm up. He wondered about Kelly Spears. If there was such a person or if that was Irwin under a different name. It seemed strange that Swallow had a girlfriend other than Carol. When Streeter finished lifting, about an hour later, he went to Frank's office and grabbed the phone book. There was no Kelly Spears listed in Denver. He decided to hit the Department of Motor Vehicles first thing in the morning. If Kelly existed and she lived in Colorado, she'd have a driver's license and DMV would give her address.

The next day started out badly. There was no record of a Kelly Spears with the Colorado DMV. That didn't help Streeter's mood as he drove to South Broadway. He decided to visit Cal rather than call. Experience had taught him that people find it harder to refuse to talk in person. Hanging up the phone is easy.

South Broadway is a major north–south artery, and in the area where he parked, near First, many of the old storefronts were being refurbished. But the neighborhood was still funky, and there were plenty of down-and-outers living there. Streeter started checking mail slots in all the first-floor doorways on the east side of the street. On the second block toward the south, he found one for A. H. Bosco. Number 211. Cal lived directly above a used-furniture store, which was next to the dive bar Mitch had mentioned.

The place smelled like an old attic as Streeter walked up the stairs. He found 211 and stood listening for a moment. No noise came from inside, so he pounded twice. Almost immediately the door swung open, and there stood Mr. Bosco. In green Army-surplus fatigues, he had the soft, cherubic features of a teenager. That effect was not what Cal intended. Clearly, he was going for bad. Wearing a scowl and sporting a weak goatee, he was a young man who wanted to be taken seriously and seldom was. Streeter could picture this guy fighting his co-workers. Bosco said nothing, but just studied the visitor. His face was framed with longish black hair and fuzzy sideburns. Pushing at his bangs, he clenched his jaw.

"My name's Streeter. Mitch called you about me. He said you'd be willing to talk about Kevin Swallow."

Bosco stepped out of his apartment and glanced up and down the hall. Then he looked back at Streeter. "Might be." His tone was stern and clipped, but too high to have any bite. "But time is money. I'm not running a fucking charity here." Coming from that voice and face, cursing sounded hopelessly out of place.

"Let's go get us some coffee and work it out," Streeter said. "I'll make good."

Cal nodded. "Caffeine's for pussies. We'll just go talk."

"Lead the way."

Bosco closed the door behind him without looking back. When they got outside, the October sun was warm. Indian-summer sun. They walked in silence. After a few blocks, Cal nodded to a bus-stop bench. When they sat down, he pulled a crumpled pack of Pall Malls from his pants and lit one.

"Look, Mr. One-Name, Mitch told me why you're here. So let's cut to it and get down to business." He sounded like he was reading from a bad script. "I think I can help you, but my life's been all fucked up lately, so this ain't gonna be a one-way street. I figure that three hundred bucks makes it two-way."

Streeter almost laughed, but he didn't want to offend Cal. "How do I know you can help me that much?"

Bosco rolled his eyes and took a drag from his Pall Mall. "No outsmarting you, huh, Einstein? Tell you what, give me half, I'll lay it out for you, and then you decide if it's worth the other half. Mitch said you're not a complete asshole."

Streeter reached into his pants pocket and pulled out three fifties from a roll. He handed them to Bosco. "Fire away, and I'll add a little extra if it's real interesting." He'd learned long ago that it's more important to make an informant feel good than to save a few bucks.

"That'll work," Cal said, stuffing the cash into his shirt pocket. "I'll make it fast. Swallow was in my cellblock for almost two years. He was one crazy motherfucker, but in that loony bin, he didn't scare anyone. And it always surprised me that he could stay out of trouble without warming up to the other cons."

"Mitch told me that only one person visited him."

Bosco nodded. "Some broad came out to see him a couple of

times. Can't remember her name but she listed herself as his wife. Tell you one thing, if she's a natural blonde, I'm your congressman."

"What do you mean?"

"Cheap wig and dark sunglasses. Never talked to any of us. We had a lot of that with visits. Guys passing hookers off as their wives or whatever. It's easy to do if you keep the guards happy. See, we were paid squat down there. I never even made thirty a year. You gotta work the cons or you'll never make ends meet. Being poor's for pussies. Inmates can get anything they want. Drugs, booze. But it all costs." He paused and studied Streeter more closely. "Mitch said you're looking for another con or a gang that took care of Swallow. You're looking in the wrong place. He didn't bother with none of them. Just go talk to that jerkoff he bunked with. He'll tell you I'm right." Cal dropped his cigarette on the ground and stepped on it. "It hadda been someone with pull that kept him comfy. Hadda been a guard that looked out for him and kept his butt hole tight and dry all those years."

Streeter winced at the allusion. "A guard? Who?"

Cal didn't respond.

"Look, you're already well into the bonus round. Just give me a name, a reason, and how to find the guy, and I'm on my way."

Bosco took out another cigarette and lit it. Then he nodded and leaned forward. "There's this one total fuckin' slob named Otis Weeks. A regular farm boy without a ounce a brains. He seemed to be about the only person that Swallow ever talked to. And he'd been there so long that he could wire anything. Like visits from a hooker, and like keeping the other cons away. It's tough picturing Weeks himself having the balls to team up with Swallow, but he could have. One way or another, he'll sure as hell know who did. My hunch is that, if you go squeeze Weeks hard enough, the guy you're after'll fall out. You better be a little cagey, though. Otis is pretty paranoid."

Streeter thought for a moment. "He still work down there?"

"No. He retired about a year ago. Thirty-two years on the job, full pension. He left right after Swallow walked. Otis lives with his mother, west of Monument. Do you believe that?" Cal shook his head in exaggerated wisdom. "Close to a two-hour drive each way to work and back, but he couldn't move out of Mommy's house. The guy's a regular swinging dick, all right. I don't have his number, but I'm sure a smart guy like you can read a phone book."

Streeter couldn't believe this phony sitting next to him used to be a prison guard. He reached back into his pants and pulled out the wad of fifties. Peeling off four more, he handed them to Bosco. "I'll take a crack at it."

Cal grabbed the money and stuffed it into his shirt pocket. The bent Pall Mall was in his mouth as he did, and smoke curled around his eyes, forcing him to wince deeply. "I guess that means we're all done here, right, tough guy?"

Streeter nodded, stood up, and looked down one more time. He wanted to tell Bosco to practice his ridiculous hard-bitten act some more in front of a mirror before taking it public. But he might need the ex-guard again. All he said was "I guess we are. Good luck there, Cal. But you might want to remember, smoking cigarettes is for pussies."

He turned and walked back to his car.

29

Otis Weeks sucked on the tiny brass hash pipe as he squinted at the television. *Jerry Springer.* "Goof wad," Otis snarled, alone in his basement rec room. Lately, that's how he lived: isolated, stoned, and honked off. Springer was pacing in front of five men who wanted to become women. Or was it women who wanted to become men? Weeks had lost track, but he liked listening to the audience react. Spasms of angry howls washed over the forms slouched onstage. If they ever held cock fights in an insane asylum, Otis figured, it would sound about like that.

"Freaks!" he yelled, turning his attention back to his drugs. He took another toke and set the pipe on the tray next to his recliner. Bending forward, he wheezed audibly. His asthma was hounding him. Smoking dope and the occasional Benson & Hedges menthol didn't help. It was so bad lately that he'd get winded tying his shoes. Although only five foot nine, he pushed the scales at close to two fifty. True, he had some mass in his shoulders and chest. But the bulk of his weight rested between his knees and his sternum, and it wasn't going anywhere.

When he brought up the recliner and put his feet on the floor, he looked around. An empty shot glass sat on the tray next to his pipe. Ginger schnapps. Twelve-ten on a Friday afternoon might be a bit early to start drinking, but Otis rationalized it a couple of ways. First, he was retired. Retired people are supposed to, if not party constantly, at least kick back most of the time. Second, it was only ginger schnapps. Barely counted as booze. Smoking the drugs he didn't even try to justify. Otis had fired up on hash or pot daily for over twenty years. He'd slipped past the DOC's random urine tests by always keeping a vial of clean pee tucked in his boot. As he used to brag to his drug source in Pueblo, "I've been holding a piss since the Nixon administration."

Suddenly, a noise from upstairs worked its way toward him. "Od-us!" A pause. "Oh, Od-us!" it repeated, louder. A car commercial popped up on the tube, so Weeks grabbed the remote and clicked it out of existence. Then he glanced at the door to the stairs and squinted for clarity. Yet another "Od-us!" tumbled down the stairs. His mother always made his name sound like a short sentence.

Slowly, he stood and moved toward the door. His thigh caught a corner of the tray and almost knocked it over. "Ehhh," he grunted. When he got there, he opened the door and looked up. Again, he squinted behind his thick glasses and frowned in concentration. Damn, he was more wasted than he thought, but he could still make out the formidable figure of his mother at the top of the stairs.

"Od-us, when are you going to town?" Lois Weeks cringed back at her son in the dark stairwell. "I need that prescription filled."

There was a nervous silence as he thought. "I got it yesterday," he finally blurted. Then he scratched at his chest through the rumpled tan DOC shirt. "It's in your medicine cabinet. I'll be up in a minute to show you."

He hadn't been out of the house in nearly five days, and he knew damned well his mother had no medicine. It was supposed to thin out her blood. Or maybe thicken it? Otis had lost track. He could see her mouth slowly drop open as she considered his answer. Lois was always bent over and leaning slightly to the side, like she was looking around a corner. With her mop of gray hair parted deeply on the left, horse lips, and dark, barren eyes, she looked like Jimmy Carter in drag. Otis didn't like her much, although he'd lived his entire fifty-four years under her roof.

Slowly, Lois began to nod as though everything was clear. Then her eyes narrowed and she drew her head back. "I'll look myself." Sounding vaguely mad, she sniffed at the air. "What's that smell?"

Otis glanced over his shoulder and then back at Lois. He knew she'd have a fit if she ever found his drugs. Still, he figured, with her circulation problems, he could repanel the entire rec room in the time it would take her to navigate the twelve steps down there. She hadn't been to the basement in years.

"Incense," he answered. "I musta told you that a hunnert times."

"What kind of insects smell like that? It's more like you're burning a bunch of tires, for Pete's sakes."

"*Incense!*" he yelled back. Can't she get anything right? "It cuts the odor from the sump pump, like I told ya. Jesus Christ!"

Lois's eyes flashed open and she nodded. "Sump pump," she repeated gravely. With that she turned and shuffled into the kitchen, shutting the door behind her. Otis stared up for a moment, and then stepped back and closed his door. He made his way through the rec room and into the little office he'd put together over the years. After closing that door behind him, he moved to his desk and eased himself into the chair. He shook his head to clear it and reminded himself to stick to just pot for a while. Hash always messed him up too much. So did the opium he flirted with from time to time.

As he opened the top drawer, several plastic eight-millimeter film containers he kept his drugs in rolled aimlessly around. He noticed the two envelopes of cash from the other night. Over twenty grand. It reminded him of Carol Irwin. Otis grabbed his pot and shut the drawer. Then he reached down to a lower drawer and opened it. His heart fluttered for an instant when he saw what was inside. Three pair of new thong panties he'd taken from Carol's dresser. Red, black, and—his personal favorite—bright green. Lying there crumpled into small wads, they looked more like lacy ribbons than clothing. Weeks took the green one and held it up just inches from his face. He leaned forward and rubbed his cheek gently against the soft silk. Then he dropped the panty back into the drawer and shut it with his knee.

He wasn't sure why he'd taken them. Maybe he just wanted a reminder of Carol. Hell, he half fell in love with her in those few hours they were together before she died. No way he wanted to see her dead. He told her she was beautiful. If she cooperated, they could maybe go off somewhere and get to know each other.

"I'd rather die of bone-marrow cancer than let you touch

me," she'd hissed back as she squirmed in the chair. "You hear me, you stupid shit kicker?"

Sitting at his desk, he felt his eyes get moist. Sure, he had to smack her a few times to get the right answers. But when he put the gag on her, he never imagined she'd panic and choke. He wasn't even in the same room when it happened. No, he didn't mean to hurt her. The term "unlucky in love" raced through his mind. So did his mother's constant assessment of him: "If there's one thing you're good at, Od-us, I've never seen any evidence of it."

He blinked against the wetness in his eyes. Still loveless and friendless. As always. And what was it that Carol had called him? "Fucking clueless!"

That last part wasn't completely true, Otis knew. He might look like just a celibate old sauce hound, but he had his moments. Made all-state as a high-school football tackle. Hell, he'd even spent a couple of winters in junior college. He liked sociology. Of course, he never finished, and that was pretty much ancient history anyhow. Still, he was no idiot, he kept reminding himself. He could rise to the occasion. That's how he tracked down Swallow and Irwin. They sure as hell never expected that. No, he told himself now, you don't want to sell Otis Weeks short.

Streeter always became slightly disoriented when he left the city. So here he was, late on a Friday afternoon, lost eight miles east of Monument. Most of the houses were too far off the road for him to see their addresses. He was on a two-lane blacktop, flat as a desk with the autumn sun searing his windshield. Screw it, he decided. Pull into the next driveway and ask for directions. But before he could, he saw forms in the distance near the side of the road. He drove another couple of hundred yards and pulled over. Two girls in their early teens stopped walking when his car began to slow down. Streeter put the old Buick into park, waited a moment, and then got out. There was a whiff of burned rubber in the air, along with a faint rumble of distant power equipment. The girls stared and then started walking again.

"Howdy," he said, working up a smile and nodding when they got to him. "I'm lost. You ladies know your way around out here?"

Once again, they both stopped in unison. Wearing jeans and T-shirts, neither of them seemed impressed with the stranger. Maybe curious, but certainly not afraid. "We sure should," the taller one said. "Lived here our whole lives." She had chopped red hair and incredibly pale skin that was highlighted with black lipstick.

"Can you tell me where Otis Weeks lives?"

At the sound of the name, both girls scrunched up their faces in forced disgust. "Not him," the tall one said.

"What's wrong?"

The talker took a step closer and lowered her country-and-Western voice. "He's nothing but a damned weirdo. None of us even talk to him." Her friend was nodding at every word. "Ain't right, an old man like that still living with his mother. *Pull-ese.* And he looks at us so funny." She shuddered and stepped back.

"Yeah, well, I need to talk to him."

"You here to buy that piano of his?" the tall one asked.

Streeter frowned. "What piano?"

The shorter girl spoke for the first time. "He got a sign out: 'Piano for sale.' It's been there for about a year. Guess they're too cheap to advertise." She turned and lifted her arm in the direction they had just come from. "His place is over there. That brown one that looks like a big old cow pie." She turned back. "Sorta like your car."

Streeter glanced at the house but resisted looking at his Buick. The girls were moving down the road behind him by the time he turned back. He got in his car, drove the half-mile to Weeks' driveway, and pulled over. During the hour-long trip down from

Denver, he was trying to think of a pretense for his visit. He was sure he was getting closer to his target and he didn't want Weeks tipped off to what he was after. The best he could come up with was the ever-popular "I'm lost." Very clever. But now he had a perfect excuse to be there. The piano. He wasn't sure what he expected to find, and he knew he wouldn't squeeze Weeks as Bosco had suggested. But he wanted to meet Otis and maybe shake him up some. Streeter would be fishing blind, but sometimes that'll catch you plenty. Sometimes it's all you've got.

Glancing at the house, he realized the little girl was right. Listing to one side, the two-story building looked more like a tractor shed sitting alone on the bare prairie. Its peeled wood was dried to a dull dung color, and the porch steps sagged badly. A faded white plank with "For sale, Spinat piano—$750" painted on it was nailed to a post at the driveway entrance.

The bounty hunter left his car at the road and walked to the front door. He gently tapped on it. Then it took over five minutes of knocking ever louder before he heard motion inside. In another minute or so, the door opened and a boxy woman in plaid shorts, a sweatshirt, and a denim baseball cap answered. She winced at her visitor, struggling to recognize him. Failing that, she looked down at the unlit cigar in her hand and scowled. "You got a match?" she asked the man in front of her.

Streeter shook his head. "I don't smoke."

The old lady raised an eyebrow and nodded. "But you used to, didn't you? I can always tell." She frowned again. "Who are you?"

"My name's Bill. I understand you have a piano for sale."

Lois studied him. "The piano. Yeah, the piano. You're the first one. We musta had . . ." Before she could finish, the lumbering form of Otis walked up behind her and coughed loudly. Both the old lady and Streeter turned to him.

"It's a beauty, mister," Otis said, pushing past Lois. "What'd you say your name was?" He held out his hand as he spoke.

Streeter looked hard at him. Weeks' eyes were dark, and blue veins wormed around them. Huge bags rested underneath. Drinker's eyes: always damp and never completely focused. Something else, too. His pupils were the size of quarters and he had that drowsy voice. A doper. Made sense, given the kind of garbage he'd been into at the state pen. "Bill," he finally answered. Then he waited a beat. "Bill Swallow."

The man in front of him dropped his jaw and his hand at the same time. He frowned and his face flushed. "I'm Otis." Then he clamped up and studied his visitor. Years of institution work had taught him one thing: patience.

Finally, Lois broke the silence. "Phil here says he wants to look at the piano. Can't sell the damned thing standing out here. Show him where it is, Od-us."

Weeks' eyes narrowed. "His name's *Bill.*" He waited a second. "Yes sir, Mr. Swallow. I'll show you the spinet. Wouldn't mind hearing you knock out a tune, either."

With that he turned and walked into the house. Lois moved behind him, and Streeter followed her. The bounty hunter was glad he'd taken lessons. He ran through his limited play list. "The Minute Waltz," "Stardust," and "Tie a Yellow Ribbon." He'd go with the waltz. The living room was dark and it smelled distinctly like mothballs. An aged black spinet stood against the far wall, and there was a metal folding chair in front of it.

"Who plays?" Streeter asked.

"No one," Lois responded. "My husband used to, but he's been dead for over twelve years. Od-us here keeps saying he'll take it up, but then, like everything else, he never follows through. I finally decided I'd rather have more room in here."

Streeter glanced at Otis, who took the insult in stride. "I see you used to work in corrections," he said, nodding to the insignia on his host's right shoulder.

Otis's eyes narrowed as he glanced down on his tan shirt. But he didn't answer.

"I had a cousin who spent a little time as a guest over at the state pen. Where'd you work, Otis?"

"Different places," he answered. A smile crept across his face and he nodded toward the piano. "Give it a shot, Mr. Swallow. See how she sounds."

The bounty hunter sat in the folding chair and stared at the keyboard. It took him almost ninety seconds to finish "The Minute Waltz." The spinet was so out of tune it sounded like he was playing under water.

"Showroom condition, ain't she, Phil?" Lois inquired.

"Yeah, right. You want seven fifty for *this*?"

"We'll take seven," Otis said. "Think you're interested?

Streeter ran his fingers gently over the keys, deep in thought. "I don't know."

"I'll help deliver it," Otis said. "You live around here?"

"North Colorado Springs, not far from the academy. About twenty-five minutes away. Let me think about it. What's your number?"

Otis took a slip of paper and pen from his shirt pocket, wrote the phone number on it, and handed it to his guest. "Mind if I get yours?"

Streeter stared at him. Weeks' eyes seemed more focused now. Those eyes were state-trained. They could stare at a wall for days without blinking. And there was more going on behind them than Streeter first thought. Otis had spent all those years dealing with the worst criminal waste the state of Colorado could produce. Even though it broke the man down, he still had a brain behind those eyes. A scared, wet brain, but it still functioned. "I'll give you a holler by Sunday if I'm interested," Streeter finally answered. "Let's leave it at that."

He got up and left. Walking down the driveway, the bounty hunter thought how he'd want to do a background check on both of the Weekses. Also, he wondered how he could get in to search the house.

Otis stood on the porch, casually scratching at a spot next to his fly. Then he stepped back into the living room, grabbed the rifle scope from a shelf near the door, walked out onto the porch again, and focused on the Buick just as it started up. He'd memorized the license plate before it was gone. One thing was dead solid certain, Weeks reasoned. Bill Swallow was totally full of shit.

30

"You wouldn't believe those two coconuts down there, Frank," Streeter said on Saturday afternoon. They were at a table in Pint's Pub, a British-style saloon on 13th Avenue, near Bail Bonds Row and the downtown police station. "Mr. Weeks has put together one hell of a life for himself. Both he and his mother. They bounce around that house like a pair of sick water buffaloes. Weeks was half demolished on booze, and the old lady looked like the queen of a trailer park on Mars. When I said my last name was Swallow, he almost lost his lunch. It really hit home. He's the man I'm after. Has to be."

Frank put down his Guinness and thought. "I talked to Mitch about him last night, and he said Weeks is pure trouble. He worked for DOC for thirty years plus and not one promotion. Sadistic, too. But you don't have any proof hooking him up to Carol."

Streeter nodded. "Carey told me Thursday that they didn't find any fresh prints at Carol's apartment. I assume Weeks'd be sharp enough to wear gloves, but it would have been nice to connect him that way. The cops are even more sure it's the same guy that pulled the other Capitol Hill burglaries."

"Not good for your theory. You better go get a little hard evidence. All you have now is speculation and a schmuck with a piano for sale who used to know Swallow. You're not gonna impress the DA with that."

"I have to get into that house and look around. If Weeks did Carol's burglary, what he took could be in there. But he won't keep it forever, and getting in is going to be next to impossible. I bet that old lady hasn't left in years, and Otis doesn't look like he gets out much, either."

"You sure you're right about Weeks?" Frank asked.

"Not a hundred percent, but there doesn't seem to be anyone else. Otis had some strong connection to Kevin in prison. Based on how Swallow skated through, I think Weeks protected him. My hunch is he was promised money for his troubles. What probably happened is that they short-changed Weeks once Swallow got out."

"Maybe. But it shouldn't have been too hard for this guard to drive to Denver, pick up a phone book, and get Irwin's address. Why didn't he go after her right from the start? I can see Swallow being hard to find, but Carol shoulda been a snap."

"I wish I had a good answer for you. That's why I've got to get into his place and see what I can turn. Either that or tail him, which could take forever. But I know I'm on the right track here. There just isn't any other track to be on."

They sat drinking in silence for a moment. Then Frank spoke. "There might be another way to shake something loose. Two places you haven't looked yet that I would definitely be interested in."

"Where?"

"Carol's apartment and her office."

Streeter sat up. "Of course. Well, not the office. It's too late for that. I already tried. I went by there early on Friday and talked to the guy who owns the building. He had her files and personal stuff moved to her apartment the day after she died. The furniture stayed, because he owned it, and he's already re-renting the office. But her apartment's another matter. Carey told me that Carol's sister came out, but she only spent a couple of minutes in there. She was more concerned with shipping the body back to Chicago. The sister left right away for the funeral. She'll be coming back in a couple of weeks to clean the apartment, Carey said. Who knows what's tucked away in there? I'd sure like a shot at it."

"Any chance you can get inside?" Frank asked.

"That'll be tough. It's still a sealed crime scene. Haney won't let me near the place, and Carey always goes by the book. No way he's going to lose his job for me." Streeter thought for a moment. "Look, I have to go meet Linda down at her place. She was at some psychologists' conference in L.A. all week, and I haven't seen her since our little tryst last Saturday. We've barely talked since then." He stood up. "You get any brilliant ideas on how to get into that apartment, let me know."

Driving to Linda's, Streeter wondered what kind of reception he'd get. She'd sounded distracted when she'd called him the night before. Especially when he told her about how his investigation was going. But he was excited to see her. That feeling melted when she met him at the door.

"Hello," she said. "It's been a while." Linda opened her arms for him to hug her, but there was no passion in either her words or her embrace.

Streeter pulled back and studied her. "Not even a little kiss? I guess absence doesn't always make the heart grow fonder."

Linda threw him a quick smile, and gave him an empty kiss. "I missed you a lot, Street. It's just that I don't know why." She walked him into the living room. "That's what bothers me. I don't know what to make of us. I sure don't know what to make of you."

"Uh-oh. Sounds like we're going to have one of those 'our-night-together-was-great-but' conversations," he said.

"Something like that. Let's have a beer and talk about it."

Linda went to the kitchen and brought back two Heinekens. She gave one of the green bottles to Streeter and they sat on the couch. Her dark-gray business clothes suited the mood.

"What's going on, Linda? Maybe you didn't fall in love last Saturday, but something happened. You sure seemed to enjoy yourself."

"Enjoyment has nothing to do with it, Street. That night was wonderful. But I've had a lot of time to think about it and I'm not sure it was such a good idea. I'm not sure that *we're* a good idea. Listen, I could really go off the deep end for a man like you. But where would I land? In Fort God? Look at you, Street. Your life. Chasing degenerates all day. You live in a bunker with . . . I don't know. How would you describe Frank? And people have a nasty habit of dropping dead when you're around. You told me yourself that you don't even like it anymore. Then along comes a Carol Irwin case and you get caught up like a child playing cops and robbers." She paused and shook her head. "There just doesn't seem to be much a future in any of it. And that's not to mention your history with women. All those disastrous relation-ships. The women you select, for God's sake. I can't see how I'd fit in, and I'm getting too old for dead-end streets. Pardon the pun."

He took a sip of beer. "That's not a very flattering summary of my life. Accurate, but not flattering. Look, I don't think either of us has to go off the high dive right away. We might have rushed things a little, but we're consenting adults and we can slow down. As for my career, I've been wrestling with that one myself. The more I get into it, the more I do things that don't leave me feeling good. Everything's about lying lately. About pretense. There's a great euphemism for you. Seems I can't just knock on the front door anymore and be square with people. That bothers me. And Irwin's case brings out the worst in what I do, with the worst kind of people. Like this jerk I talked to yesterday in Monument. You think *my* life's going nowhere."

"I didn't say that, Street. I just said I'm not sure where you're headed."

"Whatever. Carol's death has made me look long and hard at me. Particularly the decisions I've made with women and work. I'm not apologizing to anyone, but maybe what I do is a young man's game." He looked closely at her. "Still, I can't just walk away. Not from Frank and not from the business. To be honest, I have no idea where I'd go. Punch a clock for some corporation? Back to school? I'm too old to take instructions and pass tests. I'll keep examining it, but so far this is what I am." He set his beer down. "Linda, I like you a lot, but if how I live makes you that uncomfortable, maybe we ought to call it quits."

"I don't know what to do, Street. Right now, I'm just tired of thinking about it."

"Then don't. Let's go get dinner. Better yet, let's stay in and I'll cook. Now, there's a side of me you haven't seen yet. And I'll try not to talk shop, even though I'm wrestling with an incredible problem at the moment."

She took a sip of beer. "Against my better judgment, I'll ask. What problem?"

Streeter flashed a quick grin and his eyebrows shot up. "I'm at a dead end with Carol's investigation. The police are off on a whole different tangent, and it looks like the guy I'm after's going to get away. That Otis I told you about last night. I'm sure he's the perp, but I can't prove anything. If I could get into Carol's apartment for a couple of hours, I might be able to find something to link her and Swallow to Otis."

"Won't the police let you in?"

He shook his head. "Even my best source wouldn't bend the rules that far. And I can't think of any other cops who would. There doesn't seem to be anyone." Suddenly, he jerked his head back. "Wait a minute! There is one guy who owes me big-time. My newest, bestest buddy with the DPD." He turned to face her squarely. "Officer Jeff Barrows. He was out at my driveway the day of the explosion. Remember? I saved his ass, and he gave me his card when he got out of the hospital. Said if I ever needed anything to just page him."

"What can he do?"

"I'm not sure, but I can't imagine a landlord not letting a man in uniform into Carol's apartment. There must be some end run he and I can cook up together."

Linda stood up and shook her head. "Streeter, you're hopeless! Positively fucking hopeless! You just get done whining about pretense work and how you want to go to the front door and be honest with people. Then you come up with *this*? From pretense to breaking and entering is not a step in the right direction. And all on some hunch that's probably nothing but crap anyway. I don't even want to hear what you've got in mind. For God's sake, I have to work with the police."

"It's not breaking and entering." His voice rose as he spoke. "We're not going to break anything. We're just going to enter."

"And exactly what is that? Go on, put a name to it."

"It's . . . I'm not sure. It's creative investigating." His eyes widened a bit. "It's networking! People do it all the time. You probably do, too."

"Hopeless!" Linda started to move toward the front door. "Look, I don't want any dinner. I just want to take a hot bath and then catch up on some reading and my sleep. You go and play Mission Impossible or whatever your little fantasy world's called. I just don't want to hear about it anymore." She opened the door. "Goodbye, Street."

He could see that she meant it, but he was too preoccupied to respond. "I'll try to call you in a few days," was the best he could manage as he left. By the time he got to his car, all he could think about was getting back to the church and paging Barrows.

31

It was in the mid-forties and overcast as they sat down on the front stoop a few minutes before noon. When he'd answered Streeter's page the night before, Jeff Barrows had readily agreed to the meeting. But now, after hearing what the bounty hunter wanted, he wished he hadn't.

"Come on, Streeter! You have any idea what Haney'd do to me if he ever finds out about this? He'd fire me, for starters. Then he'd personally kill me." The two men were drinking coffee at the cop's tiny house in West Denver, near Sloan's Lake. "And I can't imagine what they'd do to you. You're looking at obstructing and criminal trespass, at the very least."

"Will you relax?" Streeter countered. "There's no way he'll find out. Even if the building manager tells him that a cop stopped by to get into the apartment, the guy probably won't remember your name. And you don't actually have to go in. Just open the door, unlock it, and then split. I won't leave any prints or disturb anything. No one'll ever know what you did, Jeff."

Barrows stared straight ahead, the cup in his hand dipping slightly. Even his huge shoulders sagged. He looked sad in his black turtleneck sweater. Finally, he shook his head. "I can't, man. This would end my career. There's no way we can be sure it won't get back to the department. I'm sorry, but I just can't."

Streeter glared at him. "This from the guy who said he'd do anything for me. I hesitate to remind you, but you owe me, Jeff. Actually, I don't hesitate. You *really* owe me. Who saved your sorry, by-the-book life?" Then his voice softened. "But let's put that aside for a minute. Think of Carol. She was a sick lady, but you cared about her, and her killer's going to get away. Do it for her. For the justice of it."

"Why don't you just tell Carey or Haney to go look for whatever you think's in there? Why all this spy business?"

"I talked to Carey on Friday and laid out my theory and why I'm after Weeks." Streeter paused and blew on his coffee before taking a sip. "Robert, who actually likes and respects me, thinks I'm out to lunch on this one. Just imagine how Haney'd react. He thinks I'm full of shit under any circumstances. My gut instinct is that in some weird way Carey feels protective of Weeks. Otis was a peace officer for a lot of years, and Robert thinks of him as a kindred spirit. You know, the fraternal brotherhood of officers. At any rate, he's not buying Weeks as the perp."

Jeff winced like he had severe heartburn. "Then why not ask Carol's family for permission? That'd probably get you in."

"I thought of that last night, after we talked, so I called her sister Cathy in Chicago. It seems Carol bashed me pretty good to the family over the years. Cathy barely let me finish. She said I ruined Carol's life and there's no way she'd ever help me. You can just imagine how she reacted to my story about Carol being hooked up with Swallow. She called me a few incredibly disgusting names and hung up." He shook his head. "Either you help or there's no entry. No entry, no case against that peckerhead Weeks. The choice is yours."

"Aw, hell, Streeter." Barrows stood up as he spoke. "All right! All right! I'll do it. But I'm not setting foot in there." His face tightened. "I don't think I could stand to see where she died. When did you want to go?"

"Today would be good. The manager lives right there, on the first floor. Go put on your uniform. When you talk to the guy, just get the key and say you have to check the place real quick. Then unlock it, leave it open a crack, and return the key. The whole thing'll take you about two minutes. I'll be waiting upstairs, and when you're gone, I'll go inside and see what's what.

When I leave, I'll close the door behind me and make sure it's locked. In and out, and no one'll ever know."

"Three things." Barrows stared hard at Streeter. "First, this squares us. Forever! Second, you get caught in there, you don't even know my name. Third, I don't want to hear about what you find. I don't want to know nothing." He paused. "And good luck. I mean that."

They went to Carol's apartment during the first half of the Broncos–Raiders game. If you want to deal with anyone in this town while he's totally distracted, that's the best time. Sure enough, the elderly building manager gave Barrows the key with hardly more than a glance. Jeff unlocked the door, signaled Streeter, and left. When he got inside, the bounty hunter quietly closed the door and got down to business.

Concerns about disrupting the place were unnecessary. Between the cops, the burglar, and Carol's own horrendous housekeeping, it looked like a training room for *Wrestlemania*. Streeter took a deep breath, pulled at the surgical gloves he wore, and began searching. After starting in the living room, he worked his way back through the dining area, the bathroom, the tiny kitchen, the spare bedroom, and finally Carol's room. He checked under all the furniture, all the shelves, through all the books and knickknacks, in every drawer, every corner, every closet, all her files. It took him nearly two hours. Nothing. Not one indication that Carol knew Otis Weeks, or even that she kept in touch with Swallow after the trial. Streeter was depressed and anxious when he'd finished. Had he been wrong about Otis Weeks? Hell, had he been wrong about Kevin and Carol working together? For ten minutes he sat with those thoughts on her bare mattress and stared at the wall in front of him. Then he decided to go through the whole place again. Being that wrong was not an option.

Standing up and heading back toward the living room, he rubbed sweat from his forehead. He was soaked. As he moved down the hall, he thought of how the burglar must have gotten Carol's expensive jewelry. She'd had a pearl necklace and two sets of diamond earrings that she'd cherished. They weren't anywhere in the apartment, and he couldn't imagine her selling them. Suddenly he stopped, recalling what she'd told him years ago: that she kept her most valuable jewelry wrapped in plastic and stuffed inside cereal boxes. No one who broke in would ever look there. Streeter was about to test that theory.

He went to the kitchen and grabbed the four boxes of cereal that were lying on their sides in the cupboard. On the first search, he'd paid little attention to them. Large boxes of Raisin Bran, Rice Chex, Fruit Loops, and Cap'n Crunch. The Raisin Bran was still unopened, so he turned to the other three. In the Rice Chex, nothing. Then he hit pay dirt with the Fruit Loops. Stuffed in the bottom of the half-full box was the plastic-wrapped jewelry. All three items, along with a petite gold watch. But the real treasure was inside Cap'n Crunch. Wrapped in clear plastic was a business card for StorageWorld with the number 341 scrawled on it in pencil. That and a key, presumably for locker 341. Streeter put both in his pocket, replaced the jewelry, and left the apartment.

Driving south on Washington Street to East Evans, he wondered how long Carol had had the locker. When he got to Evans, he turned right and headed west. At the intersection with Sherman, he spotted StorageWorld on the northeast corner. It was a small world. Two long cinder-block buildings stood end to end with a dozen bright-yellow overhead garage doors on both sides of each. Cryptically, the number sequence began with 311. Streeter drove to 341, on the west side of the far building. He parked and walked to the padlock on the bottom of the door. The key fit. Inside was a room about eight feet wide by seven feet high and six feet deep. It contained a wooden trunk and three large wardrobes, all packed with Carol's old clothes.

Streeter got his huge work flashlight from the Buick and returned to the locker, closing the door behind him. When he saw what was inside the trunk, he grunted with excitement. It contained all the confirmation he needed. With the exception of a few details, he'd been right about Carol and Kevin, and, subsequently, about them and Otis Weeks. Streeter stayed in the locker for over three hours, reading by flashlight and pacing. It was all there. Too bad he couldn't use any of it.

32

Bumpy gravy covered the chicken-fried steak and mashed potatoes like boiled Elmer's Glue. Tasted like it, too. Monday night meant chicken-fried steak, canned peas, Parker House rolls, and vanilla pudding for dessert. Otis grabbed the pepper and shook it furiously over his food. Ditto with the salt. That pretty well exhausted Lois's repertoire of spices. Otis toyed with the idea of adding ketchup, but decided against it. Instead he just started sawing at flank steak that had been battered and fried to just this side of a roof shingle. It didn't matter. He had the pot munchies so bad he was nearly blind with hunger.

"You say this Phil Swallow wasn't who he claimed to be?" Lois asked from across the table.

Her son nodded without looking up from his food.

"How do you know that, Od-us?"

Weeks paused and glanced at her, his jaws working the meat like a disposal. When he finally gulped it down, he rested his fork hand on the edge of the table. "Because I called up to a guy I know at Motor Vehicles this morning and found out that the plates on his car are registered to a Frank Dazzler in Denver. I also found out that there's only one Bill Swallow in Colorado and he's all of nineteen years old. Lives over in Aspen. Then I made a few calls to people I know at the Sheriff's Department up in Denver and I found out that Mr. Frank Dazzler is a bail bondsman, of all things. And he has a partner, some mutt named Streeter, who matches up with that guy that looked at the piano the other day. He's a bounty hunter." With that he started cutting another piece of meat. "A fuckin' bounty hunter."

Lois considered what he said as she slid her chair away from the table. She turned to the sink counter and grabbed an unlit cigar from an ashtray there. Turning back, she held the cigar like a pointer. "Does this Streeter have a first name?"

Otis shrugged without looking up. "None that no one up there knows. Guy thinks he's James Bond or something."

"And he told us his name's Swallow. Like your friend from work." She paused to study her cigar, then pointed it at him again. "The one who was going to put us on Easy Street when you took care of him in the pen. The one who this Streeter guy said was his cousin." Lois shook her head. "It looks like someone's on to you, Od-us. You got your armpit caught in a wringer, again."

He looked up, his jaw dropping in exasperation. "Can't you get anything right? That's not what gets caught in a wringer. Just think about it, for chrissakes."

Lois scowled, her head rising. She pulled her arm back and chucked the cigar across the table. It hit Otis in the forehead and bounced down into his plate, landing in his potatoes. "Can't *I* get anything right! Look who's talking over there. You're the big shot who said you had everything set up. You said, if you looked out for that shit-bird con, we'd see tons of money. And you're the one who told me not to worry even after he got killed. You still knew where all the money was. A simple burglary, you said. And now you're up to your eyeballs in a murder. Murder, Od-us!"

"Take it easy," he countered. "How the hell am I supposed to eat this now?" He looked back down at the brown cigar stuck in his milky food.

"The way you shovel it in, what difference does it make?"

Otis glanced back up at her. "I told you, I didn't mean to kill that woman. You read it yourself in the damned papers. She choked herself. The cops said it was an accident."

"Big deal. It's still murder, and if you get caught, your sorry ass goes to jail. Simple as that." She got up and went to a drawer in the hutch, opened it, and pulled out a fresh cigar. When she got back to her chair, she went after her son again. "So what are you going to do about Streeter?"

"I dunno." Otis shrugged. "I mean, what's he got on me? I dunno," he repeated.

Lois shook her head sadly. "My son. The man without a plan. Did you see the size of that guy? And he wasn't all lard, like you. He'll probably come down here and break you in half before he takes you in."

Otis frowned and tried to concentrate. His premeal joint made that difficult. "He don't know nothing. I was careful. There's not a damned thing anywhere that links me to Kevin Swallow or that lawyer. How could there be?" His eyes narrowed. "I was smart. No one even knows that I knew her. And the papers said that the cops think her burglary was just like a bunch of other ones around there. I planned it that way. After I saw all those Capitol Hill burglary stories, I made it look like that. Nobody knows nothing about me."

"Od-us, Od-us," Lois repeated sadly. "You talk like a sausage. The only one that don't know anything is you. Streeter knows plenty or he wouldn't a come down here. And if he knows plenty, the cops'll know it all soon enough. There must be something to link you up to that dead lawyer. I told you not to mess with her. When Swallow died, I told you to write it off and let it go at that."

"And I told you, I wasn't gonna get jerked around by them." His voice went up as he worked into the topic. "Swallow promised me about sixty thousand if I took care of him. He said he and his lawyer had it all tucked away. He said it was worth it to him for what I did. We had a deal! Hell, they were planning to cut me out and go to Mexico. Irwin, the lawyer, bragged to me about it that night."

"Great. You make a deal with a guy who's doing life for a contract murder and then you're surprised that he's full of bullshit. You can sure pick 'em, Od-us. And how much did you end up with? A couple thousand dollars?"

He looked back at his plate. "About five, I guess."

"Well, go out and enjoy it before you head over to prison. I wonder how they'll treat an ex-guard in Cañon City."

He glanced back at her. "That won't happen!" There was more fear than certainty in his voice. "I'll take care of Streeter. You've got my word on that." Then he nodded to indicate that he meant business.

"Oh, my my. Why didn't you say so earlier? Your word. I guess we'll all sleep better tonight knowing we've got your *word*."

At that, Weeks stood up and threw his napkin on the table. "There's no way in hell that I'm going down for what happened to that lawyer. I'll wait and see what Streeter comes up with. If he gets too close, I'll take care of him. I'm no killer, but if it's him or me, it's him." He frowned. "You know what I mean." Then he backed away from the table and left the room.

Lois just sat there, shaking her head. "The man without a plan," she finally repeated softly to herself. "That's my boy."

When Otis got to the basement, he was too worked up to sit. So he walked around the room, occasionally coming back to the tray by his recliner for a shot of schnapps. How *did* Streeter get wind of him? His source at the Sheriff's Department said the guy was a crack skip tracer. Otis knew it would just be a matter of time before he'd be back. What then? Weeks drained the shot glass and sat down. Could he kill Streeter face to face? It might come to that. He was positive there wasn't any link between him and Carol Irwin. Except for those few times she came to the prison, he never talked to her. Even then, she wore that stupid disguise and called herself Kelly something-or-other. Could he kill Streeter? Or anyone? He sure didn't want to. But living out his days in prison for something he didn't mean to do—well, just forget it.

He got up and walked back to his desk. The situation called for serious thought and desperate action. That meant he'd clean his .44 and smoke the last of the opium he had in the middle drawer. Sitting down, he again told himself that there was no evidence anywhere to link him to Irwin. But Streeter might have been a friend of hers. He might not need evidence. Otis remembered how he'd damned near passed out when Streeter said his name was Swallow. The bounty hunter had noticed it, too. He might come back and break Otis's spine in repayment. Screw evidence. Remember the size of his arms? Damned tree trunks. He shivered and reached into a drawer, grabbing something else he'd taken from Carol's place. As he pulled the hand grenade up for closer inspection, the guard felt calmer.

33

"I tell you, Frank, I nailed this thing cold almost from start to finish. And now I can't move on it without going to jail." Streeter was sitting across the desk from his partner at about two-thirty on Monday afternoon. "You're probably looking at charges just for hearing about it."

The bondsman considered that. "I got mixed feelings here,

Street. You breaking the law like that. Plus, you put Jeff in a box with this stunt. But I don't know that you had much of a choice. What was in that locker?"

"Diaries. Five, six years' worth of diaries. Three or four entries a week. There must have been close to fifteen books. Carol started them at Swallow's trial and she laid everything out in detail. How she hooked up with Kevin, how they hatched up all their plans. She and Swallow were totally nuts about each other. Not to mention totally nuts in general. And I won't even tell you what she wrote about yours truly. The woman despised me. They planned to kill me and then move to Mexico. Between the thirty thousand Mrs. Mallory paid Kevin, and money Carol had tucked away, they thought they could retire. They had about ninety grand, and they promised Weeks a lot of it for helping Kevin skate through the pen. But they strung him along for months once, and then finally blew him off. They thought they'd be far away before he'd find them. Evidently, Weeks didn't know exactly who Carol was until near the end, when the papers printed it. Neither of them was very impressed with Otis's brain power. The last entry was from just before she hired me."

"Did you find out who Kelly Spears was?" Frank adjusted himself in his chair.

Streeter nodded. "There was no Kelly Spears. That's the name Carol used on her visits. She was careful not to have any traceable contact with Kevin once he went away. Carol put a lot of thought and work into this. She was obsessed by it. If she'd put half that much into her practice, she'd have been rich and successful. All that energy going into blaming and planning how to get even. Like a sick child."

"Which is basically what she was." Frank paused. "That has to make you feel good about your choice of females."

The bounty hunter was silent. He thought about his conversations with Linda on the subject. Especially the last one. "Yeah, I've got a real way with the ladies. Linda and I talked about all that the other night, right before she dumped me."

"Haven't you two patched that up yet?" Frank looked pained. "I hate to see you let her get away. She's probably good for you."

"Probably. But it looks like we'll never find out." Streeter stood up, anxious. He walked around the room as he spoke. "Look, I can't worry about her right now. I'm sitting on enough information to settle this whole Irwin mess, and there's nothing I can do with it. It's nice to be vindicated, but if I can't give it to the police, I'm back where I started. Nowhere. And the cops're still chasing the wrong guy."

"You sure they can't trace anything to you?"

"I wore gloves and put everything back. Except for these." Reaching into his pants pocket, he pulled out the card and key. "It's for the locker."

Frank winced. "Good, Street. Now they got you for theft on top of all the rest. Why not go just back into the apartment and leave those things out where the cops or the sister can find them? They'll go get the diaries themselves."

Streeter shook his head. "Won't work. First of all, there's no way to get in there again. Barrows is finished. Plus, by the time they find this and check the locker, Weeks could be long gone. I shook him up pretty good the other day. He knows I'm on to him, even though he's got no idea who I am. He's going to panic and split or do something crazy. Soon." He thought for a moment. "No, I have to draw him out fast. At the bottom of the locker, I found a couple of hand grenades and a stick of dynamite. Some tools, too. Carol must have used the locker for Kevin's stuff."

"You're sure Weeks doesn't know who you are?" Frank asked.

"He thinks my name is Bill Swallow. And I parked way at the end of the driveway so he wouldn't see my license plates. Hell, the guy was so whacked out, he probably couldn't even tell my Buick from a Porsche."

"You don't want to underestimate this joker, Street. Carol did, and look what it got her. Listen, I'll be gone all afternoon and I'm meeting someone for supper. Don't do anything until I get back." The bondsman stood up and grabbed his reading glasses. "Later."

Streeter spent the afternoon practicing the piano and lifting weights. He had to think. It wasn't until eight-thirty that night that Frank walked into the loft. Streeter was sitting at the piano, listening to an Oscar Peterson tape, and staring at the keys.

"There you are, Big Guy," Frank said. "Getting some inspiration?"

Streeter looked up. "Just hearing how good this thing can sound. How was business?"

"Another day, another pain in the ass. You decide anything about your little problem with Mr. Weeks?"

He stood up. "Yeah, I did. Let's go to your office. I need to use the phone."

They walked down the stairs, but before they got to the office, Frank went to his apartment and grabbed a bottle of Johnnie Walker Red. "This could come in handy," he said as he moved behind his desk. He poured two short drinks. "So, let's hear it."

"You better make those doubles."

"I don't like the sound of that." Frank topped off the drinks and pushed a glass across the desk.

"The time for horsing around's over," Streeter began. "I'm done lying. One more 'pretense' call and I'm going over the top. So I decided to go straight at this guy. I'll call his bluff and draw him out."

"One more cliché and I'll go over the top with you. The hell you talking about?"

"I'm talking about calling Weeks and laying it all out. Let him know who I am and that I was a friend of Carol's. Tell him I know what went on with him and Swallow and what went down at Irwin's. Get him sweating. My read is that he doesn't have the stones for what he's into. I'll set up a meeting for tomorrow. Tell him, if he doesn't pay me ten grand, I'll go to the police. Ten thousand sounds like enough to keep me quiet, and yet not too much that he can't come up. Then I'll wire myself, and when we meet, I'll get as much out of him as I can. This guy's not all that bright, and I bet he slips up. That should give me something to take to Carey. Anything Weeks says could help."

Frank took a long pull from his Scotch. "Good thing we made these doubles. I don't know, Street. Even if you shake him loose, how do you explain to the police where you got your information?"

"I'll tell them I was just bluffing, guessing at all of it to see what I could get out of Weeks. Carey already knows my theory of the case."

"And what if he comes armed tomorrow?"

Streeter drained his Johnnie Walker. "We'll meet in public. Somewhere in Denver, my home turf. He's got to bite. And I'm not going up against a drug cartel here, Frank. We're talking about a day drinker who lives with his mommy and lets her push him around. You should have seen it. I don't want to underestimate him, either, but this is as safe as I can make it. He's not that dangerous."

"Yeah, well, sometimes stupid and desperate's worse than dangerous."

He knew Frank was right. "Look, this is the plan, and I'm doing it with or without your blessing. You got the recorder set up. I might as well see if I can weasel anything out of him tonight."

Frank nodded. He usually kept the small phone recorder he got at Radio Shack constantly in place. Streeter grabbed the phone and slid it close. Then he pulled a slip of paper from his shirt pocket. Reading from it, he pushed in Weeks' number.

Otis had put the wooden case for his .44 back up in its spot on the shelf when he noticed something was wrong. He'd forgotten to put the just-cleaned gun in the case. "Damn!" he muttered. Staring at the long pistol lying on the couch next to a small stack of cleaning rags, he realized that opium was too heavy to smoke if he had work to do. As he reached up and grabbed the wooden box, the phone rang. Weeks looked at it on his desk and then glanced toward the stairs. It was a couple of minutes before nine, so Lois wouldn't get the call. Past her bedtime. For a moment, he was confused. Opium's some truly heavy shit. After another two rings, he answered it.

"Yeah." He spoke weakly into the receiver. Calls at that time of night were unheard of at the Weekses' house.

Nothing came from the other end at first. Finally, "I didn't wake you up, did I?"

Otis struggled to recall where he'd heard the voice before.

"I say, you weren't passed out, were you?"

Weeks shook his head and gave up trying to remember. "Obviously not."

"It's Bill Swallow. I came out to look at your piano the other day."

Streeter, the guy from Denver. The name jolted his opium haze, and his head started clearing. "Right, right. *Swallow.* You made up your mind yet?"

"About a lot of things. You don't sound too good, Otis. Feeling a little under the weather tonight?"

"I'm okay. What'd you decide?"

"That it's time to cut the crap." Streeter spoke in clear, authoritative tones. "You know I'm not Bill Swallow. That was clear the minute I said the name. It's not important who I am. But what is important is that you listen real close. I know all about you. About you and Kevin and what you did at Carol Irwin's place. You didn't mean to kill her, but she's still dead. You're up Shit Creek and I've got the paddle." He waited, hoping Weeks would acknowledge something. "What do you think of that?"

Otis shook his head, his mind clearing. The guy was probably recording the conversation.

"I said, what do you think of all this, Otis?"

"All what? So far, I got no idea what you're talking about. Who the fuck's this Carol Irwin?"

"Oh, I see." Streeter turned it up a notch and put anger in his voice. "I'm all wet here, huh? Maybe I'll have this little chat with a friend of mine at the Denver PD. If you don't know what I'm talking about, then I must be dealing to the wrong guy. Let's just say good night." Again, silence from the other end. "Good night, Otis. Detective Carey's the one you'll be dealing with. Bob's a good man. I'm sure you two'll hit off."

"So you know everything. What'm I supposed to do about that?" Weeks knew Streeter wasn't joking.

"You admit you know what I'm talking about?" Streeter wished he hadn't said that. "Admit" was too obvious.

"What do you want?" Weeks' voice was getting more sure.

"I want to see you again. Isn't that nice?" No response. "Tomorrow. And this time you're the one who's going to be shopping."

"Yeah? What is it I'm buying?"

"Peace of mind, Otis. Your peace of mind and my silence."

Weeks frowned as he let go of the big question: "How much will it cost?"

Streeter smiled. Otis wasn't incriminating himself on the phone, but at least he'd show up tomorrow. "Ten thousand. Take it from what you found at Carol's place."

"Where do we meet?"

"In Denver. South Denver, someplace neutral. The bar at the Broker Restaurant, just off I-25. At noon, when people are around. I want everyone to be nice and safe. Do you know Denver? Can you find the Broker all right?"

Otis had no idea where it was. "Sure. But noon won't work. I'll need time to get my spending money together. Make it the bar there in twenty-four hours. Nine o'clock tomorrow night. There'll still be plenty of people there then."

Streeter looked at Frank across the desk and made a sour face. "Nine o'clock?"

"That's the deal, buster. I can't do it before then." Otis felt in control. "And how can I be sure that I'll have complete peace of mind? For all I know, I'll be hearing from you every couple of weeks with more to sell me."

"You'll just have to trust me. I don't want to go through this again. Ten grand's a lot of money, and I wasn't that close to those people. This is a one-time proposition. Everything's been priced to move, and all sales are final. Trust me, Otis. What choice do you have?"

"I suppose none." He thought he sounded convinced. "And we'll both be alone? You don't have any help on this, do you?"

"Just me."

"If your name's not Bill, what do I call you besides 'cock-sucker'?"

"Names aren't important here. We're just a couple of guys out for a beer on a Tuesday night. Until tomorrow."

Weeks hung up without responding. Streeter turned off the tape recorder and looked over to Frank. "Guy's no idiot. He didn't give up a thing. Probably suspected I was recording."

"He was a peace officer, Street," his partner said. "Trained to be cautious. Don't expect much more than that tomorrow night."

"You're probably right. I'll call Terry Nathan and see if he'll sit in the parking lot and photograph Weeks coming and going. And I'd like you to be in the bar, as close to us as you can, to try and listen in. Even if he doesn't say anything good, I'll be able to place him at the Broker and verify that we spoke. I'll have the money, which could give us prints, and I'll have you guys to back up what I did. That might give the police probable cause to search Weeks' place."

"What if he doesn't show?"

Streeter shrugged. "Then I call him again and we start over. All I can do is what I can do."

Otis looked down at the gun he'd just cleaned. A .44, a hand grenade, and who knows what else he'd take? Kevin had talked about rigging traps during their long talks in the pen. There was a lot of planning to do between now and noon on Tuesday. That's when he'd make his move against Streeter. No way he'd meet the man at some bar and just hand over half Carol's money. Hell, he'd probably come wired. Weeks walked back out to the rec room and flopped down on the recliner. He poured himself two fingers of ginger schnapps, knowing he had a lot of work ahead of him. One crack, that's all he'd have at the bounty hunter. He'd have to kill him then. The schnapps burned nicely as it went down his throat. This whole nightmare would be history by about one the next afternoon. So would Mr. Streeter.

34

Otis ate a big breakfast that morning and washed it down with three cups of stiff black coffee. He'd been up most of the night working out his plans. Back and forth between the basement and the garage, he'd carefully assembled all that he'd need. By now, he was going for both Streeter and Frank Dazzler. Around 2:00 A.M., he decided that Streeter must have told his partner everything. Weeks' friend at the Sheriff's Department said the two men were inseparable. That was the word he used. Which meant that what one of them knew they both knew. It wouldn't do any good to take out one of them only to get nailed for it when the other went to the cops.

"You look like dog do, Od-us." Lois stared at him from across the table. "What's the matter? Didn't you sleep?"

He looked back, working a piece of bacon fried hard as beef jerky. Suddenly, he stopped chewing. "That's about how I feel. I was up most of last night thinking about all sorts of stuff. I'm heading to Denver today to pay a visit to this Streeter character. I gotta find out what he's up to. Talk some sense into the guy." That said, he returned his attention to the food.

"Like how you talked sense into Carol Irwin, Od-us?" She grabbed a yellow Bic lighter and put fire to the cigar in her mouth. "We all know how well that one went."

He looked up again. "No, not like that. I just want to find out what he's after and get him off my case." No need to tell her much. "I'll be back for supper."

"Figure you can outsmart this one, huh?" She looked closely at him through a bluish-white cloud of cigar smoke. Then she mellowed. "Son, you can't battle wits with another adult human being. You're unarmed in that department. That should be clear even to you. Now, just what is it you're up to today?"

Weeks sat back in his chair, gnawing the last of his breakfast. "I'm not sure yet, but I have to talk to him. Whatever his game is, it's between me and him. It don't involve you."

She put the cigar down. "If you end up in jail or dead, I got nothing. Sad to say, you're the only family I got. And I sure can't run this place by myself. Let's face it, Od-us, you were born to screw up and you pretty much always done just that. When the Good Lord was handin' out the higher traits like looks and brains and such, you musta been in the john. But you're all I got left, son."

He pulled his chair back and stood up, looking genuinely pained. "You think I'm happy with the way things turned out? Hell, no. But I'm in deep shit with Streeter, and there's no way I'm going to spend the rest of my life locked up. Now, I'm taking off for Denver and that's that. I'll be back in time for supper, like always. Tuesday night. Meat loaf, right?" He turned and started to walk out of the room.

Lois sat there watching. Nodding slowly, she wiped a tear away with her hand.

The three White Crosses he'd taken began to kick in as Otis walked into the garage. Coffee and amphetamines would counter the lack of sleep and the brown hash he'd toked just before his morning shower. If the speed made him too jangled, he had a bottle of schnapps and more hash in the car. Getting the right mind-set was no small trick, and heading up to Denver straight and sober never occurred to him. He went through the cardboard box on his workbench one last time before putting it in his Sentra's trunk. Masking tape, fishing line, pliers, wire cutters, hand grenade, hunting knife, several pairs of handcuffs, Super Glue, putty, rope, a flashlight. It was all there, even though he knew half of it probably wouldn't be needed.

When he'd placed the box in the trunk, he turned to the propane tank in the corner of the garage. Not really necessary, but if he wanted a big explosion, it would help. As he bent over to lift the tank, Otis cursed. Empty. He'd been meaning to fill it for over a month. Too late now. Glancing around the room, he noticed a five-gallon gas can back near the bench. That'd do. He made sure the top was on tight and then put it in the trunk.

Standing behind the car, he spotted his reflection in a wall mirror by the door. Otis was wearing an orange hunting hat, green plaid pants, and an old Miller Lite T-shirt. "Less Filling— Tastes Great," argued bright-red letters over his huge belly. Should he change? No, he didn't want to go back into the house and maybe face Lois again. Instead he grabbed the tan windbreaker from a wall hook and put it on. He got into the Sentra and checked his supplies. A shiny nine-millimeter handgun sat next to the schnapps bottle on the passenger's seat. He'd decided on the nine, the .44 being too large to handle easily. His brass pipe was in the open ashtray on the dash. He didn't want to go to hash that morning, but he was out of pot. With two more White Crosses in his pants pocket, Otis figured he was ready for whatever lay ahead. His body shuddered from a random speed rush, and he started the engine.

Driving north on I-25, he had to keep slowing down his car. The White Crosses pulsed through him, and his right foot kept pressing to the floorboards. He worked the ginger schnapps like it was Evian. By the time he hit Denver, he was a twisted mass of energy, rage, and confusion. But was he ever awake. His eyes bulged like a lizard's, and it'd be days, he realized, before he'd sleep again.

Frank was doing the *Rocky Mountain News* crossword puzzle and eating a tuna-fish sandwich at his desk when he heard women going into the gym down the hall. He looked up. Was the noon karate class letting out already? Then he remembered the special gender-awareness presentation set for that day. Frank thought of how he was aware of their gender every time he watched the ladies go to work out. No need to teach that, so he turned back to his puzzle.

As he drove past the church, Otis finally managed to hit the right tone. Loose and confident, yet focused nicely. He slowed down to read the signs: "Dazzler's Bail Bonds" on the right; on the left, "Womyn's Workout Space." Whatever that was. There was a smaller sign he couldn't make out. He drove to the corner, took a left, and pulled over. After he parked, he took one more pull of schnapps and stuffed the nine into his waistband. When his feet hit the pavement, he felt light and primed. He walked back to the church, wondering if both his targets would be there. When he got to the front door, he read the small sign. "Noon, today: Removing the gender bias from MIME."

He walked into the church and followed the arrow to the bonds office on the right. Just before he entered, Otis put his hand on the nine above his fly. Then he spun into the room, pulling the gun out as he did. Frank didn't hear him at first.

When he looked up, Weeks was standing in front of his desk, waving the small gun at him. The two men stared at each other without speaking. Otis finally broke the ice. "Are you Dazzler?"

"In that outfit, you're no slouch yourself," Frank deadpanned, setting down his paper. "Yeah, I'm Frank Dazzler. What's this all about?"

Otis glanced down and realized how bad he looked. "Where's Streeter?"

"Be back in an hour. Why don't you put that thing down and we'll wait for him?"

Otis's eyes shot around the room. No way he could sit still in there for that long. "We're going for a ride. Get up." He tipped the gun slightly.

"What the hell's this all about?" Frank was getting mad. Then it dawned on him. "Your name wouldn't happen to be Otis Weeks? How the hell did you find us?"

"Don't worry about that. Just get up! Where's your car? You're driving."

Frank rose slowly, keeping even eye contact. "Where to?"

"To wherever the fuck I say." He held the gun higher.

"When Streeter gets back we can all sit down and straighten this out. Why not just put the gun away and I'll go get us some coffee."

Otis shook from the speed and blinked. Standing still for any length of time was out of the question. "We're going to hop in your car and take a drive. Then we're going to call back here in an hour and have Streeter meet us. We'll leave a note, so he sticks by the phone. Now, where's your car?"

Behind the thick glasses, Weeks' bloodshot eyes were wide. Anger and fear. Frank knew, if he didn't hurry, the guy'd do something crazy. "Out front."

That calmed Weeks. He looked at the reading glasses and a cellular phone sitting on the desk next to Frank's food. "Bring the phone with you," he ordered.

Frank reached down and grabbed it. Suddenly, Weeks stepped forward, picked up a coffee mug on the desk, and brought it down hard on the glasses. They smashed, and part of the frame slid off the desk.

"Hey! The hell you do that for?" Dazzler moved, but Otis poked the gun at him.

"So your partner knows I'm serious. Let's go." He stepped aside to let Frank out.

"Aren't you forgetting something, Robin Hood?" Frank asked. The gunman frowned, puzzled. "You said you wanted to leave a note. Remember?"

" 'Course I do. I was getting to it." He nodded at the desk. "Write something."

The bondsman grabbed a pen and notepad from the top drawer and then bent over to where his face was just inches above the paper. Squinting hard without his glasses, he scrawled: "Street, I'm with Otis Weeks and he seems rather upset. Call my cell phone right away. F." Finished, he looked up. "You want to read it?"

Otis shook his head. "Let's just go."

They moved into the hallway. Otis walked a couple feet behind Frank, the gun held up close to his chest. Suddenly, a side door from the gym opened. A thin man in a black full-body leotard, a black bowler hat, and chalk-white face makeup stepped out between them.

Weeks let out a grunt and then, "What the hell?" He moved his gun back and forth between Frank and the stranger. The mime stayed true to his profession, silently throwing his hands back—palms out—to shoulder level. His mouth shot open in exaggerated shock. Otis turned to Frank. "What's this?"

"He's a mime. Didn't you read the sign out front?"

Otis's frown deepened as he glanced at the door and then back. "So what's that mean? Is he like a retard?"

"A mime," Frank repeated. "As in pantomime. You know, street performers who pretend they can't talk so they can wave their arms around and piss everyone off. Some people think it's funny. They're the retards."

Clearly, Otis didn't get it, but he knew the mime was trouble. "You can't talk?" he asked. "Then listen. I'm not leaving you here. You're coming with us. If you understand, nod." Ever the performer, he bobbed his head wildly, his face twisted in concern.

"They can talk and they can hear," Frank interrupted. "Least I think they can. Clamming up like that's just part of their act. Can't you leave the poor guy here?"

"No way. He'll be on the phone to 911 before we get started. Come on, let's all of us get going." Otis waved the gun to indicate the mime should walk in front of him. For his part, the silent one held up his hands like a robbery victim and moved ahead. "Hey, asshole, cut the drama," Weeks snarled.

When they got to Frank's Mark IV, Weeks ordered Dazzler behind the wheel; the mime would ride shotgun, and he himself would cover both from the back seat. He said to drive around the block, to where his Sentra was parked. Once there, he told Frank to pull right alongside, stop, and pop his trunk. Then he leaned forward in his seat. "Cut the engine and give me the keys," he said to the driver. "I gotta get something out of my car and I don't want you running off."

Frank did as he was told. Otis jumped out of the Mark IV and walked to his Sentra. He got the box with his tools and the gas can, and put both in the trunk of Dazzler's car. That done, he returned to the back seat and returned the keys to Frank.

"Just head north up Brighton Boulevard to where it leaves town. We're going to the country." Then he turned to the mime. "Hey, dickface, aren't you going to pretend to clap your hands or something? Not so funny anymore, is it?"

Frank drove about four miles. The farther they went, the

more open spaces appeared between industrial buildings and small shops. Right before they crossed into Adams County, Otis ordered him to take a left, south of Riverside Cemetery. Vaguely nauseous from the drugs and schnapps, and not used to being in the back, Weeks was getting carsick. To ease the pressure, he leaned forward and let one rip quietly into the seat.

In front, Frank looked around, his nose wrinkled in disgust. "So which one of you two had the napalm for breakfast?" he asked as he rolled his window down. He glanced at the mime, whose face was scrunched up elaborately, and then into his rearview mirror. "Shooting us is one thing, Weeks, but there's no need for torture."

"Quit whining," Weeks answered. By now, he'd had enough of the drive himself. "Pull over there behind that empty shed." He pointed his free hand to a rusting tool barn in an open field at the end of a driveway. "That'll give us privacy."

Frank obeyed. When he stopped, the Mark IV was hidden from view from the road by the shed and there was nothing but expansive, open fields on the other three sides. He cut the engine and waited for more instructions.

Otis looked around, pleased with his progress. "Pop the trunk, and then both you two get out." When all three were standing next to the car, Weeks waved the nine to indicate they should stand back a few feet. They obliged, and he went to the trunk. He studied the cardboard box. Bending over, he grabbed three pairs of handcuffs and the masking tape from it. He put the tape on top of the car and then nodded to the inside. "Get in the back seat," he ordered. "Both of you." As they did, Otis shivered from another speed rush and belched.

In the back of the Mark IV, his captives waited. Weeks got into the front on the passenger side and knelt, facing the back seat. He tossed the cuffs back. "Each of you cuff one wrist to the door handle, and then cuff yourselves together with the last pair. Now!" He moved the gun between them.

They did as he instructed, and when they were done, Frank spoke. "I hope you got the keys handy."

"Don't worry about that. The way I'm going to rig up this car, you guys ain't going anywhere for a while." Then he took the cell phone from the floor and set it on the seat top. He tucked his nine back into his waist and got out. He went to the trunk again and in a couple of minutes returned to the front seat. After placing the masking tape, the fishing line, and the hand grenade on the driver's seat, Otis closed that door. Only the front passenger door remained open.

Finally realizing what was happening, the mime broke his silence with a loud "Hey!" From behind the driver's seat, he spoke. "You're actually going to kill us? I didn't do nothing." He sat up, looking back and forth between his wrists and those of the man next to him, his eyes wide in terror. His voice was high and screechy.

The other two men studied him. Otis grinned. "He can talk! How 'bout that? You finally figured it out, huh, Whitey?"

"Calm down, pal," Frank told the mime. "He's not gonna kill no one." Then he turned to the man in the front seat. "What now?"

"We wait for your partner to call. Then I'll invite him out here to chat. I'll set up the car with a surprise. Don't worry, none of you'll feel a thing." He got out and went to the trunk again. When he returned, he had the gas can with him, and he set it on the floor under the steering wheel. Seeing that, the mime made a gurgling sound and again fell silent. "This is a trick your friend Swallow taught me," Weeks continued. "Lucky thing I found the grenade over at Carol's place."

"But I didn't do nothing," the mime interjected, speaking to Otis.

Weeks stared at him. "You know, I liked you better when you didn't talk. You got a voice on you makes me wish I was deaf. Put a lid on it and I won't have to kick the shit out of you."

Frank turned back to the mime and shrugged. "Sorry about all this. Looks like you were in the wrong place at the wrong time. What's your name?"

The man in black stared at him, his mouth wide open. Then he turned away, retreating back into silence.

"That's better," came from the front. "Guy's a gamer to the end." Otis pulled a couple feet of fishing line from the spool and tied an end to the driver's door handle. Then he unraveled about four more feet and broke it off. He tied the other end to the pull ring on the side of the grenade. "I'll have it set so's when Streeter opens the door to get you he'll pull the pin out. Ba-boom. Gas and all. Like I said, no one'll feel a thing."

"What makes you think he'll come running out here? Nothing in it for him."

Weeks faced Frank again. "Because he's such a true-blue guy. He'll want to save you. Look at all he went through for Irwin." He nodded. "Oh yeah, I can read the papers, too. And he's still trying to avenge her, which is why he's after me. Streeter'll come running because I got something he wants. You."

"Don't count on it. He's not stupid."

"Probably not. But he's got a blind spot for loyalty."

They sat there for about twenty minutes. Otis chattered away on mindless topics, his teeth grinding incessantly from the amphetamines. The effects of the alcohol and hash were by now completely overtaken by the speed. Suddenly, the cell phone rang. Everyone stared at it as it rang again. Weeks picked it up and pulled out the small antenna. "Good of you to call," he said into it, winking at Frank as he spoke.

"What's going on?" Streeter yelled. "I thought we were meeting tonight."

"Calm down, dipshit. Change of plans. I've got your partner out here and we were hoping you'd join us."

"Where are you?"

Weeks gave him directions. "Do hurry," he said when he finished. "Someone would like to see you right quick." With that he shoved the phone in front of Frank's mouth. "Say howdy."

"Stay put, Street!" Dazzler yelled. "It's a trap!"

Otis pulled the phone back with his right hand and reached over the seat with his left hand clenched in a fist. He smashed Frank in the side of his face, as the mime watched in silent terror. Putting the receiver back to his mouth, Weeks said, "Don't let that stop you, Streeter. We'll be waiting."

"I'll be there in fifteen minutes. Don't do anything stupid." Then he hung up.

"I told you he'd come." Otis pushed the antenna in and let the phone drop to the seat. "I better get busy here so we're all set up for him." He took the masking tape and pulled off a piece for Frank's mouth. Then he stuck it across the seat top. "I can wait for that, Frank." He turned to the other passenger. "Guess I'll have to tape you up, too. But that can wait until I'm outside. Streeter won't be here for a while."

The mime threw his head back a bit. "Bite me," was all he said.

35

Streeter hung up and went to the loft to get his .38. Then he made a quick call to Terry Nathan for backup. Terry's secretary said he had gone to Boulder to see a client and wouldn't be back for about two hours. The bounty hunter knew he couldn't wait that long, so he headed down to the Buick and left for Brighton Boulevard. As he drove, he wondered how the prison guard had ever located the church. How he even found out who Streeter and Frank were. Sort that out later. Rolling three stop signs, and two lights, he still took over fifteen minutes to get to Riverside

Cemetery. As he turned west, he thought of Frank. He hit the accelerator and flew around a UPS panel truck. Playing Mission Impossible, as Linda put it, was about to get his best friend killed. He couldn't let that happen.

"I better finish up here and get moving," Otis said as he got on his knees in the driver's seat and faced the open passenger door. "Don't want to be around when he gets here." He held the grenade, tied to the fishing line, in his left hand as he propped himself up with his right on the seat next to him. "Tape this to the door here, so when Streeter opens it the pin comes out, and the car blows."

Frank studied him. "What if Street comes through one of the back doors?"

"They'll be locked, with the windows rolled up. The only way he can get in is through a front door. Either one'll set her off. I've got enough fishing line to let me slide on outta the car, yet I'll keep it tight, so when the door opens the pin gets pulled. By the time he figures out what he did, it'll be too late. He'll only have a few seconds to react."

"What if he sees the line and doesn't bite?"

"That's an excellent question, Frank." Otis was now on all fours, his knees on the console between the front seats, his hands on the passenger side. He shuddered silently from the speed before answering. "First of all, this line's damned near invisible. I figure he'll be in such a hurry to get you out, he won't see it. But even if he does, I'll be waiting in the shed over there. If he don't go for it, I'll shoot him and take care of you two myself. I appreciate your concern, Frank, but I got her covered."

Another huge speed rush shivered through Otis as he worked his way closer to the passenger door. That caused his hip to swing hard into the steering wheel, setting off the horn. A harsh blast of noise filled the car and startled Weeks. He shot straight up, causing an unfortunate series of events to occur. His head smacked into the ceiling, knocking him nearly unconscious. The quick motion also yanked hard at the line, pulling the ring pin from the grenade in his hand. Weeks then tumbled wildly down toward the passenger door. As he crashed into the floor, his left shoulder smashed into it with such force that he let out a scream of pain. But he held on to the grenade and ended up with it wedged between his shoulder and the floor well next to the door. Miraculously, it was wedged so tightly that the release bar stayed clamped shut in his hand, keeping it deactivated. In the commotion, the nine-mil fell off the seat and landed on the floor under Otis's chest.

When the horn went off, Frank and the mime lunged forward. They saw the tail end of the bizarre sequence. It was quiet for a minute before Otis screamed again. Then, "Jesus damn, my shoulder hurts! I think I broke it!"

Frank and the mime, still handcuffed, turned to look at each other. The mime's mouth flew open in confusion, but he didn't speak. Then they both turned back to Otis. About all they could see of him over the front seat was his wide green plaid rear end sticking up, pointing at them. When he landed on his face and shoulder, his hips and butt followed, and his knees rested on the passenger seat.

"If it's broke, get up off of it." Frank stated what seemed obvious.

Otis, his head turned sharply to the right, responded through teeth clenched nearly shut by his weird position. "I can't. The damned grenade's right under it and the pin came out. If I move at all, it'll go off. It's right behind my head. I'm holding that bar thing on the side shut, but if I get up, it gets released."

"Great, Otis." Frank thought for a moment. "Can't you reach it with your right hand? It looks free from here. Maybe you could throw it way the hell out in the field by the time it blows?"

Weeks considered that option. "I don't think I can get to it fast enough," came the jangled response. "My damned left shoulder's busted, and by the time I move off the grenade and grab it with my good hand, it'll be too late."

"It's probably just dislocated, but don't move. When Streeter gets here, he can pull the grenade out and toss it. Stay still." He turned to the mime. "You got any brilliant ideas?" he asked the man cuffed to him.

The mime glanced at him and shook his head emphatically. Then he turned again to face the plaid butt on the other side of the seat.

"And you people wonder why everyone hates you so much," Frank said loudly. Turning back to Otis, he asked, "What the hell are you on that has you shaking and grinding your teeth like that?"

Through clenched jaws, "White Cross. Keeps me sharp. On top of things."

"Jesus. If this is sharp, I'd hate to see how you operate when you're straight."

By the time Streeter got to the drive leading to the shed, his mouth was dry, his shirt laced with sweat. He slammed on the brakes, skidding past the drive. Then he shoved the Buick into reverse. When he got into position, he put it in low and blasted toward the shed. Once there, he parked near the small building and jumped out. With the .38 in both hands, he moved carefully along the side of the shed. Before he turned the corner, he listened closely. Nothing but distant road sounds. He came around to the back, the gun at shoulder level. About twenty feet in front of him, Frank's white Mark IV sat with the open front door facing him. On the ground next to the car lay an orange hunting cap. Just inside, he could see the top of a head with thinning sandy hair. Otis, his butt in the air. One of Weeks' arms dangled outside the car while the other appeared to be jammed up near the side of his head.

From the back seat, Frank saw him spin around the corner.

"Street!" he yelled as he leaned in that direction. "Get over here fast!"

The bounty hunter walked to the Lincoln. "What the hell happened?" He nodded at the head on the floor. "Is he dead?"

"No," Frank returned. "But he sure screwed up." By now, his partner was just outside the car door from where he sat. "He was rigging a trip wire to a hand grenade, but he's so trashed on speed that he messed up. The grenade's under his shoulder and the pin's out. You gotta get it and toss it away from here."

Streeter glanced in at the mime on the other side of his partner and frowned.

"Don't even ask," Frank said. "I'll tell you about him later. Weeks has us cuffed back here so we can't leave."

Setting his gun on the car roof, Streeter knelt down by Otis. "You awake?" he asked the head on the car floor.

"Get this thing out of here," Weeks answered. "My shoulder's busted, and if I don't get off it soon, I'm fucked. This grenade's gonna slip any time now."

"Relax. I should just cut them loose in back and leave you here." He looked around Weeks' head. When he spotted the top of the grenade just behind his neck, he reached in and nearly touched it. Then he glanced off toward the front of the car.

"Come on, man!" Otis could feel the speed still jerking through his system.

"This is how we'll do it," Streeter finally said. "When I count three, you pull your head and shoulder back as much as you can. I'll grab the grenade and throw it out front." He looked at Frank. "Get down back there." Then to Otis. "You understand, Weeks? The count of three."

"Yeah, yeah. Just do it."

In the back seat, Frank and the mime extended their legs forward and lay on the seat as low as possible.

"Here goes," Streeter said. He leaned in so his face was about ten inches over Weeks' head. "One! Two! Three!"

Otis shifted, not much, but enough, so most of the grenade was visible and it rolled slightly forward, activated. Streeter quickly grabbed the thing. Then he jumped to his feet and threw it about thirty yards into the shrub grass in the open field. It rolled wildly for a couple of seconds before it blew. By that time, Streeter had dropped to the ground, facedown. The explosion shook the earth. Dirt, stones, and grass flew in all directions, and even the heavy Mark IV seemed to hop. It was so loud that all four men had an immediate ringing in their ears. But when the dust began to settle, they were all alive. Slowly, Streeter stood up, shaking dirt from his hair and working his jaw. He looked into the back seat. Both men were sitting up. Frank was gingerly moving his head around to get his neck limber.

"Everyone all right back there?" Streeter asked, leaning in the rear window.

"My head hurts, but I'll live," his partner answered. The mime kept opening and shutting his mouth dramatically, as if to get his ears to pop. He looked right at Streeter, nodded, but said nothing.

The bounty hunter looked over the front hood of the Mark IV, which was covered with dust. Off in the distance, he heard the low wail of a siren approaching from the southeast, the way he'd just come. A harsh burn smell filled the air.

Suddenly, right in front of him, Otis's chubby, awkward form stumbled out of the car. He almost fell, but caught himself. When he spun to face Streeter, the shiny nine-mil was planted in his right hand. His left hand was nearly immobile by his side, since that shoulder still hurt. Streeter glanced at his own .38, which was on the car top, about four feet away.

Weeks saw the look and hollered, "Don't try it, asshole! Lock your hands behind your head and move away! Slow and easy!" His voice was shaky but he held the gun still.

Streeter did neither. "Weeks, don't you ever give up? Listen to those sirens. The police'll find this place in a few minutes. Grenade blasts tend to get people's attention. Give it up!"

Otis reached laboriously across his body with his left hand and grabbed the .38 from the hood. Without looking back, he then tossed it on the ground behind him. The nine was still trained on Streeter. Weeks held it at about chest level, his arm bent. But he didn't seem to know what to do next.

"You're in enough trouble," Streeter continued, still not moving away from the car. "Don't add another murder on top of all the other charges."

"Another murder," Otis repeated. "I got nothing to lose, man." He nodded and pulled the trigger.

Seconds before that, Frank had yanked hard with his left hand, forcing the mime close to him. That gave him a sliver of room to navigate in the back seat. In one quick motion, the bondsman shot his head out the window and rammed the top of it into Otis's gun hand as he fired. That pushed the nine-millimeter off to the left and up as Weeks squeezed the trigger. The slug whistled past Streeter's head.

Otis was deeply dazed by the move. In the confusion, Streeter stepped forward and grabbed his right wrist just above the nine. He forced that hand down and held it there like a vise. Weeks screamed and shivered visibly one more time from the speed, a pained look in his eyes. He panicked and hugged off another round. This time the slug hit flesh: Otis's right foot, almost directly in the middle. His mouth dropped open and his eyes rolled back behind his glasses. Then he dropped straight down into an unconscious pile of plaid and tan.

Frank and Streeter stared at the man on the ground. From deep in the car, the mime bobbed his head to get a look, too.

"Do you believe this guy?" Streeter asked, still looking down. Then he turned and leaned in Frank's window. "Thanks."

"Right. Just find the keys and get us out of these damned

cuffs. I spent enough time hooked up to Harpo back here."

The siren was getting close. Mechanics at a nearby garage had called 911 when they heard the explosion, although nobody knew exactly where it came from. The police car sped down the road past the shed, but the driver must have seen the remaining dust from the explosion: he turned around and came back.

Inside the Mark IV, Frank turned to the man next to him. "We're going to be okay, pal. Sorry you had to get dragged into all this."

The mime sat up indignantly. Then, in a dull monotone, he repeated an earlier comment. "Bite me." With that, he turned away.

Frank looked back out his window. "Guy's a regular talking fool once you get him going, Street."

36

Streeter was on the phone to Terry Blue Nathan. "This should do it. Haney and the boys went down to Weeks' place last night, after he got our statements. You should have seen them trying to drag words out of that crazy mime. I thought Haney'd shoot the guy." He smiled to himself as he sat behind Frank's desk. "Anyhow, the cops went to Weeks' house and found stuff from Carol's. VCR, cash, some letters. Even a few pair of panties, according to Carey. How about that, Terry? Looks like Otis is going to be back with DOC, but on the other side of the bars.

"I guess it was pretty sad down there. Lois, the mother, took it hard. She and Weeks seemed so pathetic to me. An old boozer living in his mother's basement. The two of them always snarling at each other. But now she's alone. Her boy lived with her for fifty-some years and now he's gone. Poor thing's pretty upset. 'Course, Otis isn't feeling too good himself, with a bullet clean through his foot."

"That ought to slow him down," Terry said.

"Better his foot than my head. Frank saved me on that one."

"Tell me, Street, how'd you know he was your man?"

"Followed a hunch. At least that's what I told Haney. He seemed to believe me, too. I'll give you all the gory details tonight."

"Berardi's, on 17th, right?"

"Eight o'clock, about two hours from now. See you then."

When he hung up, Streeter returned to the loft to practice the piano. About a half-hour later, Frank yelled up the stairs.

"Someone here to see you." His voice was followed by the sound of footsteps. Streeter glanced over from the piano keyboard and was stunned to see Linda Parnell walk into the loft. She had her glasses on, and her hair was up in a ponytail near the top of her head.

"Don't let me disturb you," she said, nodding toward the piano.

"You always disturb me," he responded. "You can't help it."

Wearing a light-gray pantsuit and white blouse, Linda looked prim but soft. Streeter wondered how she managed that. He stood up and took a step toward her, but neither of them spoke. He glanced at the green sweatpants and tan T-shirt he was wearing. No shoes or socks. Suddenly, he felt self-conscious. "This is sure awkward," he finally said. "Can I get you anything? Coffee, pop, a double boilermaker?"

She flashed him a grin. "Coffee'll be fine." Then she looked slowly around the room. "This is nice, Street. Books, movie posters, a baby grand. The whole works." She looked back at him. "Very comfortable but sort of elegant."

"And you were expecting something like Hitler's bunker in the final days."

"No, I didn't know what to expect. Come on, Street. I wasn't that hard on you." They both fell silent again. She spoke first. "I talked to Frank for a while. He came out of yesterday in good form."

"He always does." Streeter walked to the kitchen and started putting water in the coffee maker. "It'll take more than handcuffs, a grenade, and a boorish mime to stop Frank Dazzler." He turned to face her. "I finally think I can describe him, though."

"What?"

"Saturday, you asked me to describe Frank. While you were critiquing my life. Remember? Well, he's the best friend I ever had, and that's going some. After what we went through yesterday, I wouldn't trade that old war-horse for any twenty grownups and a real career."

She considered that as he went back to the coffee. "I said a lot of harsh things. Maybe I panicked last week when I realized how much I cared for you."

"Right!" He stopped to look at her. "Why is it that every time a woman tells me she cares about me, it's followed by a kick in the ass and a 'Get out of my life'? I liked it better before you started caring. The sex was sensational."

"You get your ass kicked often?"

"I've got my share of foot marks. For a lot of different reasons."

Linda walked to the table between the living room and the kitchen and sat down. "I meant a lot of what I said last Saturday, but I overdid it. Can we try to talk about it again? I promise not to call you hopeless."

He went around to her side of the table and sat next to her. "But I *am* hopeless. That's pretty clear after these last few days. I can't blame you for not wanting to be part of all this. Tossing crime scenes, shaking down guys, bullshitting half the county. Then nearly getting Frank killed. It turned out okay, but next time I play Rambo I might not be so lucky."

"Come on, cowboy." She pulled her head back. "Your life's not *that* hairy."

He studied her in silence for a moment. "I always feel obligated to explain myself to you. I'm a big boy and this is how I am. Still, I end up wanting you to understand me and trying to impress you at the same time. It's that high-school thing I always feel around you." He paused. "Listen to me. You've got me using the F-word in every other sentence. Exactly why are you here, Linda?"

"We have a saying in therapy. 'Great sex is the best reason to stay together.' "

"Really?"

"No, but we should." She shook her head slowly. "I'm not sure why I'm here. It's just that I hated the way we left it and I missed you. That's all. Maybe I should go."

He leaned in to her. "You know, if you weren't so edgy and I wasn't so flaky, we might have shot at hammering something out for ourselves here."

"That was pure poetry," she said. "You really should write greeting cards for a living."

"So I've been told." He stood up. "Look, in about an hour, I'm going to dinner with Frank and a friend of mine named Terry Nathan. His partner's ex-wife, too. Why don't you join us? I promise that we'll actually eat this time. And who knows? If we're still talking at the end of the night, we could slip back here and I'll give you a tour of the place."

"I'd like that, Street." She stood up and moved toward him. "I'm starving, and I can always use another tour."